LUCK

GERT HOFMANN

LUCK

TRANSLATED FROM THE GERMAN BY
MICHAEL HOFMANN

A NEW DIRECTIONS BOOK

*The translator would like to thank Paul Muldoon
for the loan of a phrase,
and Eva Hofmann for her vigilance and tact*

Published by arrangement with The Harvill Press, London, and Carl Hanser Verlag, Munich.
Originally published under the title Das Glück

Manufactured in the United States of America.
New Directions Books are printed on acid-free paper.
First published clothbound by New Directions in 2002.
Published simultaneously in Canada by Penguin Canada Books, Ltd.

Library of Congress Cataloging-in-Publication Data

Hofmann, Gert.
[Glèuck. English]
Luck / Gert Hofmann ; translated from the German by Michael Hofmann.
p. cm.
ISBN 0-8112-1502-4 (alk. paper)
I. Hofmann, Michael, 1957 Aug. 25- II. Title.
PT2668.O376 G5513 2002
833'.914--dc21
2002003556

New Directions Books are published for James Laughlin
by New Directions Publishing Corporation
80 Eighth Avenue, New York 10011

LUCK

1

By the time Father started packing, it had been light for ages. The birds were all over the garden, stuffing themselves on our worms. Father was standing in his favourite place, in front of the window. He wasn't happy, though.

This is a sad day, he said, the heavens should be weeping!

And then he was quiet again. We were in his study, with my sister standing between us. She pressed her nose against the glass and made a greasy mark. Every so often, someone walked past, preceded by the sound of their footsteps. Some said hello, or waved up at us. My sister was right next to me. She hadn't washed yet. Her arms were full of a half a dozen or so dolls that she was clutching to herself. All her nails were chewed, especially the ones on her left hand. Mother was already up too, but she was in her room. She hadn't gone to the office, because it was a Saturday and she was expecting Herr Herkenrath, who wanted to marry her. She was probably making herself beautiful for him. Father, who was naturally beautiful, said: That primping and preening won't do any good! She can preenand primp all she likes.

And what are we going to do now? asked my sister.

Ha, said Father, that's always the question! There's a writer, I forget his name now . . .

Do you mean Thomas Mann? my sister asked.

Never mind the name! In essence, said Father, there was only one difference between him and me. He was a bit taller. Then Father was going to say something else, but he forgot it. He and my sister and I had got ourselves ready to go out together for

3

the last time. But then he suddenly put his walking stick down again. He unbuttoned his jacket and sat down. He was relieved "to get the weight off his feet". He spread his legs as far as he could. Not a pleasant sight for any onlookers, I freely admit, he said, but how else is a man to sit? Then he tweaked at a hair in his beard, and said: The weather, unless I'm mistaken . . .

What about the weather? asked my sister, and Father said: There's this pressure, at least I feel it! I have a sense of something hanging over me.

And what about me? asked my sister, Is it hanging over me too?

Yes, said Father, it's hanging over you too, but up to a point, up to a point! Then he took a deep breath and said: I feel I'm being driven into the ground, if you take my meaning. He looked at his watch, because there was still a lot to be done. But he was ready. He had his beret in his hand, his stick, and so on. That was the one he went on walks with. He liked swinging it around, only not in the house. He didn't want anything getting *smashed to smithereens*. He had got into the habit of swinging his stick around many, many years ago, when he had still been happy. There, he said, pointing to the corner by the window, that is the corner I used to sit in, and you used to come and sit, one of you on each knee.

And then? asked my sister.

Then I used to give you rides, and I was happy too, he said. As he was a creature of habit, his walking stick always had to accompany him. Without it, he felt like he "didn't exist". It was a length of smooth linden wood. He had peeled it and sharpened it, long before our time. So I can hit back, he said, if I'm set upon.

And where will you hit them?

4

Where do you think? About their heads!

And then?

Then, he said, there'll be a couple of villains less in the world!

The handle of his stick was worn and dark, "because dark, not light, is the natural colour of things in this world". Then he laid his stick aside, and fiddled with his beret. It was the kind of beret that artists liked to wear. He had *stolen* it.

A writer I have quite a lot of time for also had a beret, he said. He didn't wear it much, though, so no one knows.

Just you, said my sister, right?

Yes, said Father, just me!

A mourning ribbon was fixed to his beret, you could see it from some way off. It wasn't long and thin, the way they mostly are, but short and broad. That made his grief more visible. When my sister saw the mourning ribbon for the first time, she asked: Has anyone died?

Father shook his head and said: No, not yet! Is someone going to? she asked, and he said: It's a sign.

A sign of what?

Of the fact that, after protracted suffering, my marriage with your mother has—barring some miracle—gone on, said Father, and gave a little tug at the mourning ribbon.

He was much given to sweating. When he sweated, it was on his forehead and his palms. They were always damp. Just like they were today, because it turned out to be a bright, warm, universal sort of day, in May, 1960. Then again, it wasn't so warm that he absolutely had to sweat. Father reached for his handkerchief and said: Misfortune is approaching! Then he pointed in various directions, and asked: Will it be from here? From here? From here? He didn't know yet. It would be a surprise. With some effort, he got up and walked—crept—across the room. He reached the window and looked out. The moving van would come up this street—the Jakobsstrasse—to fetch us, only we couldn't see it yet. It would come to a stop outside our door, and stay there for a little while. For the time being, it was still safely in its garage. But never fear, said Father, it will come, just as surely as we're standing here now, when we should be making tracks. The front gardens on either side were dry, *unseasonably dry*, he said. When I went into the kitchen and ran the cold tap, there was only a thin trickle. Father would stand beside me and watch the trickle. Sometimes he held his finger-tip under it, and said: Look, now I'm going to toughen myself up! At other times, he couldn't even drag himself as far as the kitchen, he said he was too exhausted. The real reason was that he didn't want to run into Mother, because he didn't know what sort of expression he should put on, and what he should say to her. Because that's always the question when you run into your wife in the corridor: What sort of expression do you put on, he said. When he sat sweating at his desk and I asked: Don't you want to come to the kitchen with me and cool your hands, Mother isn't around! he said: You're younger than me, and you need it more, because your blood is warmer and circulates more quickly. You go and do it for me! When I came back from the tap, and he asked: Well, how was it? I said: Oh, there was just a trickle! And it was lukewarm!

I can't say I'm surprised, Father would say, and, because Mother was divorcing him: The whole world is out of kilter!

Being a writer of a kind, he was given to poetic turns of phrase, so we often couldn't understand him. He would generally be leaning against the wall in his favourite corner. There was a postcard from Switzerland hanging that he'd framed and used to look at a lot. And as he looked, he would say: Yes, addressed to me! It was handwritten, and came from Thomas Mann. Years ago, Father had written to him once and told him he wasn't getting on too well with a novel that was going to be called *The Magic Table*, and Thomas Mann had written back, saying he wasn't getting on too well with his novel that was going to be called *Felix Krull: Confessions of a Confidence Trickster* either. Father showed the postcard to everyone, regardless of whether they wanted to see it or not. He had always meant to write back, but before he got around to it, Thomas Mann had died. A pity, said Father, now he'll always think of me as discourteous! Perhaps he might have written to me again. At least I've got the one! There are people who have a great deal on their minds!

You mean like you? my sister asked, and Father said:

Yes, like me!

As he didn't know how things would develop with Mother, he often assembled us in his study when he wanted to talk to us, and locked the door. Then he would give us advice that he had garnered *in the course of a stupid life*. Be sure to take a good look at the world in which I put you in a moment of weakness, and you arrived pretty promptly too. And at the times, which are ours to share, if only for a year or two. Because you must know that world and time go together, you don't get one without the other. So be open to everything, because now something new is beginning, for you and for me, he said cheerfully to me. At any rate, he wanted to appear cheerful. Did you understand?

Which bit, asked my sister, the bit about being open?

Yes.

No, said my sister, not really!

From one particular day on—it threatened rain to begin with, but later turned out fine—he spoke to me as to a grown-up. He even straightened his tie for me, if he happened to be wearing one. Then he would take me by the arm and say: Do you have a moment, young man! and pull me into his room. My sister tagged along unasked. Then we stood around for a long time, scuffing the furniture. Because he had forgotten by now whatever he had wanted to say to me, he didn't say much, something like: Well, why not! or: Was there anything else? If he wanted to talk to me for longer, he didn't just launch into it now, he gave some thought to how he was going to put it. I wasn't to misunderstand him. He even permitted interruptions. You want to say something, don't you? he would ask, I can see it in your face. Well, spit it out! I don't want you to be able to say later on that your father never let you get a word in edgeways, and that you had a mute and oppressed childhood.

It wasn't important, I said.

Everything my boy wants to say is important! Come on, out with it! he said.

And what about what I want to say, do I have to spit that out too? asked my sister.

Certainly, said Father, albeit . . . Well, he said, up to a point.

2

The day he moved out with me and Herr Herkenrath arrived to take his place—so that there are no vacancies in the wedded world, he said—I got up early. I couldn't stay in bed any longer. I went into the kitchen and stood around there for a long time. Then my sister turned up.

Are you really moving out? she asked me.

Yes, I said, today!

And when are you coming back? she asked, and I said: Never!

Then we both stood around for a while. After a time we heard Father at his window. He liked looking out at the trees. They were green now. Soon we would leave all that behind, the walls and the floor and the windows. (But also the *smell* of the floor, the *smell* of the window, and the *feel* of the room.) Father's room was even more untidy than it always was. When his door was open, Mother would avert her eyes as she walked past. She couldn't stand the sight of so much disorder.

And yet she once felt so happy here, said Father sadly. Can you remember how happy she used to feel here?

How happy was that? my sister asked.

Very happy, said Father, oh, very happy! How often she would stand here by the window and look out and ...

And?

And feel happy, said Father. Then he rested his forehead against the windowpane and left another mark on it. He had already sorted out a few things for the move and piled them up by the door. Now we had to climb over them, making sure we didn't trip and injure ourselves.

You'll have to pick your feet up, said Father.

As high as this? asked my sister, lifting her foot.

No, he said, even higher!

Of course, we weren't going to take everything with us. Mother, sister and Herr Herkenrath wanted something for themselves too, and so all that was staying here. For days now, Father had been crouched in his corner, wondering: What am I going to take with me into my new life?

I said: I don't know either!

So you don't know either, he said. Then he sat down in a different corner, and asked: What shall I leave here? He was yawning a lot, but he was still giving lessons. Because no school

would employ him without a diploma—without a bit of *bumf,*
he said—he only got to teach those pupils who had failed their
exams. They didn't matter so much. Father lay back in his
rocking chair and waited for pupils. Not many came any more.
Word had got around that he was leaving, only no one knew
when. He had banished us to our room and shut the door, so that
his pupil wouldn't hear our noise and be distracted by it.
We stood by the window in our room and waited for him. Father
stood in his room, waiting as well. He looked by turns at the
street and his watch, and exclaimed: Talk about punctuality! The
books he needed for the lesson were all spread out on his desk.
Some were already open, so that he wouldn't need to look for his
place, but could start straight away, and now the pupil hadn't
turned up. Father kept throwing the window open and leaning
out to see him maybe coming round the corner. But
he simply refused to come round the corner. At other times, it
was Father who forgot about a lesson. Instead of waiting for his
pupil, he went for a quick turn round the block. Then, on his
walk, he would forget all about his lesson. And so there would be
the pupil, having washed his hands at home and all smelling of
lilac soap, sitting in Father's study, waiting. We had let him in
and asked him to sit down. We wanted to keep him company,
and stood beside him. The pupil asked: Is it your father who's
supposed to be giving me lessons? and my sister said: I think so.

Is his English good? asked the pupil, and my sister said: Not
really.

Then how can he teach me if he doesn't know himself? asked
the pupil, and my sister said: I think he needs the money!

Doesn't he have any then? asked the pupil, and my sister said:
Not enough!

When is he finally going to come? asked the pupil, Do you

think he's forgotten? and my sister, who didn't want him to go, said: Perhaps he's on his way now! But the pupil didn't have the patience to wait for Father to return, and left. Of course taking with him the money for the lesson. That lovely money, Father said sadly, and now he's taken it away again! I thought he was coming tomorrow.

Sometimes it was Father who wasn't in the mood, and he wouldn't open the door when a pupil rang or knocked. The pupil would call out: Hello, is nobody home? And then, instead of getting up and opening the door, Father would put his finger to his lips, and we had to be quiet. After a while, we would hear the pupil go back down the stairs and out of the front door. There, now we'll have a bit of peace, said Father contentedly.

Aren't you giving lessons any more? my sister asked.

Not today, Father said, I have more important things on my mind today! or again: I'm too exhausted today!

Often Mother didn't even notice how exhausted Father was, and that he'd been forced to cancel a lesson. She was sitting in her office. Or, of late, with Herr Herkenrath, to ask him about something important. In her room the window was open, to let in the air. Air, she cried, aren't we lucky to have it, especially fresh air! Sometimes we would hear her laugh, and not know what it was about. Father didn't laugh much any more, he tended to shake his head instead.

Will you listen to her! he cried. I think too much, he said. When we asked: What about? he didn't say: About death! which was what he usually said, but: About money! And he lay in his cane rocker and rocked. That gave his heart little jolts, which was beneficial for him. To us he called: Step back, step back! Not so close! He was afraid our little tootsies might get caught under the rocker, and he said: You can lose one of those little toes of yours just like that, and then what? You'll be crippled for life, and I'll have to support you. That was why we had to stand as far back as the wall, to let him *rock to his heart's content.* He wanted us to start learning something useful soon, so that he wouldn't have to go on feeding us for so long, but could finally retire. And what will I be able to do then? he asked.

Then you'll be able to lean right back and let yourself rock to your heart's content.

That's right, he said.

Next door, Mother was laughing again. Each time something struck her as particularly funny, she laughed from her belly, otherwise it was just from her throat. Then Father would say: She's shrieking. She was making fun of him and his plight as a writer. We listened, in case Mother should shriek again, but she didn't. As men, Father said to me, try as we may, we often find ourselves unable to follow the creeping progress of a thought, as it were, through the windings of the female brain.

Instead of going into town with us on our last day together, Father had stretched out once more, inasmuch as it's possible to stretch out on a rocking chair. His good jacket that he had put on for my teachers was all crumpled. He brushed it with his fingertips, and looked sadly at the creases. Then he looked up at the ceiling, which had a couple of cracks in it, and said: Interesting!

What is? asked my sister.

What might be behind those cracks.

Is there something behind them?

Now, if only one knew, said Father. Instead of finally getting on with his packing, he was studying the cracks. In the time we'd been living there, they had grown steadily longer. But who could have guessed they would ever get *that* long! Father shook his head. Then he started going on about the cracks again, about how something should have been *done* about them. And now it was too late. He sighed once more, and then he forgot about the cracks.

He hadn't spoken to Mother for a long time, not *properly* at any rate. But then she hadn't spoken to him either. They avoided each other. When one was in the kitchen, the other wouldn't even go in there, but go back to their room and close the door. When Mother came home from work in the evening, she would sometimes forget that she wasn't supposed to be speaking to Father any more. She would point to a saucepan, and say: This is what I'm cooking for you tonight! Then she would tie on her apron, and start cooking supper. Father was always the last one to come to the table, he wanted to show us that he wasn't *greedy*, and didn't really need anything. His shirtsleeves were rolled up, and he was preoccupied. During supper, he hardly looked up once. Finally, he would say some sentence, I forget what it was. And that would be it. Sometimes he pushed his bowl across to Mother and ask: Does anyone want this? Mother would get such a shock at being addressed by him that she would have to *collect* herself.

Did you just say something to me? she asked. Oh no, she cried, I don't want that, and she pushed the bowl away again. Sometimes she would add: I seem to have lost my appetite!

I sat pressed up against my sister, so that I could feel her warmth and she could feel mine. Whenever Father and Mother spoke for any length of time, we would breathe more easily. Now they're talking again, we would think, but then one of them would merely nod, and the silence would start again. Because Father was given to mockery, he said: We like to economise on air here. If only every household did as we do . . .

Isn't there enough to go round? my sister asked, and Father laughed and said: Once things get to such a pass in a family, it's pretty much all up.

The air too?

The air too.

And the water?

Everything! Father exclaimed impatiently, everything is! After that, he would be silent once more, and *eaten up with things.* Even Mother, who used to be so fond of talking, now said only what seemed essential to her, such as: I won't be in for supper tonight. You'll have to fend for yourselves! or: I'm having all your washing collected tomorrow. I'm not going to do it any more! Sometimes she—or Father—would accidentally say something that she—or he—would straight away regret, because it sounded too conciliatory, something like: Warm weather we're having! or: Really windy out! The other would merely nod in response but not say anything, or at the most: Wasn't it windy yesterday too? And then, unfortunately, the other didn't pursue the subject, but just said: I expect you're right. That's why it was so quiet at home now, you could "hear the mice chattering". If someone, even with good hearing, passed our house, they wouldn't be able to tell if we were in or out, there was no sign of life. My sister sat in the corner, with her dolls in her lap. She could stand the silence least, and kept looking from one to the other. She even looked at me too. Say something, she said, and then, very quietly, Please. She wanted Father and Mother to talk to one another at last, because then she would see that they still loved each other. But they simply wouldn't talk. After they hadn't been talking for a while, my sister lost her temper. She put her dolls down and stood between

14

them. Now, she said, you're to start talking to each other! Or she took Father by the hand, pulled him across to Mother and said: Why don't you reply when Mummy says something to you? She just said something to you!

It must have been very quiet, Father said then.

She did! cried my sister, I heard her! Isn't that right, you said something to Father? she said to Mother.

I'm happy to talk to anyone who'll listen to me, said Mother. If someone wants to listen and give me an answer, then let them. If not, then it's their loss!

Did you hear? my sister said to Father, Now you should answer!

He doesn't have to, said Mother, it's up to him what he does! I don't care!

Well then, said Father, if you don't care, I don't see why I should make the effort!

Of course you shouldn't, said Mother, I'd be the last person to try and force you to talk to me! And then there was silence again. Outside, a moving van drove by, somebody was moving out. And sometimes someone crossed the street, and went into the house next door. We heard the creak of the hinges and then the slam. Then my sister for the last time took Mother's hand and said: Now say something, please! But Mother shook her head and said: There's nothing that remains to be said within these four walls! Everything's been said! And now let go of my hand!

When my sister didn't let go of Mother's hand, Father cried: Let go of her hand this minute! and stamped his foot. At that, my sister did let go. Father was going to say something else, but then he didn't. Outside, the sun climbed higher. The sky was cloudless, at least the bit of it that we could see. Now, as you see, the sun is at its zenith, he said, but never fear, it will come down again!

Both Father and Mother still spoke to us. One day they might speak more to my sister, and the next more to me. Both preferred speaking to us alone, without the other being present. When Father wanted to speak to us and Mother was in the room, he pulled us into his study. It smelled of cigarette smoke there, or cigar when he was flush. Father quietly closed the door behind us. There, he said, now we can talk! To aid the flow of blood to his brain, he massaged his temples. Unfortunately, it doesn't do much good, things are too bad for that. Then he would talk about Thomas Mann a bit. I'm more the man of letters, he said, whereas he's more of the novelist. No, he said, I'm both really! What else, he asked, wasn't there anything else? Oh yes, he said, he had a sweet tooth as well!

When he couldn't think of anything else to say, he let go of our hands and threw open the door.

Have you finished now? asked my sister, and Father said: You're never really finished when you're talking to your loved ones!

But we can go now, can't we?

Yes, go, he said, go to your mother! It makes her jealous when you spend too much time in my room. Don't tell her what I told you.

And what did you tell us? asked my sister.

Keep it to yourselves, he said.

All right, we said, and went off to Mother or out into the garden. The weather was still fine then. Anyone who had eyes in their head and cared to use them couldn't help seeing things flowering and burgeoning. Only my sister didn't see anything. Father wore a white shirt and spotted socks. He had spent a long time looking for them. He said: They're artist's socks! They show me for the cheerful person I am! He stood by the window, softly drumming on the glass with his fingers. Sometimes he scratched at it, and thought about the book he was going to write. The thing I'm working on is going to be another *Magic Mountain,* he said. No, a whole range of *Magic Mountains*! Sometimes he looked at us out in the garden, and nodded to us. He didn't talk to Mother because she didn't talk to him. He didn't want her thinking he couldn't live without her.

Well, asked my sister, and can you?

What a question, said Father, and stood up very straight.

Can you? asked my sister.

I suppose not, he said.

That was in May or June. Because Mother had given up checking, we had given up washing our knees. Sometimes Father came in. He looked down at us for a long time and said: You're letting yourselves go!

Is that bad? my sister asked, and Father said: It's the beginning of the end! The end of one form of existence, behind it, he said, is a different one.

What different one? asked my sister, and Father said: One we don't talk about! It was the season for June bugs, but they were late this year. The world, Father said, is all confused, even the creepy-crawlies don't come when they're supposed to. My sister had been waiting for the June bugs for a long time. She wanted to catch one, and had got Mother to give her a shoebox. She had got a nest ready for them, and now they weren't coming. So I said: Come along! and we went into Father's study without knocking. We wanted to go into town at last. Maybe Father wanted to go too, he just wasn't sure any more. First he rubbed the top of his head and then one of his ribs. He would have liked to leap to his feet, only he couldn't do that kind of thing any more. Instead, he said: For the moment, I'm sitting down! He was coming up to fifty, and was too old for us. Fifty, he said, whoever would have thought it? Just look away for a moment, and you're already an old man.

Are you an old man? asked my sister.

Well, said Father, maybe not quite an old man, but . . .

My sister leaned against the wall. She was impatient to go out. When are we going? she asked, I'm so bored! Then she did the worst thing she could have done: she went to Mother. I was feeling bored myself, so I went off after her.

3

Mother was a beautiful woman, and she worked in the office at Scharschmidt's. Because she brought home a little money that way, it meant Father didn't have to write quite so much. Sadly, she was a little on the plump side. Apparently, it wasn't from overeating, it was something to do with her glands. When we asked after her glands, Father said: She keeps them tucked away somewhere! In the mornings she smelled of lemon soap, and in the evenings of perfume. When my sister wanted a sniff, she would say: Can I have a go! and went in with her nose. Mother would say: Stop that nonsense! and push her away. Often Father didn't have any money in his purse. It was made out of velvet. Then Mother would look in her drawer and find him a bank-note. But seeing as they had now grown apart, she didn't go looking in her drawer any more, she said: I haven't any myself! But that was a lie, she always had some. Sometimes he just needed *an eentsy weentsy one*, but Mother said: I don't even have that! Then Father said: Oh, come to think of it, I don't need one after all. Then, a couple of days later, he forgot he didn't, and asked her again.

Because Herr Herkenrath was coming, Mother was sitting in front of the mirror with her back to us. She didn't turn round to look, she knew it was us. As she was just re-drawing her eyebrows, she needed to concentrate so she didn't make a mistake, and she wasn't able to talk to us for a long time. She didn't really have any eyebrows. She had shaved them off, and needed to draw them in with a pencil every morning. Poor Mother, not having any eyebrows, said my sister when Mother wasn't around, and Father shook his head and said: It's the fashion of our lamentable epoch, to which she has enslaved herself!

And what's that supposed to mean? asked my sister, and Father said: She does everything the way everyone else does!

When Mother made a mistake because of us, she cried: Oh, you make such a nuisance of yourselves! Just look at me! Then she had to wipe away the line, but it couldn't be done. Well, so there you are again, she said as we entered the room.

Yes, said my sister, here we are.

And what are you up to now?

We're not up to anything, said my sister. We're just standing around.

And do you have to do that in my room?

No, said my sister. A minute ago we were standing in Father's room.

And what were you up to there?

Just talking.

About me?

No, said my sister, not about anything! Then she thought for a moment and said: Father won't tell us how old he is.

Did you ask him?

No.

Then ask him, said Mother, ask him!

He still won't tell us.

Mother laughed and said: I'm not surprised. He's a vain character. At least he has his vain side.

What about you? asked my sister. How old are you?

Mother put her eyebrow pencil away. But she wouldn't tell us either. Maybe later, when we were a bit older and wiser. When we asked her a second time: How old are you? she said: It isn't done to ask a lady her age. It's her own sweet secret. She didn't even like to talk to us about our age, as it had implications for her own. Another year older, you poor things, she said, when it was our birthday and we wanted to celebrate. What was there to celebrate? Then she went right up to the mirror to look at all the little wrinkles. She plucked out a little hair. Has your Father remembered he's moving out today?

He's remembered, said my sister.

And does he remember where he's moving to?

I think so!

Did he refer to it?

He did a funny gulp.

When?

When he was drinking coffee.

So he drank coffee?

Yes.

Did he have something to eat with it?

Yes, he did.

A roll?

Three!

Did you get them for him?

He got them himself, very early.

Has he packed?

Not yet.

And why not?

He's still thinking about what to take.

Well, I'd like him to get it over with. Because I don't want him here any more, said Mother. There, she said, and now I'd like to be left in peace for a minute so I can collect my thoughts. Off you go, shoo!

My sister wasn't yet ready to leave Mother in peace. She sat down. Do I have to shoo as well? she asked.

The pair of you!

Then my sister clutched her leg and said: I can't walk!

What can't you do?

It hurts here, said my sister. Ooh, it hurts so much!

What is it now, for goodness sake?

My sister thought for a moment. Then she said: My foot!

Which one?

This one, I think, she said and stretched out her leg.

Mother put down her lipstick and finally looked up. So you're starting that again, she said. Then she told my sister to move her chair up next to hers, but careful not to scratch the parquet. After that, my sister had to lay the foot she claimed was hurting on Mother's lap so that Mother could take her shoe off for her. She had to pull it quite firmly because my sister made no attempt to help. She had to be very careful as she took the shoe off, because otherwise my sister screamed like a stuck pig. In the end, she had to move her foot around a couple of times and wiggle her toes. She wiggled them around for quite a long time.

Does that hurt? asked Mother.

I don't know, said my sister.

Look at me and be truthful. Does it hurt?

Not much.

Then there's nothing the matter with you, said Mother, and you're just malingering.

What's that?

Something very bad, said Mother. Then she put the shoe back on. She was pretty fed up.

Well, we'd best be going then, we said.

Father had his beret on; that way he knew where it was. He was sitting at his desk, but not working. It was just impossible to get him going, that's how unhappy he was.

Are we going to his stupid school now or not? asked my sister.

In a minute, he said, in a minute!

Or maybe he was fifty-five and just didn't admit it. When my sister tugged at his sleeve and said: I want to ask you something, but you have to tell me the truth! he said: Very well. Then she asked: How old are you *really*? and Father said: I'm a certain age, in a manner of speaking. In another sense, I'm already dead.

But you're still walking around!

It only looks that way, said Father. That was all we could get out of him. Now he got to his feet. He would rather have leapt up, but his leaping wasn't too good any more.

Are we going into town now? asked my sister.

What for?

I thought you wanted to say goodbye.

Who to?

To your friends.

I don't need to go into town for that, said Father. Let them come here.

All of them?

All of them, he said. But first of all I must take a look at something. Then he went into the bathroom and stood in front of the mirror, and we followed him. He switched on the wall-light; we were right behind him. Strange, he said, it doesn't even show!

What doesn't? asked my sister.

My age, said Father. There's not a fold or wrinkle to be seen! Isn't that extraordinary! Look, he said, and plucked at the skin on his face. You could look for weeks and not see one, not even with a magnifying glass! Then he turned round in front of the mirror and tried to look at the back of his head. Nor from behind either, he said.

Can you see the back of your head? asked my sister.

Only the devil can see himself from behind, said Father and laughed. Then he switched off the light, and we left the bathroom. Then Father had an idea. It had come to him in front of the mirror, that was where he had some of his best ideas. Once I've made a note of it, I'll just straighten my beret, and we'll be off, he said.

To school?

Where else? he said. It had got a bit warmer in his room, and it was a bit close as well. Father sat down at his desk and cleared himself a space. There, he said, now! Then he took his penknife out of his pocket and sharpened a pencil. Now I can write anything, he said, farewell letters, for example. But then he didn't write a farewell letter, he didn't write anything at all.

Well, said my sister, can't you manage anything?

In a minute, said Father, in a minute! He was sitting on his study chair and had gone quite red. Intellectual effort does that, he said. Then there was a long silence.

You look like you're straining on the john, my sister said suddenly.

What's that?

As if you're pushing.

And then Father even started groaning too, but still nothing came. A car drove down the street. A bird came along and sat down, bouncing on a twig. My sister was indescribably bored. She looked round again. Are you taking all that with you, or will you leave some of it here? she asked.

I'm leaving most of it here, said Father.

Will it go to that stupid man, then?

You'd better ask your Mother. She's the one who'll be distributing it.

Who to?

To you and to him. She's the one who'll be lavishing her gifts on him.

And what will happen to the desk?

I don't know yet.

And the wastepaper basket?

He can have that.

Then where will you throw your waste paper?

I'll buy myself a new one.

Do you have the money for that?

I'll have to earn it.

How?

I'll have to sit down at my desk and write something.

Do you have a desk?

I'll buy myself one.

What about the big trunk? asked my sister, What are you doing with the big trunk?

That's coming with me!

Will you carry it by hand or on your back? my sister asked, Tell me: in your hand or on your back? but Father was once more immersed in himself, and didn't reply. I stood by the window, thinking about the moving van. It was coming this evening, at seven o'clock. Maybe it would still be light, or maybe it would already be dark. Then I thought about our departure, with my satchel on my back. I would walk out of the house with Father, if, that is . . . If Father and Mother really did separate and the moving van really did come and Father really did get into it with me and Mother really went and stood by Herr Herkenrath and said goodbye—or rather, farewell, said Father— and waved, and stayed behind, really stayed behind.

4

We lived, where we'd always lived, on the second floor of 1 Jakobsstrasse. There were wood pigeons there. They sat on our roof and shat on everything. My sister would call to them: Coo coo coo! Come on, little baby pigeons! Father would throw open a window and shout: Begone, monstrous brood! That was on our last day, when we were about to go into town. Father just wanted to smoke a cigarette first. He had put one in his mouth, and wanted to light it, but there wasn't anything. There ought to be a match somewhere, he said, as he looked for one. He referred to his room as *the sweatshop*, and the window was *my peephole into the world.* If someone asked him what his plans were now, he said: I don't have that many any more! He had to walk over to the window a lot to look out. When he drew the curtain, he said: Now the hole's boarded up again!

The other hole that Father had was his imagination. They were trying to board that up as well, but he wasn't going to let them. When a newspaper returned a story of his, he hurriedly put it in an envelope and sent it to a different one. He would have liked to be more productive, he just didn't have the ideas. He said: I'm a martyr to the air-pressure and to my epoch! No, he cried, it's not really mine at all! He used to be skinny and slender, and had wangled his way through the war, now he was wangling his way *through the other thing*. He leaned against the wall, it was more comfortable than standing.

See what happens to your nice jacket when you lean like that? said my sister, and beat it a little.

I know, said Father, beat all the dirt out of it! Beat me while you're at it. I'm afraid I deserve it.

The back as well? she asked.

Wherever seems appropriate, said Father, I won't mind! When my sister had finished, he cried: Was I really that dirty! Well, let that be a lesson to me to take better care of myself! And then he leaned right back against the wall and dirtied his jacket again. In the mornings, when Mother was at the office and Father *quickly wanted to get something down on paper*, he said he always used to write in the mornings as well! and bemoaned the emptiness of his head. He knocked at it, and said: Nothing, nothing, nothing at all! At noon Mother came home, but there was just a little snack. When she was back in the office, Father said: A man needs to unwind from time to time, and he stretched out on his cane rocker. He swore because it had got so tight of late. Sometimes he would hit his head against the wall, or his legs dangled in the air. Often he was angry with *the politics that the wretched* weltgeist *had poured out over us while no one was watching. We were better off without it.* Professionally, he was in a mess, we realized that, by and by. I read somewhere that at my age, you're supposed to be at the height of your powers, he said, and where am I? Up to my neck in the . . .

Papa! cried my sister, You're not supposed to say that word!

I didn't say it, said Father, I just thought it. I hope there's no law against that!

His desk was littered with bits of paper, but he got nowhere. In the time since Mother had made the acquaintance of Herr Herkenrath, Father had started three novels. Instances of sedentary incapacity, he called them, and wondered whether, given the circumstances, he had *any claim to being called a writer at all.* My sister and I stood so close to him, we could feel his warmth. We could feel his fear too, but we could do nothing to help him. It wasn't really a job, he just didn't admit it. For a job, said Mother, it involves too much sitting around! When she asked him if he didn't have anything to do, he sat up straight and cried: Now what's that supposed to mean? Then he pointed to a book that happened to be lying around, and said: Not content with reading that sort of thing, I'm also planning to write it!

When will that be? asked my sister.

Very soon, he said. Well, isn't that something?

But you're not reading it, said my sister. You're just turning the pages.

At the moment, I may be turning the pages, said Father. But at the same time I'm doing something which is incomparably more important. I'm thinking about it!

When my sister then asked: Which bit of it? he shrugged his shoulders and said: Whatever takes my fancy! He had in fact written some stuff sometimes, but it hadn't been printed or else it hadn't *caught on.* I'm going to give it up, he sometimes said. He had *made mistakes* in his life. When we asked him: How many mistakes? he said: I've stopped counting them! and when we asked: And have you stopped making them now? he said: No, I make new ones! For instance, he had spent too long at university, far too long. And in the end, he had even forgotten to take his exams, and now it was too late. All his contemporaries had taken theirs, and had found niches for themselves, only Father hadn't. So, to try and catch up, he had quickly got married to Mother, moved in with her, and then . . . He had no profession. He was a writer, and needed to go for lots of long walks, sometimes with a stick, sometimes without. At home he just got in the way. In the morning he would look at the newspaper and exclaim what a pack of lies. At noon Mother would come back with her shopping bag. Instead of putting her feet up a bit, she had to make something to eat right away.

Father lay back in his cane rocker and rocked, that way he could get a better sense of reality. In fact, he should have known it already, he was certainly old enough. But he still didn't know it, and was surprised at himself. As he rocked, he was given to falling asleep. He would never admit it though; he always said he was thinking. Or that he had been thinking, and needed to recover. Sometimes he was crouched in his *thinking corner*, where there was nothing behind him. Because all unpleasant surprises come at you from behind, he said, that's how you can tell what they are! We had to economize on everything. That's why he ate so little too: so that Mother couldn't turn around one day and say he'd reduced her to *penury*. I'd sooner live on air, he said.

Can people live on air? asked my sister.

I can, said Father. In the course of endless, deeply humiliating years, it's something I would say I've mastered! For two weeks now, he'd stopped coming to table with us at mealtimes, Mother would keep staring at his plate. When she sent us in to fetch him, he said: No thank you, I don't need anything!

But don't you have to eat? asked my sister.

I can manage without, he said, and we went back to Mother. She had the window open as always. She was standing by the stove, tasting. (She pretended she was only stirring.) Well, she asked, when she'd gulped it down, does Sir not want to come to the table? What's his story today?

He's lost his appetite, we said.

Ha, exclaimed Mother, I wish! While she and my sister and I tied on our napkins and started shovelling—tripe and onions or bangers and mash or mince—Father crept off into the remotest corner of his study. He couldn't stand to hear the clink of eating irons, and the smell of food made him ill. He listened as we spooned up the broth and chopped up the meat, and waited impatiently for Mother and my sister and me to be finished and leave the kitchen. We were always in a rush anyway, seeing as Mother had to go back to the office. But that doesn't bother me, I eat like a bird anyway, she said, and ran out of the house. Then there was silence again. God knows what Father was up to, and what was on his mind! Finally, there was the creak of a floorboard in his room. He had stood up and was emerging slowly, very, very slowly from his *philosophical corner*. He was covered with cigarette ash. Because Mother wouldn't give him anything to eat, he was forced to poison himself with tobacco! Slowly he shuffled down the corridor and stuck his head round the door of the kitchen. He needed to be sure it was empty. He took the saucepan with the food in it, and a knife and fork and plate, and settled down at the table. Now he had it all to himself: the chairs, the tablecloth, the whole table and, of course, all the food. Because Mother had loved him once, and had had two children with him (us!), she still cooked for him as well, and left him the best bits. She had wrapped a dishcloth round the saucepan to keep it nice and warm. Father tasted it, and then ate two or three plates full, so he could go on writing and bring money into the house and not collapse. Occasionally he would eat straight from the pot, that way he saved Mother from having to wash up. Sometimes I joined him, sometimes with a book. I was reading *The Treasure on Silver Lake*. *"And where,"* I read aloud, *"is Silver Lake?" "I don't know either. I expect Brinkley won't tell us until he's decided who's going to be in the party. He wouldn't want to give away the secret."*

What's that? said Father, cupping his ear.

He mustn't give away his secret.

I should think not, said Father. He hadn't been paying attention. There was silence in the room, in the house, in the universe. My sister had gone down into the garden to build an orphanage. I moved up close to Father. He was soft and warm. For a long time we didn't talk. What's that, he asked suddenly, did you say something?

No, I said, nothing.

I thought I heard you speak?

No, I said, I was completely quiet.

Father looked at his empty plate. Then he picked up a spoon, and gave it one final scrape. After that he got up and began to clear the table. Now it looked as though Father hadn't eaten anything, as though he'd completely given up eating. But that wasn't the case. Father ate as much as he'd always eaten, perhaps even more, but he did it without us. He was just as fat as always too, he couldn't understand it. How is it possible with all my worries, he would sometimes say, they ought to be gnawing away at me! I suppose they're affecting my heart instead. Then he forgot to clear away his empty plate, and went back to his study. I picked up *Silver Lake*, and went after him, so he wouldn't be so alone. Then we hunkered down there side by side, Father on his cane rocker, me on my stool. From time to time, he shook his head and muttered something. That was about the size of it now. I could hear his breath coming and going, he was given to puffing. Sometimes he had a little tickle in his throat and coughed. That comes from smoking, and it bodes no good, he said to me. That's what Dr Heidenreich had told him, so he'd stopped going to him. I took up my book again. *"In any case,"* I read, *"the matter is fraught with danger!"* *"Why?"* *"Think of the Redskins."* *"But there's only two of them who live there, the grandson and the great-grandson of the man who sketched the map. A couple of bullets will take care of them."* *"If that's all it is,"* he said. Father's eyes were closed, but he wasn't sleeping. If I asked him a question, he said: You ask too many questions! Is this an Inquisition or something? or: Stop quizzing me! Then he would yawn again. If I still wanted to ask him a question, he said: We've had talking already today. Let's try the other thing for a change.

What other thing?

Silence, said Father, and closed his eyes. I hunkered down on my chair, while he reclined on his cane rocker. He was silent. I had *Silver Lake* on my lap, I would browse in it from time to time. We stared into space, each in his own direction. Because it was warm, and he'd had so much to eat, Father was apt to fall asleep. You noticed it from the sudden silence. It extended to the garden too, and way past the edge of our town. I looked at Father. His eyelids had stopped blinking. How could he be so still, it was as if he was already dead! (Of course I didn't say that, I just looked.) His limbs were extended as far as they would go, arms, feet, everything. His neck was fatty and close to me. He didn't have much of a one really. His eyes were tight shut, as if for keeps, and his mouth gaped open. A little dribble of spit had emerged from one corner of it and was running down his chin, slowly, though, very very slowly. What a shame, I thought. Then I panicked and cried: Father, what's the matter? Why won't you talk? I bent down over him and grabbed him by the shoulder. It was thick and soft and seemed swollen. For a long time I shook Father, but he didn't stir. My heart almost stopped. But in the end, Father wasn't dead, he opened his eyes and said: What are you nudging me for? Did you say something? and when I said: No, I didn't say anything! he cried: Then stop shouting like that, you pestilence! Can't you see I'm thinking!

Weren't you sleeping? I asked.

Me and sleep in the middle of the day, cried Father, whoever heard of such a thing? At the most, I might try to draw a little strength for what's in store for me.

What's in store for you?

Father inclined his head and said: Oh, this and that, but nothing pleasant, I'm sure! Don't imagine my day is over! It's only just beginning! Can't you see that my brain is always occupied? Now whatever it was, you've driven it away. Pity, because whatever it was won't come back. If I asked what sort of thing could it have been, he would make a sweeping gesture and say: Something about the totality of the circumstances in which we've been placed, you and I, my poor lad! Or he would say: About what is plummeting towards me with ever-increasing velocity. And when I asked what was plummeting towards him, he would say: Nothing pleasant, so best keep *shtum* and not ask! Then he dozed on into the afternoon, *which was now at hand.*

*

It meant that he didn't sleep well at night. He tossed and turned. Sometimes he got up and went into the kitchen for a glass of water. It had to be ice cold, so he ran the tap until he had woken us all up.

It hadn't been like that earlier, before Herr Herkenrath. Then Father had always slept soundly and not run the tap. When he finished a *little essay* or a story, we would celebrate it for at least one evening. First he drew the curtain to let in the light. Then he blinked and yawned and rubbed his eyes. He had been cloistered in his *sweatshop* for days on end, and written till his fingers were sore. Now he reappeared in our midst, looking thoroughly spiritual. His remaining hair had all been pulled over to one side, so he didn't have to bother to part it. Round his neck was a silk kerchief from his salad days. His feet were in slippers. In spite of that, he looked rather taller than usual. He emerged into the corridor, and called out: Hello, anybody there? Have I been deserted? When we burst out of the nursery, he took hold of us by our arms. Just think, he said, I've finished a piece! Now we'll enjoy ourselves!

What will we have? cried my sister, and Father said: Party time! and hauled us into his room.

He had put away his pencil, now he wanted to *treat* himself. First off, he put *something Egyptian between his teeth*. Once it was lit, he sat down, with his feet apart. My sister and I had to sit down too. Then Mother was summoned. She was in the kitchen or in her room, and cried: Do I have to? She had her hands full, what with trying to hold everything together. Father was terribly courteous to her. He even stood up again, and said: Yes, we have to, I'm sorry! When Mother came in, she had to sit down right away too, whether she liked it or not. Are you sitting comfortably? asked Father. Do you have some support for your back?

I don't need any support for my back, said Mother. I'm not that ancient.

I suppose I'm not either, said Father, and brought her a cushion just the same. He shoved it behind her and she was more comfortable. Then my sister and I had to huddle together on one chair, and pay close attention, because now he was going to tell us something. First of all, he always told us how he'd had to *wrestle* with his new opusculum. Of course, Father would rather have written something else, maybe a bit more like *The Magic Mountain*, but for the time being he couldn't come up with anything of that sort. At any rate, the torment was over for now.

Then what, asked my sister, what will happen next?

That made Father sad. Then, he said, my article will appear in an obscure part of the newspaper, where no one will see it.

Why not? asked my sister, and Father, instead of saying: Because the world is against me, with a sudden burst of insight, said: Because it's not very good!

Oh come, said Mother, who hadn't met Herr Herkenrath yet, and was still talking to Father and needed to comfort him: I'm sure a few people will read it!

Yes, some swine will bury his snotty nose in it for a few seconds to be able to make fun of it, said Father. I know what people are like!

I'm sure a few people will enjoy it, said Mother.

A few, a very few, said Father. Then he got the flashlight out of the kitchen cupboard, and sent my sister and me down to the cellar to get a bottle of champagne, and we all celebrated his article anyway. Mother held her glass aloft and cried: Here's to your next piece! It would be nice if it could be a bit longer!

That was the last thing I'll ever write, said Father gloomily. I'm through with writing! He had had two glasses to drink and was pink as though he'd been running. Then something occurred to him. He clapped his hands and cried: All right, that's enough of that! and he packed me and my sister off to bed.

But it's still light, said my sister, and Father said: No talking back! It'll get dark whether you like it or not!

But we're not tired, we said.

I don't care if you're tired or not, said Father, scram! Then he got to his feet. He was swaying a bit. Once you're in bed, you'll feel tired soon enough. He took Mother by the hand—he hadn't taken her by the hand for weeks now—and dragged her into the bedroom, even though it really was still very light outside. Anyway, we didn't go to bed, but hung around instead. When we had hung around long enough, we went up to the bedroom door, behind which we could hear Father and Mother. We knocked quietly. Father and Mother didn't answer. When we knocked harder, Father cried: Don't bother us! Go away! We want to go to sleep! And shut your bedroom door behind you! Then he groaned and cried: Such pests, these children! Then he got up and turned the key in the lock. Now we'll have a bit of peace, he said, and returned to bed and Mother. It was a little darker outside, but Father and Mother just couldn't get to sleep. Mother in particular kept tossing and turning. Oh, why don't you just forget it, she said! You can see it won't go!

It will, it will, grunted Father obstinately, it's got to!

Maybe it'll work tomorrow morning, said Mother. Sometimes it's like that!

But Father wasn't having it. No, he cried, I'd rather jump out of the window! He kept on trying it. We had lain down in our beds, leaving the door ajar. It was dusk outside. We could hear our parents for a long time yet.

5

Before Father took us to school on the last day, he said: I'll just tidy up quickly!

Oh God, said my sister, that too!

Don't worry, said Father, it'll be quick!

In fact, instead of tidying up, he made an even bigger mess. Mother called out from the kitchen: Careful, he's tidying up!

Father put a book away in the wrong place and said: That's the secret organization that things find for themselves! Sometimes he had his beret on his head, sometimes it was next to him. Sometimes it had *topped itself* and *leapt to the ground*. Father looked at it a long time, and shook his head. Then he pointed at it and said: There! and we had to pick it up.

Are we going then? asked my sister.

I'm still hesitating, he said, for reasons that an intelligent person may readily imagine.

Why?

Because they'll come the moment I turn my back!

Who will?

Those who want to say goodbye, who do you think? he said. They'll all want to wish me well. After all, I haven't lived half my life here for nothing. I'm as famous here as a six-legged dog. Did no one ring?

No.

Did you listen carefully?

I think I did.

I think I did, I think I did, cried Father, that's not good enough! But then again, I suppose you could be right! Maybe they're still on their way here!

Do they know you're getting a divorce?

I'm not getting a divorce. She is.

Then do they know she's getting a divorce, and you're moving out?

News like that gets around, said Father. In the morning, one person knows it, but that's just the beginning. At lunchtime, maybe ten people will know it. By the end of the day, it's the whole town!

You mean the whole town is talking about you and Mother separating?

Of course I do!

And that she's putting you out on the street!

Yes, he said, the whole town! Then he started playing with his beret again. When it was lying on the floor again, and my sister stooped to pick it up, he said: Leave it, if that's where it wants to be! Because he was an author, he always had a pencil to hand, or in his pocket. Sometimes he licked the tip of it. We should have been gone ages ago, but he still wasn't ready. Inwardly, he said, I'm ready, and I can prove it! And suddenly he stood there, booted and spurred. He reached for his walking stick. He had put on his beret so that his bald spot—your darling little patch! Mother had used to call it when she was still in love with him—was invisible. Watch out, he said, off we crawl!

And then?

We'll accomplish whatever remains to be accomplished. Then we'll come back.

And?

Pack, hop into the moving van and never show our faces in these parts again, at least not in this life. But before that . . .

Yes?

. . . spit on our palms, and break a leg, said Father and stood in the doorway. He cupped a hand to his ear and listened.

Why aren't we going now? asked my sister.

Because I think I hear something. There's someone coming up the stairs.

What for?

He'll be wanting to wish me well, said Father. Then we listened some more, for rather a long time.

So why doesn't he press the bell and wish it to you? asked my sister after a while.

Probably because I was mistaken, said Father. I'm afraid that just now there isn't anybody who wants to wish me well. They don't care what becomes of me. Father walked up and down. After sitting—*hunkering down*—he needed to get used to walking again, and he made his boots creak. Outside, the day was changing. It was, above all, brightening. Let's go to school then, he said. Otherwise I'll forget what I still need to accomplish.

What's that?

Something beginning with "g", I made a mental note of it in here, said Father, tapping his brow. Instead of at last getting himself going, he sat down again. The whole world disgusted him, because no one wanted to say goodbye. He hadn't even left, and already he was forgotten. The way his room looked too! My sister started wailing. Are you pulling her hair? cried Father, come on, I want the truth!

I didn't pull anything, I said, she must have pulled it herself.

Scoundrel, said Father, this is no time for that sort of thing! Then he froze. He put his hand to his head and asked: Time for what? He thought. He said: Nothing at all, nothing, nothing! He looked at his watch. It was almost nine o'clock, and the thing was that he'd forgotten where he was supposed to be going with us. School, naturally, but then what? He stood there, the way he always stood, with two fingers pressed against his temple, but he didn't find the answer. Strange, he said, and took off his beret with the mourning ribbon. He fiddled with it a bit.

What are we doing now? asked my sister.

Just a minute, said Father, just a minute. His arms dangled and he stood there looking perplexed. Was it important? He padded quietly across his study. His handkerchief peeped out of his top pocket, the yellow and blue one, the prettiest one he had. He had laced his boots up tightly so they creaked nicely. He held his pipe in his hand for a long time, then jammed it between his teeth. It was already filled, and all it needed was a match. Where could he find a match? Lost, surrounded by empty space, he stood in the middle of the room. He seemed to have got smaller. Strange, he said, wasn't I just about to . . . ? I must have forgotten! It's something to do with my upping sticks and leaving. Well, maybe it'll come to me in a minute! When he saw that it wasn't about to come to him in a minute, he put his pipe in his jacket pocket. Now, son, he said, let's take another gander through the old town! Keep your eyes peeled! Maybe you'll see something you won't want to forget, something to take to Russdorf with you. Then he laboriously bent down and loosened his laces, so that his toes could breathe, specifically the little one on the right. Maybe he was thinking about his life, how it was passing and how it ought to have passed, of the novel he had wanted to write, and, even though he would have earned a lot of money from it, hadn't written, and of his manky teeth. He pulled back his upper lip and said: The third one on the right! Oh yes, the third one on the right! Well, I'm not the only artist who's had trouble with his teeth. One particular colleague even *died* under the dentist!

My sister had already heard all about his tooth, and she wasn't listening. She said: Are we going then?

I was hoping someone might still come to say goodbye and wish me well, said Father.

Are we going or not? asked my sister.

Let's go, he said, and we walked off.

6

When Father felt like talking *on the hoof,* he mostly talked to himself. I would ask him: What did you say? and he would reply: That wasn't meant for your ears, it was for me! Then he would tell himself where he was going, what he happened to be thinking about, what he could see, hear, smell, etcetera, if he happened to be thinking or smelling anything. Now he said: This is your last hurrah in that institution, no one knows what will happen next! and I said: No.

Life, Father said, is a step into the unknown! and I said: I know!

How do you know? asked Father.

You told me so once.

In that case, lead on, he said.

Next came my sister with her dolls. Father said: Quick sticks! and trailed his cane. Everything will be different now, he said, and took it in his other hand. It trailed just as nicely there. Actually he had meant to write something before she put him out, just as Thomas Mann had managed to dash off *something Egyptian* following *The Magic Mountain.* In his head it was almost complete, he said, in his head! But then that Herkenrath ran into her, and I have become distracted, and *my magic mountain* is stuck in an inaccessible corner of my brain. Then again, I'm hardly surprised, it's one of the tricks that existence plays on us . . . He walked along on the cobbled part of the road, not the tarmacked part. It makes for better hopping, he said, skipping from stone to stone. He couldn't always leap, his legs weren't long enough. Now he wanted to get *the last bit of official business* over with, after that it was the turn of *the other thing*. He wanted to try *to talk your Mother round*. When we asked: Talk her round to what? he said: To a conciliatory conversation, which may take a long time! and when my sister asked: How long? he said: Hours,   perhaps   days.   But if it takes several days, then you won't be able to move out today, said my sister. Then you'd still be there tomorrow.

True, said Father, then I'd still be here tomorrow!

You mean you'd still be sitting around tomorrow? asked my sister, and Father replied: Yes, I'd still be sitting around tomorrow!

In any case, he meant to conduct that one *last, deadly, or, to put it no higher, decisive conversation—decisive for her, deadly for me!*—with Mother today. When my sister asked: What are you going to say to her? he said: I don't know yet! and he carried on skipping. A   shoe   was   pinching   him   again,   *not the proverbial one, the left one*, he said. When he had loosened it a bit, the right one started playing up. The fact of the matter was that he didn't *want* to walk, and that's why they pinched him. But I do need to extricate myself from this predicament, he said, it's high time I did! Then he stuck his finger up in the air and said: Do you hear that?

Hear what?

The time passing!

But you can't hear that, can you?

It just so happens that sometimes you can, said Father, especially when you grow older. You need to keep perfectly still,

41

he said, and stopped for a moment. We were as quiet as mice, and listened. Did you hear it? he asked.

I did, said my sister.

What about you, my boy? Father asked me, and to please him, I said: So did I! (In actual fact, it wasn't till much later that I could hear time passing.) Because they gave protection from the morning sun, we walked along under trees. A lot of them were blooming, and some of them smelled as well. Father looked up at the sky, there was always something worth studying up there. Because, as a writer, it was his job to put everything into words, he said: A fine little day!

What? asked my sister, and Father repeated: A fine little day!

Fine I can see, said my sister, but why *little*?

It sets off fine to a tee, said Father, and then we saw Herr Schröder-Jahn in the distance, and he said: Well, here we go!

Herr Schröder-Jahn was in shirtsleeves and gleaming black waistcoat. He was wearing a wide-brimmed hat, which shielded his skull from the sun. He was carrying a packet of candles, meant, said Father, to light him through his old days. Because he was on the other side of the road, he waved to us. In order to save energy in the heat, he used only one finger to do so. He wasn't sure yet whether he would cross the road to us or not. He was wondering if it was worth it. It's up to him, said Father, let him chance it! When Herr Schröder-Jahn did finally come towards us, Father groaned softly. He doesn't have a clue yet, he said, we'll have to break it to him.

And why am I not moving out? asked my sister.

When a family breaks up, the daughter stays with the mother, that's accepted practice, said Father. Now there's no escape! He's coming.

But then Herr Schröder-Jahn wasn't coming after all, he

stopped at the curb. Father waved to him a bit. If the mountain won't go to Mohammed, then the Prophet will just have to cross the street to the idiot on the other side, he said under his breath. Come on, little ones, let's tell him the sorry news, while it's still warm, and he can take it home to his wife. Let's bid him good morning for the last time!

We crossed the street towards Herr Schröder-Jahn, Father leading the way. Because my legs are the longest, at least until you grow up and yours perhaps grow even longer, said my short-legged Father. Morning, he said.

Morning, replied Herr Schröder-Jahn.

Nice weather, said Father, tipping his beret.

Herr Schröder-Jahn did not touch his hat. Then he saw something that shocked him. What's that you've got stuck on your beret, he asked, I can't quite make it out. He pointed at the mourning band.

A conventional reminder of *sic transit,* said Father, tweaking at it.

In the family?

Yes, but distant, distant.

Was it in the paper? Ought I to have known about it?

Only a very few people outside the family circle know, and they're widely scattered.

Are we talking overseas?

Kind of thing.

America?

New Zealand, in fact.

That's a bit of a ways.

It's on the distaff side, said Father. Best not talk about it! Then he scribbled some indecipherable marks on the pavement with his walking stick. Herr Schröder-Jahn followed its movements, and tried to decipher the marks, but couldn't. Then Father drew himself up to his full height, such as it was, and said loud and clear that he had a bit of news for him. I didn't really want to tell anyone, he said. You're the first to hear about it.

Really? said Herr Schröder-Jahn. Then he came a little closer and asked: Is it that you've written something new, or were maybe just planning to?

Father was a little embarrassed, because he had so few ideas. He made no reply. Then he summoned up all his strength, and said: It's the family! Marriage, living together, the household, it's finito. We're getting divorced.

Herr Schröder-Jahn was stunned. He exclaimed: You don't say!

We're leaving tonight, junior and myself, said Father. He drew a line hard across the ground with his stick, and said: Wardrobes empty, shelves bare, everything gone, gone, gone! This one, he said, pointing at me, is coming with me. No, she's staying, he said and pointed to my sister, but it doesn't matter so much in her case, she's much less aware still of what's going on around her. Not that she's unintelligent, quite the opposite. Isn't that right? said Father, and my sister asked: What am I meant to be less aware of? You find us, said Father, on a round of farewell visits, a melancholy task. This one, he said, and pointed to me again, will have to bite down hard and go to school for the last time. He has to be taken off the register by someone with, as it were, parental authority, meaning myself. I have an idea he won't be sorry to leave: his reports have not been the best. Well, the boy tries hard, that's all that can be expected of him. Presumably he too will become an artist in due course, something where brain-power is not the be-all and end-all. We're on our way to collect his papers, so they don't just gather dust!

Herr Schröder-Jahn jabbed his stick into the pavement. But

these are sensational developments, he said. He had parted his legs, as though they had sprouted from the ground in just that position. He was full of questions. What in God's name will become of the little ones? he asked for example, and pointed at us.

They will be rent asunder, said Father, each will go his own way.

And Madame? asked Herr Schröder-Jahn, Didn't I see her only last week?

Perfectly possible!

Then who will take your place at table, to say nothing of the marital bed?

I don't know the gentleman yet, said Father, he's being presented to me this evening.

By her?

In person.

And who, said Herr Schröder-Jahn, meaning to go on with his questioning, but then Father drew a final double line on the pavement with his stick, and said: I won't divulge any more, because the decisive conversation has yet to take place. Perhaps she will reconsider, and stay with the children and me.

When do you expect her decision?

I should say in six or seven hours from now, said Father, looking at his watch. Much will depend on the solicitors we will unleash at one another. That's it, he said, and didn't even offer Herr Schröder-Jahn his hand, maybe it was too sweaty. Then we just left him standing, and simply walked away. Well, now his curiosity has been satisfied for the moment, said Father, we've put so much news his way, it'll take him months to digest it all. And what more can a man ask for? And now, on, he cried, on on!

*

The post office was painted yellow and was usually shut. Then we would stand in front of it and knock on the door and Father would call out: Isn't anyone there? When he had shouted for long enough, he said: Just like Thomas Mann! How often he used to walk to the post office in the Poschinger Strasse, only to find there was no mail for him! I was so sure there was something waiting for me today, I had that twitch in my nose! he said, and we went home again. The next day we tried again, went up to the counter, if it was open, and Father said: Ah, there you are again!

The postman said: I'm always here, doing my job! and Father, not wanting to start an argument, changed the subject and said: Have you got something for me today? Sadly, there often wasn't anything for him. I can see I'll have to start writing letters to myself, to give this fellow something to give me, he said to us, he'd rather hang on to it all himself. Sometimes Father said: Now everything's going to be different! He had entered a competition. Lest the whole town get to hear of his triumph, he entered the number of his postbox. Unfortunately, he didn't win. Sometimes he would get one of his stories returned to him as an "unsolicited manuscript". Then he would take a deep breath and say: Ignoramuses! Bloody fools! Rascals! Oh well, he said, Thomas Mann's first book was rejected five times, before someone took it! So let's not waste words about it, and he stuffed his poor manuscript into his jacket pocket. It peeped out sadly all the way home. When my sister asked: Don't you want to check what's in the envelope? he said: I know what's in it, after all, I put it there myself! He knew the publishers always managed to find fault with his things, and he couldn't stand to read the rejections. Then he would say to the postman: I don't need it today, that thing you were going to give me. Just leave it there. I'll collect it tomorrow.

But for Heaven's sake, why won't you take it? cried the post-man. What am I supposed to do with it? but Father called back: Tomorrow, tomorrow! and was already at the door. Because he felt a profound distaste for any rejected manuscript, he would refuse to go back to the post office for weeks, and his lovely story languished in his postbox all alone, where it even cost him money. Once his story had lain around in the post office for long enough—Father called it *ageing*—he summoned us one day and said: All right, I think it's ready! We're going to collect it today! Then he put on his artist's beret, and we went to get it. We walked very slowly, so we could turn back in case Father had a change of heart. At the post office, he rapped on the floor with his linden stick so that they would know it was us, and would come out and serve us at last. Then he would ask if anything of a more propitious nature hadn't by chance arrived for him. But nothing else had. Sadly, Father stood by the counter and asked: Are you certain?

The postman replied: Certainly, I'm certain! and Father said: It has been known for mistakes to be made!

Not by me!

Then it must have got lost, I can think of no other explanation for it, said Father, and we went home again. Even on our last day, there was nothing for him. When he heard that, Father fell into a temper and shouted: Right, well you can kindly take my name off that box of yours! The postman didn't understand to begin with. Cross me off! Cross me off! cried Father. I'm leaving, I don't need your post any more. Then, before the postman could ask: Where would you like it forwarded to? we were already out on the street, the *Saturday street*, as Father said. Take a look around so you know what you're leaving behind, he said to me, and my sister asked: Shall I take a look around too?

You're staying here, said Father, you're not leaving anything behind!

So we stood on the street and looked about us one last time. Well, so there was the post office! And there it would remain, at least for some time to come. When it was gone, there would be another one, or maybe none at all. It was still painted yellow, that was all that could be said about it. Right, said Father, let's put it behind us! and we went on. When my sister asked whether Mother *really* wanted to get rid of him, and *take the other man*, he said: It certainly looks that way!

They had already divided up the family between them, on a Sunday morning in April. It had all happened very quickly. We were sitting at the breakfast table, each of us had a plate of croissants in front of us. Father had one with ham as well. He had one hand over his heart, to feel whether it was still beating. It was, but only feebly! When we wanted to say something, he called: Ssh, I can't hear it! The sun was already high in the sky, and Father and Mother still hadn't spoken to one another. We sensed they would never speak to each other in the living room, so we sat out on the veranda. Father preferred to talk outside because there was more air, and Mother because she could see people. Admittedly never many, we were only a small town. We sat down as before, pressed tightly together. In the same physical positions, but with different emotions, since the time has now come for speech, said Father. His cup was empty. Mother had made cocoa for us, she had taken rather a long time about it. Now she poured it out. My sister couldn't restrain herself and drank hers immediately. I waited for the skin to form. Father drank his coffee sugarsweet and *male strength*. That way he would die sooner, and find peace. Because a coffee like that, no one would survive long! It's never a tragedy in any case, he said, least of all in mine, and he pushed his cup around on the table. He looked at Mother, as though about to ask her a question. He didn't ask it, it was no longer necessary. Every-thing had been decided, only it hadn't been announced. Father and Mother would separate, and we would go our different ways. I would stay with Father, and my sister with Mother and Herr Herkenrath. When my sister heard that she was to stay with Herkenrath, she started to cry.

I don't want to be with him, she said.

Doesn't matter what you want, I said, you have to!

So that Mother couldn't say he just sat around the whole time, Father stood up and went into a corner. He seemed exactly the same as ever, but he wasn't. He was different inside, and to look at too. His shirt was unbuttoned. He had white hairs on his chest which he had never shown us, and now we saw them anyway. He was past caring. He didn't want to separate from Mother, he just didn't want to admit it.

To show that he was no longer present, inside, he fetched his walking stick. I'm a traveller, with one foot I'm already far away, he said, standing by the door. He swung his stick. But I'll strike back, if I have to. Will you help me strike back? he asked us.

Yes, I replied, and my sister said yes as well.

Good, said Father, very good! and he put the stick back in the corner. Other than that, we didn't do much talking on the day that Mother and Father decided to separate for ever. I had gone into our room and was thinking how it used to be before, on Sundays, after breakfast. When it had been to his liking, Father's trousers would be unbuttoned, at least one button and sometimes two. He had eaten too much, without appetite, he had *forced it down*. Because I'm a man of conscience, I eat con-

49

scientiously, not for pleasure, he said. For me, it's brute necessity that forces a man to dangle his nose over a plate from time to time. It's just to postpone his final collapse.

And then what? asked my sister.

Then there's no more appetite either, said Father. Then they'll give his nose one final wipe and stuff him under the lawn, which will be the place for him.

At mealtimes my sister sat between Mother and me, facing Father. He had his silk kerchief on. Sadly, he'd spattered it with something, he just didn't know it yet. We would have to tell him. My sister was clinging on to Mother's hand, her left, the one that Mother didn't need so much when she was plying her spoon. She had recently met Herr Herkenrath, and got her old spring hat out of the wardrobe. (Father said she'd *dusted it off.*) It had lain there the whole time on the top shelf, surrounded by other ancient gear. Mother had got a little older herself, but not too old. When my sister asked: Too old for what? she replied: For living! and looked provocatively at Father. The hat was already yellow. Mother imagined it would make her appear younger. That's why she was wearing it again. She stood in front of the mirror and said: A pretty hat, ooh yes! And because the weather was fine too, she said: I might as well just keep it on! Then I'll have straw on my head, others just have their heads stuffed full of it! She untucked her remaining curls. Father put his hand to his heart when he saw the curls. He stood next to her, looking a little more shrivelled than usual. Wasn't there something else we had to talk about? he asked.

I believe so, said Mother, sitting upright.

Ah yes, said Father, now I remember! and he sat down too. Then they pulled their chairs a long way apart, and talked about Herr Herkenrath.

7

Even on my last day of school, Father was talking about him, but he didn't say his name. Each time the name should have come, he spat on the ground and then trod on it.

What are you doing that for? asked my sister, Why are you spitting like that? and Father replied: Was I spitting?

Yes, said my sister, and you keep doing it! and Father said: I must have had a bad taste in my mouth! or: There was something I had to get rid of!

Even if he was only thinking about Herr Herkenrath, I knew it right away. He put his hand on his heart, or he wrinkled up his nose. He would happily have murdered him, but that was against the law. And Father didn't even know Herr Herkenrath, who had never *introduced himself* to him. Mother knew Herr Herkenrath better, from Stein the grocer's, where he sometimes bought himself a bottle of beer or a packet of liquorice, which he liked to suck in the office or on his way to work. When they bumped into each other in the shop, Herr Herkenrath was terribly polite to Mother. He said: After you, please! and let her go ahead of him. Then he waited to see what things she bought. When she bought something he knew, he would say: Excellent, a wise purchase! When she was finished shopping, he went up to the counter and bought exactly the same things, but in smaller quantities, because he didn't have a family—so many mouths to feed, Mother said. If she bought a pound of tomatoes, he bought half a pound, if she bought a sack of salt, he bought one too, but in a smaller size. Then they would stand there chatting, over their respective sacks of salt. Mother would tell us all about it later, when she got home. Often she was so late that Father would have lost his appetite, and wouldn't want anything to eat. But then he did anyway. When he had gone back to his desk afterwards, to read the paper, or cross out a few lines, and we were alone in the kitchen with Mother, we asked her: Where were you before supper?

Oh, said Mother, I was chatting to someone.

Man or woman? asked my sister, and Mother replied: With a gentleman I bumped into in the shop.

What, again? asked my sister.

Yes, again!

And what's his name? asked my sister, and Mother said: How am I supposed to know the names of everyone in the shop?

But you were chatting for a jolly long time, said my sister.

Oh God, said Mother, it's easy to get caught up in a conversation, especially if you lead such a boring life in other respects, and you happen to meet someone you like.

So you like him?

We share the same opinions on many subjects, said Mother. She must have said that to Herr Herkenrath the next time they met.

And what makes you think we share the same opinions? asked Herr Herkenrath.

The fact that we both buy tomatoes and salt, said Mother.

Ah, so that's what you mean, said Herr Herkenrath earnestly. Then they were once more standing around together, caught up in their conversation. It seems to me that he talks a little slowly, Mother said once, like most men, but there's a good side to that too. He thinks deeply before he opens his mouth, as opposed to you two.

I think before I open my mouth, said my sister, and I said: But not deeply enough!

Herr Herkenrath was older than Mother, but only by three years. He was much younger than Father, who was already a fossil. He had a brisk gait and an upright carriage. My God, said Mother, when I think of some men!

What men? asked my sister.

Some other men I know, she said.

Sometimes they looked at each other for no reason, first Herr Herkenrath looked at Mother, then Mother looked at Herr Herkenrath. Then they both looked away, preferably into space. They looked at each other covertly too, out of the corners of their eyes. Then each of them hoped the other would say something, but neither of them did. It turned out that they shared the same taste in many things. Once they were even wearing the same shoes, she the ladies' version, he the gents'. Mother was the first to notice.

Look! she exclaimed, and she slid her foot forward.

What is it? he asked.

Our shoes!

Well I never! exclaimed Herr Herkenrath, and he slid his forward too.

Of all the thousands of different shoes there must be in the world, what a coincidence, said Mother, and Herr Herkenrath said: Some things are more than a concidence!

Do you think so? asked Mother.

Since that time, she always wore the shoes when she thought she might run into Herr Herkenrath. She hoped he would be wearing his too.

Is it all right to do that? asked my sister.

What is it I'm not allowed to do now? asked Mother. Who could find it in them to put an end to such a harmless amusement? What else does life have to offer me?

She was now seeing Herr Herkenrath fairly regularly. Maybe she'd seen him before too, but she hadn't taken him in then. Now she was taking him in. When she got home, we would be standing in the doorway, calling: Well? And did you see him?

I bumped into him. By chance, she said.

And what shoes was he wearing?

My ones, of course, she said. By now she was talking to Herr Herkenrath a lot, and Herr Herkenrath was talking to her a lot too.

Is he really interested, seeing as you have such a boring life? asked my sister.

He seems to listen, she said.

Once he confessed to her that he might have liked to be *something artistic* like a painter and decorator. Now Herr Herkenrath was pushing forty, and it was too late. He was an office worker.

Oh, said Mother, an office worker! Well, they can be important too.

Certainly can, said Herr Herkenrath, and he described his office job to her.

Because Mother was so fixated on his voice, she forgot to listen to what he told her, so she was unable to tell us much about his work. They are equally necessary, painters and decorators and office workers, said Herr Herkenrath, and Mother said: Too true! Once she came home in high excitement. She had run into him in his work clothes, a black, buttoned-up office coat. That was what he wore when he processed the files that a one-armed office-boy left on his desk every morning. Each time Herr Herkenrath got to the end of a file, he put a lump of sugar in his mouth and took a sip of coffee from his thermos flask, which he called his *secret weapon*. He was known to take the odd mouthful of beer, but never before lunchtime, he was quite inflexible about that. But he needed something to help him get through life. While Father was in his room reclining on his cane rocker, thinking about his work, Mother was on the kitchen chair, putting us in the picture. She didn't really want us in the picture, but there was no one else around, and she liked hearing the sound of her own voice. There I was just buying some cinnamon for my stewed apples, she said, and I walked smack into him. She was still quite out of breath.

Accidentally or on purpose? asked my sister, and Mother took a deep breath to tell us everything, but then the door opened and in came Father. He had his sleeves rolled up, and was about to ask: Are we not eating today? when he heard the name Herkenrath, and not for the first time either.

Him again, he said.

Father didn't know him personally, and didn't want to. But he could do nothing about the fact that Mother and Herr Herkenrath had bumped into each other, and were growing closer. Now Herr Herkenrath was part of his life, not to be got rid of. He was standing next to him, *a man with great big feet.* So Father now took a deep breath, twisted a hair in his beard, and began to make fun of the man. He began with the name. When he heard it, he raised his eyebrows and said: What did you say the fellow was called?

Herkenrath, I believe, said Mother.

Say that again?

Herkenrath!

Father said: I see! and pretended he had heard it for the first time.

Don't play the fool, said Mother. You know perfectly well what his name is!

I've never heard the name before, as true as I'm standing here, said Father, and sat down. He winked at us. Sometimes he pretended he'd misheard the name, and called him *Heldenrath*.

Oh, exclaimed Mother, you know that's not his name!

She would have preferred to talk about something else, but Father wouldn't let go. Sometimes he would come charging into the kitchen, in a state of high excitement, claiming that Herr Herdenlahm was outside and wanted to see Mother, he missed her so badly. Then he ran out into the corridor and called down: Don't be shy, my dear Herdenlahm, she's expecting you! Or he tore open the window and shouted: Heldenlahm, Heldenlahm, why won't you come up? Straight into the lounge, the wife's waiting! My sister and I ran over to the window and looked down. Of course we didn't see Herr Herkenrath, because he wasn't there. But we too pretended he was standing outside, and shouted: Hello, Herr Herdenlahm! Mummy's waiting! She was sitting on the kitchen stool, shaking her head.

You should be ashamed of yourself, being so tactless in front of the children, she said. What are they going to think of you?

But Father wasn't ashamed of himself. He felt sad. He kept thinking of the many walks that Mother went on with Herr Herkenrath. But instead of being sad and subdued, Father was all boisterous and merry. I believe he answers to Benno, that Herr Heldenglanz, just like a fox terrier I used to know. Clever animal. Though if I'm to believe what I'm told, he's an uncommonly stupid man, he said, when he was alone with the two of us. Mother had gone *round the block*, but would be back soon, because she'd promised to give my sister a goodnight kiss. Benno! exclaimed Father, Isn't that a disgusting name?

Very disgusting, said my sister.

And what do you think? Father asked me. Or do you like it? I wanted to please Father, so I said: Disgusting! too.

To begin with, Mother and Herr Herkenrath used to walk up and down outside Stein the grocer's. She said: He has such a soft jacket! because she sometimes happened to brush against it.

Isn't Father's jacket soft too? asked my sister, and Mother said: Not noticeably! She couldn't stand on the street with him for very long, because otherwise *tongues would start to wag.* So she walked round Stein's with him, which took about ten minutes. Later on, she went with Herr Herkenrath to a park a little further afield, and *took a turn there.* He was wearing his grey double-breasted suit, grey was always becoming. With it he wore his shiny booties, which were allegedly very soft as well, and smelled of shoe-polish. That showed that they were well looked after. His boots scraped across the paving stones. One can hear him miles away, said Father, like an old carthorse! But far be it from me to give an opinion, he said, thank God I don't know the gentleman! and he took notes towards something that *was certain one day to become a novel, and what a novel at that!* He had bought green writing paper specially, because green was the *colour of hope,* and Thomas Mann had used green paper too. For reasons we didn't understand, Father never wrote his book.

Well, that was predictable enough, said Mother, who talked about Father a lot, often to herself. When my sister asked: And why does she talk to herself? Father replied: A woman needs to talk about everything, otherwise she doesn't take it in properly! That was why Mother talked so much about Herr Herkenrath as well. One time, when it was raining, she had to go up to his two-room apartment on the Volkerschlachtstrasse, otherwise she would have got soaked. Herr Herkenrath showed her round everywhere. He was wearing his double-breasted suit, and called the apartment his *digs*. Then he made coffee for Mother, and got milk and sugar out of the cupboard. The milk was unfortunately off, however. He himself didn't drink coffee in the evening. He didn't want to overstrain his heart.

I, said Mother, know a man who has that very problem!

Really, said Herr Herkenrath, and who might that be? but Mother gestured and said: Oh, some distant relation!

Herr Herkenrath was standing in front of the window, to catch the light. He was apprehensive because he thought he was expected to entertain Mother now. She wasn't even listening, however, being too excited herself. Herr Herkenrath had had no success with women, there was something lacking in him. He didn't spark off anything in them.

What sort of thing should you spark off? asked Mother, and Herr Herkenrath replied: Feelings, that sort of thing.

That always takes a while with we women, said Mother. You need to be patient.

For the moment, he had collected many issues of something that he was storing in his low-boy.

Let me show you, he said.

There was a purple curtain in front of the low-boy, which he was going to pull aside. Unfortunately he forgot, Mother told us, and she was going to say something else when Father appeared.

Has supper been cancelled tonight? he asked, and Mother, who had been much kinder to him since meeting Herr Herkenrath, said: It's all in hand! and quickly she produced it: the rough board with the bread, the butter, the sausage, and the hard and soft cheeses. Father rubbed his brow, and then his hands, and said to us: You mustn't keep tormenting Mother about this gentleman whose name I keep forgetting. She barely knows him herself.

Of course I know him, said Mother, why should I deny it? It happens to be the case that in the course of a lifetime one makes a certain number of acquaintances, all of them more or less superficial! and my sister said: That's right, you only saw him once, from a distance.

Be that as it may, it's a wholly innocent acquaintance, of the sort that everyone makes by the score. If you like, she said to Father, I'll invite him round, and that way you can see for yourself how innocent our relationship is!

You mean invite him here, to our apartment? asked Father. Why not?

Father thought about it. Don't invite him on my account, that would only lead to misunderstandings, he said. I'm perfectly capable of picturing him for myself. Besides, I have so much to do at the moment. I couldn't leave my desk, and that would seem rude of me.

Please yourself, said Mother, it was only a suggestion! Just so you see I have nothing to hide from anyone!

I saw something in the paper about one of those so-called innocent relationships, said Father. A man lost a button off his trousers, and a girl who happened to live in the same building, offered to sew it back on for him and had just knelt down in front of him when the man's wife . . .

You should be ashamed of such tastelessness in front of the children, if you're not ashamed in front of me! cried Mother, Ugh, ugh, ugh! Then she leapt up and ran to her room, slamming the door behind her. For three days she wouldn't speak to Father, not a word. She was hardly ever home in the evenings. She was always nicely dressed, much more nicely than before, in case she ran into Herr Herkenrath in the shops or on the street. She put on make-up first thing, to look *fresh and youthful.* Father couldn't fail to notice, and said: That Herrenglanz must be dear to her heart! Certainly he's costing us a packet! Of course, my sister had to run and tell Mother he'd said that. Then Mother said: But it's not his money! I'd rather hack off one of my fingers than spend a single penny piece of your Father's on the little pleasures that are all I have left!

She bought herself nylons and lotions and a new lipstick because the old one *didn't work any more.* Father toyed with his knife and asked: Wonder what she's doing now? Sitting in front of the mirror? Is she smearing that new lipstick all over her face?

Yes, said my sister, on her lips!

I wonder how she does it, said Father, I couldn't if you paid me! Don't you know where the redness in lipstick comes from? What do they teach you at school? It's distilled from the blood of lice, in Paris, that's where they make the stuff!

Mother now spent even longer in front of the mirror, and we stood next to her, and my sister asked: Do you really need all those pencils? And Mother replied: Every self-respecting woman does!

Will I need some too one day? asked my sister, and Mother replied: Yes, but not for a long long time!

She was bored now, both at work and at home. To feel her misery less keenly, she went out even more, saying: Just going round the block!

Are you going by Herr Herkenrath's place?

I'll be back in a jiffy!

Are you just going to check if he's there?

Oh, he won't be there, said Mother. He'll still be at work, earn-ing money, as a man ought to be doing. Then she kissed my sister on the cheek, sometimes on both cheeks. She didn't kiss me much any more. Then she was on her way out, but we heard Father getting up from his rocking chair next door. He wanted to have a talk with Mother at last. What, he probably meant to ask her, is going to become of us? Surely you don't intend to tear the children apart, and abandon me after so many years? But Mother had already shut the door behind her, and left the apartment.

Once Mother had gone, Father and my sister and I stood around for a long time. My sister let her arms hang, while Father clenched his fists. I had gone over to the door, but my arms and hands were no different to how they were usually. Later on, Father unclenched his fists, and we went over to the window. The street was deserted. There were no more birds left in the garden or on the trees. Below us, Mother was just emerging from the house, wearing her spring hat. Not content with going for hour-long promenades with a complete stranger, she even goes and puts her hat on for him! said Father. He stepped back from the window. He didn't want to be seen by her, nor did he want to see her.

Do you think the hat doesn't suit her? asked my sister. Do you think she shouldn't wear one?

Oh, she can do what she likes, he said, and went to his desk. He shuffled a few pieces of paper around. Weeks later, Father was still standing by his desk, shaking his head. Not content with putting a hat on for the gentleman, he said, now she wants to go and marry him!

Marry him! I cried.

Isn't she married already? asked my sister. Is she allowed to do it a second time?

In this world, people can do as they please, so long as they're not caught, said Father. He'd had it up to here with his *Magic Table* and had given up writing in favour of smoking. He sat in front of his ashtray and exclaimed: Ash and debris! My sister had something in her mouth that she was chewing. One day she would choke on it for sure. What are you eating now? asked Father. Well, what is it?

She's not eating anything, I replied. She's only chewing.

Well, what's she chewing?

Paper.

Not again! cried Father and groaned. She's practically got through a whole stationery business, he said. Spit it out, he cried, spit it out! My sister spat it all out, there was masses of it. She had to pick it up, roll it in a piece of newspaper and drop it in the bin. Father said: What a life for the poor creature, away from the vigilant eye of a good mother! But she's got other fish to fry. Oh, what a life it is we lead! Well, can't be helped! Soon be over!

Because we were going to my school, Father adjusted his mourning beret. His fingertips were stained brown.

Let's see, said my sister, and Father said: You've seen them before!

Well, I want to see them again!

Father stopped. There you are, he said, and he let us see them again.

Yuck, said my sister. They stink too!

His scalp was itchy. All goes to show that a man's out of step, he said. Or that he's not living in harmony with the helpmate he's supposed to be living in harmony with. The sun climbed higher. Today we're in for something, he said, I mean in terms of Fahrenheit and Centigrade! His hand trembled ever so slightly as he stroked our cheeks. Once, my sister said to me, as quietly as she could: But Mother's already married!

You can do it twice if you run away from the first, I said.

What first? she asked.

Father, I replied.

8

Then it was summer—and with a vengeance! Father pointed to the sky, and said: Well, what do you say? Summer was coming out of the gardens. There were one or two corners that it hadn't quite reached yet, but it was expected there too. Because of Herr Herkenrath, Father had failed to take in the summer. I have enough things to worry about, he said. And now it was there, just the same. This air, Father said, is summer air, these gardens are summer gardens, these girls are . . .

Summer girls? asked my sister.

I suppose so, he said. They were in thin dresses and short-sleeved blouses. When my sister walked in front of me, I could see her swinging her arms. They were terribly thin, much thinner than my arms. Sometimes Father felt them and exclaimed: She's all skin and bones! And he shook his head. Now we were on our way to my summer school, in fact we could already smell it. Father hadn't smelled any sort of school for years—for centuries, he said—he didn't have to go to one any more. Mother, when we asked about her school, said: Don't bother me with that! My sister didn't know the smell of school *yet*, but she soon would. I knew what a school smelled like, and I wouldn't forget it. Father was now in the lead, and he thought he ought to say something, but he didn't know what. He couldn't come up with any *sentences*, only *words*. Sometimes only single words, like: Well! or: Maybe! or: Maybe not!

We hoped there'd be more to come, but there wasn't more to come. That was at Schimmel's the newsagent's, when we went up to the door. My sister said: Good morning, and Father said: Nice weather we're having!

No nicer than yesterday's, replied Herr Schimmel.

Oh, said Father, much nicer! Then he asked: Would you allow an old customer just to reach into your . . .

Into my till? joked Herr Schimmel.

No, said Father, into your display. If I don't buy it, I promise I'll replace it, good as new.

Oh go on, help yourself then, said Herr Schimmel.

Father walked up to the newspaper display. Then he pulled out today's paper, and slowly leafed through it, reading the headlines and looking at the pictures. When he'd made his hands nice and dirty, he looked reproachfully at Herr Schimmel, and said: Printer's ink! He wiped his hands on his trousers. They need to go in the wash anyway, he said. Then he looked to see if anyone in the area had been murdered of late, that always interested him. Wives doing away with their husbands, or husbands doing away with their wives. Occasionally, someone did away with themselves. But today there wasn't anything like that.

Do you want the paper then, or don't you? asked Herr Schimmel, folding it up again, but much more tidily.

Father shook his head. It's too thick for me today, he said. I don't have the time.

You! exclaimed Herr Schimmel, Since when don't you have the time?

Since I'm moving, replied Father.

Where're you moving to?

64

To the open spaces where men are men. Me and the young fellow here, said Father, pointing at me. He needs his freedom
as well.

And where do you go to find freedom?

Berlin, of course!

Berlin?

Berlin! It's all too small here.

What about the rest of the family? What's going to happen
to them?

They can stay where they lay, said Father, I'm just taking
the boy with me. Now I'm sure you're anxious to hear more,
but I'm not telling you any more. Maybe it'll be in tomorrow's
paper. I just wanted to see if I could find any reference to it
already. But I can see it won't be till tomorrow.

What's happening tomorrow? You moving?

What else? said Father. Then Herr Schimmel saw the mourning ribbon, and that of course gave him a shock. He asked: Is
everything all right with you? and Father said: I can't talk about
it, it's too personal! I know you'll forgive me if I don't say any
more than that. Then he touched his beret, said: Well, that was
all! and we said goodbye and went on our way.

My sister was quite bewildered. Since when are you going to
Berlin? she asked. I thought you were going to Russdorf.

That's true, said Father, maybe I am going to Russdorf. But
I reserve the right to change my destination at any time.

To Berlin?

For instance.

Or to Africa?

Africa too.

But you've never been to Africa.

That's all in the future, said Father, and we moved on. The factories here used to pollute everything and make everybody sick. But that's not an episode I care to dwell on now, said Father softly, and my sister asked: Are you talking to yourself again, or are you talking to us? and Father replied: I'm talking to anyone who's capable of listening and understanding.

And what if there isn't anyone, asked my sister, what if . . . ? Why do you always lock yourself up in your room? she asked later, and Father said: That way I can be sure of remaining in the best society. Then he attacked his beard, as though he'd hidden something in it that he wanted to show us now. Sometimes he found a hair that was longer than all the others, which made it good for tweaking at. After a certain amount of wheezing, he said: Anyway, I have a career! And he took a deep breath, and said: I'm a writer, after all!

Why?

Now that's enough, said Father. Then he crumpled, and said: It's a fatal error, because of course writing isn't a career, but something you put your foot in if you don't know what to do with your life.

Did you put your foot in it?

I did, said Father sadly. Then we went on. As a young man, I crossed the wrong box when I was asked: What would you like to become? he said, and tweaked at a long moustache hair. A lot of them were grey. Since Mother had come to know Herr Herkenrath, and to love him, some were even white. That meant that people could no longer identify him at a distance by his beard. Now they identified him by his voice, which they would always be able to identify him by, or at least for a while yet. He was staring at the ground. That signified: I am about to say something, which might be something truthful, or it might be a joke. When we had waited for long enough, we asked him: Well, what is it you want to say? and he replied: Sentences, more and more sentences! Do you know what is meant by a career? he asked.

No.

A career, Father said, is the leg on which a man limps through his life, with his hands in his pockets. Like this, he said, putting all his weight on one leg. It made him stand crookedly. You stand there, and you support yourself on your career, said Father, who had no career. Then he looked at his watch again. The time, the time! he exclaimed, and looked guiltily at us. You're growing up too quickly, my poor little mites! What's going to become of you?

Oh, said my sister, something or other!

As we walked along side by side on our last day together, our arms brushed against each other. Pardon me, young man, said Father. Then he looked at me and said: It won't be easy, but we'll manage! I'll need to teach you a few things yet, to make a complete little human being of you, in spite of all the unpleasantnesses that are coming towards us. I think I'll get along with you very well when I'm a single man again. Then he looked at the ground and quietly asked: We shall get along together, shan't we? And now, said Father, we are going to your school for a concluding bit of business. But before that, I'm going to dive into my pocket . . .

How can you dive into your pocket? asked my sister, It's much too small.

So I don't feel I haven't . . .

There's no need, I said.

. . . I haven't done enough for you, he said. So that you don't come away from the present turmoil completely empty-handed. Not that you won't anyway: come away empty-handed, I mean, said Father, and smiled at us. Then he reached into his trouser pocket and fished out his last two 50-pfennig pieces, and pressed one of them into each of our hands. A luck-penny, he said, so mind you don't lose it! And don't show your Mother, no need for her to know on what lavish a scale I entertain you!

Then we turned a corner, and there in front of us was the school. School, said Father, is always the ugliest building in the world for the person concerned. He slowed down so that we could let its aspect sink in. They have succeeded in distilling the oppressiveness of a hundred million lessons in that one single sight, you really have to hand it to them. A sight that, furthermore, smells. Or can you not smell it?

My sister wanted to please Father, and said she could smell it. As for me, I had said yes to him so many times, this time I just said: Maybe.

The school was a building all by itself on the edge of town. That was where they meant it to be. There was a bit of grass growing round it, but we had trampled that underfoot. As always when I was approaching school, I had *a feeling*. Because my sister wasn't going to school yet, she didn't have the feeling. Father no longer had the feeling. He said: I've got over it! Later, I wouldn't have it any more either.

Father and my sister and I walked across the schoolyard. Because of all the chestnuts and sycamores around it, it was dark and almost cool. Father said: It's poetic! The corners of it were regularly peed in, you could smell that. There were no electric lights, all the bulbs had been successfully smashed by stones. On the side of it where I'd played football—never, never, never again!—the centre line, penalty boxes and goals were all drawn on the ground with chalk. The school was named after Hindenburg. The windows of the classrooms were open, to let in the air. As a courteous man—*with courtesy you can keep the rabble at a distance*—Father greeted everyone he knew. He knew quite a lot of people. Because he did such a lot of strolling around in his life, the others greeted him back too. Sometimes he made mistakes. He would greet someone familiarly, then afterwards shake his head and say: No, not him! And then the next one was upon us already, and Father said: Yes, but him! and he greeted the man with his upraised walking stick. The day, he claimed, could not be more suitable for a little ramble in the woods and meads, wouldn't you agree? Then he pointed to his mourning ribbon, and was about to fabricate some lie about it, for instance that his brother—he didn't have a brother—had fallen off the roof while feeding the pigeons. But as Father hoped to spare us his more detailed fabrications, he just said: A distant relative! I hope all is as it should be with you!

So far as I know it is, replied the other.

With me too, said Father, except for one small matter that ideally I wouldn't bother you with at all. As of today, he said, and stopped, my wife and I are going our separate ways. If she goes East, I go West. The upshot of it all is that I'm taking sonny-my-lad here to school for the last time. His stint here is at an end. I'm taking him off the register, and moving to Wüstenbrand with him.

To where?

To Wüstenbrand, said Father, where life is cheap and the air is clean, or was it the other way round, I can never remember. Then he explained to the man how to get to Wüstenbrand, in case he ever wanted to visit us there. I've not yet had the pleasure myself, but I've had it described to me. Come and see us once we're established, he said. But I bet you won't!

Oh I will, I will, said the other, I'd love to!

Then we were once more standing around. Suddenly Father pointed to me and said: I'm sending him to school there, so he can spend the last years of his martyrdom in the flatland. He will never see his birthplace again.

Another family breaking up!

But I'm leaving her behind, said Father, pointing to my sister. She's getting a new father, someone by the name of Höllenrath. I can't offer a description of him, I'm afraid, we haven't been introduced as yet. Although the boy claims to have clapped eyes on him, he said, laying his hand on my shoulder. He gave me a shake and said: Tell him you've seen the fellow!

I've seen him, I think, I said.

Don't be shy, said Father. Tell the gentleman what he looks like! and I said: I've forgotten!

I'm not surprised, said Father. Whenever you ask him about something, he can't remember. I wouldn't even have mentioned it, only the fellow is presenting himself to us today, if he remembers, that is. I'm supposed to have seen him too, but I really can't remember. He made no particular impression on me, only on my wife. Now we're all dying to see what he looks like! Then Father drew a circle with his stick, and said: No, I don't know him! and put a line through the circle. He's no stranger to my wife, though, he said, she sometimes visits him in the evening. He's said to live on the Völkerschlachtstrasse, and to draw a regular income, payable monthly. Which of course speaks in his favour. They are supposed to have known each other for some time. Not as long as she and I of course, but even so! I expect the whole town has seen them creeping into each other in all sorts of nooks and crannies, only I never did, because my work keeps me chained to my desk. I'm writing something at the moment, he lied.

What's that?

I can't discuss it yet, but it'll be something very fine. Begins with an "n".

Nonsense verse?

Of course not, said Father, a novel! Did you know about the divorce? he asked.

I'm gobsmacked.

I expect most people will be, said Father, but that's how it is with love. It turns up one night, hits you hard, and sneaks off at the earliest opportunity, leaving no trace of its former self. She even managed to keep him a secret from me for a long time, but today she's letting him loose. Today we may view him and appraise him, so we know what sort of hands she has placed herself in. And now you must excuse us, said Father. No school waits for ever. All right, he said, tipping his beret. See you in the next life, if there is one, and we're both invited, he said pleasantly. All right then, chop chop! He jabbed us merrily in the ribs, and we left the man standing there.

Now why are you moving to Wüstenbrand all of a sudden? asked my sister.

I just hit upon that while I was speaking, said Father. Some of my best ideas come to me like that.

I'm sure, she said, but why *really*?

We'll see soon enough where I finish up, said Father. At the school gates, he greeted a couple more pupils. I hung back, so they wouldn't think I was with him. Now mind you behave your-selves nicely, and always do your homework, and don't blot your copybooks, Father said to them.

Did you know them? asked my sister.

Probably not, said Father, but now they know me, and they'll never forget me! The dishonest ribbon bothered him now, and he took off his beret. Then we stood in front of the school building, taking great gulps of air. That's something you can never get enough of, as long as you're overground, I have to agree with your Mother about that, said Father, and pushed me in to the school. My sister entered willingly. Lessons were still going on. One class kept breaking into song, but the teacher wouldn't let them. He rapped on his desk with his baton, and they had to start all over again. Because I was leaving, I hadn't been to school for three days, I'd hung around at home. I thought that if I did that, then they wouldn't quarrel so much. They quarrelled just the same. This is the last time you're setting foot in your school, Father told me. So take a good look at everything to keep a memory of it, and don't go through life without leaving your mark, like the Hottentot! That's the worst thing you can do: Not leave your mark!

What sort of mark? asked my sister.

Just a mark, it doesn't matter what sort, said Father, and we climbed the school steps. The janitor had waxed them so we'd break a few legs between us. The stench was in every corner. We passed Senior Master Schindler—my sister said: Senile Master—standing outside his classroom not able to go in yet, because some other Senior Master was still occupying it. Herr Schindler had his books under his arm, and was waiting for the bell. Father slipped past him, then he pointed at me with his stick and said: That's my eldest, if I'm correctly informed. Do you remember, he used to be in your class. I imagine you would have remarked on his lack of interest. From now on you've no longer any need to worry about him. I'm taking him abroad, we've booked our passage from Hamburg. Now we're just gazing up at the sky and hoping this weather will hold. Neither of us is terribly keen on a stormy passage.

Is that so? said Herr Schindler. He was lost for words, because Father had so unexpectedly addressed him. Then he saw the mourning ribbon.

A fleeting acquaintance, neither a blood-relative nor an in-law, explained Father. Altogether a bad egg in fact, not worth shedding a single tear over.

Is that so? said Herr Schindler again, then we left him behind.

There's a scintillating conversationalist, said Father.

But you're not going abroad, are you? asked my sister, and Father replied: You never know until you get there!

Herr Schindler watched us till we turned the corner. Father nodded happily. The two of us will have a high old time once we've got through these formalities. A new life, he said, winking at me. His hair was going fast. A bachelor existence, he said, smacking his lips.

And Mother? asked my sister.

Mother, said Father, will have a high old time as well, and eat apple pie every day. Then she won't miss us. And he quickly lit another cigarette, that was all he could think of to do. So he could smoke better, he had put on his beret again. He had pulled it down over one ear, it looked almost cosmopolitan. As if he was a traveller, who had just dropped in on us. He took a couple of puffs and said: Smoking doesn't help either! You feel like disappearing into clouds of smoke, so that reality can't find you the next time it goes looking. And so you smoke like a . . .

Chimney? asked my sister.

Like a fish, said Father. We were now outside the headmaster's study. From time to time a pupil came by, probably wondering who the fat man was who was standing so sadly next to me and smoking. I moved away from Father again.

Let's go in, then it'll all be over and done with, he said, not going in. He didn't feel beautiful enough yet, and adjusted his appearance. Because the way a man feels, after a while becomes the way he looks, he said. I don't know if that's your experience as well?

It is mine, said my sister, and I said: Let's go in!

One shouldn't rush into misfortune, one should calmly sit back and let it approach, he said, like this, and he demonstrated how.

And then?

Wait and see what form it takes this time, said Father. He looked down at his shoes, he could hardly see the tips of them past his belly. As always he put them out every night with the other shoes that Mother had to polish, but she didn't polish them any more. And I, said Father, I have too much on my plate to be doing with polishing shoes! At least I've put on my best shirt, he said. He tugged at the collar, and cried: In celebration of the day, as your Mother always used to say in the days when she still spoke to me. And had baked us a crumb cake, and began to saw it into small, but just portions. But we hardly need to waste words on my shirt, it's plainly visible after all. When going, he said, for the last time, through a region where one has once pitched camp for good, or so one had supposed . . . Would you rather walk on the left or the right of me? he asked.

The left, I said.

Good, well let's keep it like that in future, said Father. Let's go inside then, he said, but made no move. We can do what we like, the moment of farewell is approaching, he said. Half the town will want to beat a path to our door, to shake us by the hand and say how much they will miss us. We will tell them how much we always enjoyed their stupid chatter, and how much . . .

Why don't we *really* go into the headmaster's study? asked my sister, and I asked: Will you tell them the truth, or will you cook up some story again?

What truth do you mean? asked Father.

That you're getting a divorce.

Truth, said Father, is a curious growth. But we find ourselves in a school, where truth is not on the curriculum. At any rate, they will be gobsmacked to hear that you're leaving them.

We went up to the headmaster's door, Father swaying slightly. His walk was curious. First he took a short step, then a long one. It looked like hopscotch. Why are you walking like that? asked my sister.

Like what? he asked.

In that funny way!

Oh, said Father, I don't walk in a funny way! I walk like everybody else walks. Just like everybody else, he said, and he knocked on the door. A woman's voice called: Enter!

9

I didn't say goodbye to the class, I didn't want to interrupt the lesson. I didn't want to see them again anyway, I didn't even want to *smell* them. I heard the familiar voices of Malz and Jässing and Hirschberg. They were reciting something. They were *supposed to be reciting something*, but they hadn't learned it properly. In the headmaster's office, Father stood next to me, my sister stood behind us. He had taken off his beret and held it completely still. He was leaning against the wall, for *structural reasons*, as he always said. He didn't talk much. He didn't even compliment the secretary on her blouse. He really was getting on. He said: We're leaving, the young fellow and I! Then he had them get out my files, and shoved them in his pocket. When we were ready to say goodbye, the secretary wasn't in the office, so we pushed off without saying goodbye. Then the thirty-four steps, I counted them. The whole school would know I was leaving.

On the way back, Father walked in the middle, that was a welcome bit of variety.

You know how it is when you want to speak, and you can't quite think of anything to say? he asked. The expression is: I've got it on the tip of my tongue! but that's not accurate at all! It would be better to say: It's floating around in the room or on the street somewhere. At any rate, it's not a nice condition to find oneself in! At least the cat's been let out of the bag, or wherever else it's been. Let them know, who cares! When the moving van draws up, they'll know anyway!

What are we doing now? she asked.

I have a task to perform.

Anything important?

It could well be important, said Father. Then we walked right out of town, and into the Hoher Hain.

Is it much further? asked my sister, when we were in the Hoher Hain. She didn't like walking with so many dolls. When she was younger, Father used to carry my sister and her dolls, but now she was too heavy. We walked on, sometimes we had grass underfoot, sometimes dirt. The shoes Father had on looked sad. He had given the right one a dab with a cloth, but not the left. If he tried hard, he could still just about reach the right one without having to take it off.

76

And can you not reach the left? asked my sister.

There is an obstruction between me and the left.

What?

Oh, what do you think gets in the way? said Father. A protuberance which has cost me a lot of money.

Is it the thing that you have to hold in to do up your trousers? asked my sister, and Father replied: That could well be! Now we were standing on the Hoher Hain, where the railway tracks were. The path got narrower. On, on! called Father, driving us on with his walking stick. He'd had an idea.

What idea? asked my sister, and he replied: You'll see presently!

Something beginning with an A or a B?

Neither.

Is it something good or something bad?

Something good, said Father. Something to surprise your Mother with.

Ooh yes, said my sister.

Do you think she deserves it? asked Father, and my sister said again: Ooh yes!

Right, said Father, let's give her a surprise then!

What with?

Father stopped. He needed a lot of air when he was climbing. When he finally had enough, he elaborated. I'm thinking, he said, of presenting her with a bouquet of flowers. She's very keen on her flowers. It needn't be expensive. We could just pick them. Then we could put them in her room when she's not looking. Then she'll walk in and see the flowers, and at first she won't believe it. And then she'll have to believe it!

Believe what?

That we're thinking of her and giving her flowers, said Father. What do you reckon to lupins?

But they never keep!

Maybe, maybe not, said Father. Handled with care, they will keep, just like anything else that's handled with care.

They droop and they wither, I said. It's a law of nature, but Father shook his head. There's an exception to every law, he said. I don't believe in laws of nature that set artificial limits to lupins and me, and that try to tell us that we don't keep. If you treat something lovingly, it will keep!

We walked along the railway embankment. The ballast crunched under our feet. Father had taken off his jacket and folded it over his arm, and so he strode through Nature. He left us in a safe place on the siding, far away from the tracks. We had to promise that we wouldn't leave the spot, and would wait for him there. Then our fat Father took his stick and clambered even higher, we could hear him puffing away. Up at the top, he plucked a huge armful of flowers for Mother, at extreme risk to life and limb, as he called down to us. But he returned safely. In his left hand he carried his walking stick, in his right the lupins. He had leapt across the tracks three times, and the train hadn't hit him once. We helped him back onto the path. He held out his flowers for us to smell.

They don't have a smell, said my sister, and they won't keep either!

Thereupon Father pulled my sister right up close to him, looked deeply and shortsightedly into her eyes, and said: This time they will!

Do you mean they won't droop?

Not this time, because we will have faith in them!

It was such a beautiful day, that last day! We hauled the lupins home. We meant to produce them at exactly the right moment, and give them to Mother. Now it was Father's turn to haul

78

them, now my sister's, now mine. If he was lugging them and we happened to run into an acquaintance, he would wave the lupins aloft. Sometimes the other person would wave back. Or else Father would thrust them up in the air, and call out something. Often he just called out: Lupins! I had to carry his jacket, I draped it over my shoulders. Father was sweating a lot. By the time we were back in the Jakobsstrasse, he was panting and begging for a glass of water, a nice tall one! When we first wanted to run the tap a while, he cried: I can't wait that long! and he drank it all in one go. It was quite lukewarm. Then he said: There! and he got into his slippers, as though he would be staying here for ages. Mother was in her room, we could hear her humming. Father went into the kitchen, and got the blue vase. He jammed the lupins into it. Now pay attention, he said, and he put the vase down on our table in the nursery. And he looked hard at the lupins.

Now what? said my sister.

Sit still and keep your eyes open, then you'll see for yourself, said Father, and he paraded up and down in front of the lupins on his short legs. He had clasped his hands behind his back. Then he stopped in front of them. They were already beginning to droop. Watch me now, he said, I'm going to put a spell on them! See how it's done, it may come in handy in later life! Then he waved his hands around a bit, and muttered something. All that's needed is faith, he said, Anyway, you can always try it, it doesn't cost anything! Then he went into his study, as though he wasn't leaving at all. We were on our own again.

And stood around, and pressed our noses against the window onto the garden again. Before long we wouldn't be together any more. My sister would still be here, but where would I be? We told one another we weren't waiting for anything, but in fact we were waiting for Herr Herkenrath, who was getting Mother. When we asked Father: What does he look like? he replied: Like a rhinoceros! A rhinoceros, he explained, is a mammal that . . .

I know, I know! said my sister, and when she asked: And why does he look like a rhinoceros? then Father didn't have an answer, except to say: That's just what you say in a situation like this!

He only knew Herr Herkenrath from what Mother had said about him, and now that was a little time ago, because lately she didn't talk about him at all. When his name came up, she said: Don't know the man! or: Who's that you're talking about? But that was a lie. Of course Mother knew Herr Herkenrath, she just wouldn't let on any more. Father might have nodded to him too on the odd occasion before he realized that he was his *personal nemesis*. Today he would have to hand over his study and Mother to him. When we asked him who would get to keep the furniture, he said: That remains to be discussed! When my sister said she wouldn't mind seeing what Herr Herkenrath looked like, Father said she'd be seeing plenty of him soon enough. Then he thought for a while and said she'd probably seen him already, "a thoroughly repulsive person". My sister couldn't remember, though. Now I was standing at the window next to her, hoping he would turn up. We wondered what he *actually* looked like, whether he was round or square, still with his own hair, or already without. My sister was chewing paper again. She shut her eyes and imagined him to herself. While she was doing that, she pressed herself against me.

Not so close, I said, and shoved her away.

I'm not close at all, she said.

Yes, I said, you are so!

Rubbish, she said, I'm not at all! and she kept coming in closer. Her heart beat a little bit faster than mine. She pressed her nose against the windowpane and said: I'm going to run away! and when I asked: Why? she sometimes replied: Because I hate him so! and sometimes: Just because! When I asked: And where will you run away to? she said: I don't know yet! And what about you, she asked, what will you do?

I'm getting out of here anyway, I said, and then Mother walked in.

She said to my sister: No fuss now please! and pulled the blue summer dress over her head. First she had to put her arms in the sleeves, and then her head went through the neck-hole. It was her prettiest dress. Mother wanted her to look her best for Herr Herkenrath. Then she went away again. When she had gone, my sister spat on the dress. First she spat on the sleeves, then she spat on the front. She wouldn't have minded spitting on the back as well, but she couldn't swivel her head that far round.

When I asked: What are you doing that for? she replied: Just because!

Don't you mean anything by it? I asked, and she said: Yes, I do, but I'm not telling you!

When we had been standing around for long enough, we went in to Mother. We didn't even knock.

Well, said Mother, what is it this time? and my sister said: I've got a question! and Mother said: Go on!

I have to warn you, it's a difficult question, said my sister, and Mother said: Just keep it brief!

Are you going to marry that stupid man? asked my sister, I mean: are you really?

If you're referring to Herr Herkenrath, and if he's agreeable, then yes, I am, said Mother.

Is he agreeable?

It looks like it.

But aren't you married already?

That can be fixed.

And then what will happen to Father?

Don't worry your head about him, said Mother, he's got a lively imagination, I'm sure he'll think of something.

And what if he can't think of anything? asked my sister, but Mother waved her hand impatiently and said: He's bound to think of something, I'm quite convinced of that.

But if he can't, said my sister, what if he really can't?

Because she wanted my sister to make a favourable impression upon Herr Herkenrath, Mother went in the cupboard, and fished out a couple of ribbons for her. She said: I'm getting to be too old for ribbons! and she began tying one in my sister's hair, a blue one. But my sister didn't want the blue one, she wanted the red one instead. So Mother gave her the red one, and my sister asked: Is that for the benefit of the Herdenschwein?

Oi, said Mother, if I catch you saying that again! and my sister said: Sorry, my tongue slipped!

You want to look pretty, don't you? asked Mother.

Yes, but not for the Herkenschlange, said my sister under her breath, and Mother asked: Sorry, what was that?, and my sister said: Oh, nothing! and Mother said: I bet you like the red one!

No, I don't want the red one either, said my sister, and she was going to pull the red one out of her hair as well, but she caught sight of herself in the mirror, and she came over all coy. She pulled it a little this way and that, and she looked at herself for a long time. She thought she looked so beautiful that she couldn't bring herself to pull it off. She kept on looking at herself. Until Mother said: There, that's enough! and we had to go back in our room. My sister made a beeline for the mirror, while I went over to the window. I was thinking about my bicycle. My suitcases weren't packed yet, but they half were. One of them had clothes in it, the other one had school stuff. Because Herr Herkenrath wasn't coming until evening—like a thief he's sneaking into my home under cover of darkness, said Father—we looked up at the sky a lot, and hoped the time was passing. But on that particular day, it didn't pass at all. My God, how life drags on! Father would often exclaim, and look at his two watches. Either we were staring out of the window or into space. Thank God Father walked in. In the course of his tidying up—*scavenging*—he'd come across his green silk neckerchief, and put it on. Now he wanted to show it to us.

How do I look? he asked, and my sister asked: Aren't you packing? and he said: If I don't pack, who will do it for me?

So you are moving out? asked my sister, and he replied: That's up to your Mother!

And he's going too? asked my sister, nodding at me.

That too is up to her, said Father, everything is up to her! He had sat down on a chair, and his expression was thunderous. Because now something else had happened.

Something good or bad or in between? asked my sister, and Father replied: Something bad! He heaved one or two sighs. At first he didn't want to tell us, but then he told us. It's ridiculous, he said, but then, ever since she decided to divorce me, everything that's befallen me has been ridiculous. The latest thing is: I can't remember the reasons for her to stay and not leave me. Isn't that unbelievable? But I know there are reasons, I had them all laid out in my head, one after the other. And now, with the moving van at the gate . . .

But the moving van isn't at the gate at all yet, have a look! cried my sister, and dragged him over to the window. She

83

pointed to the empty street, but Father said: Yes, but it'll come any minute!

And what if it doesn't come?

Oh, said Father, it'll come, it'll come! He got out his handkerchief and mopped his brow. If only Mother would leave him a little more time! Then one or other of his reasons might come back to him. But I can't do it on my own, he said, couldn't you help me? Then he ran through our room and looked at my suitcases. What will happen to all the flotsam and jetsam that no one wants? he cried. I'll chuck it out of the window! Then he wanted to explain something to us, and he elaborated. The situation, he said, in which your parents find themselves . . . The situation Mother has put me in . . . Father looked at the floor, the better to brood over his situation. The hole I have been plunged into . . . The grave, he said. Then he walked around some more. Do you notice anything? he asked me, and when I replied: What do you mean? he said: You see, you don't notice anything at all. You don't notice the day dragging on? Do you know what I called that in one of my books?

No, what?

"Pyrite eternity", he said.

Well, said my sister, and did it sell?

I crossed it out, he said. Then he went into his study, and we were on our own again. We shuddered as we imagined Herr Herkenrath breaking into our apartment. The two or three times we might have seen him, we were standing by the window, just like now. I had only seen him from behind, my sister, she claimed, from the side as well. She was probably fibbing. She probably hadn't seen him at all, just *imagined* him. When I asked her: So what does he look like from the side? she couldn't manage a description at all, and said: Just like an ordinary guy!

And what does an ordinary guy look like?

Like the Herkenschwein.

Then what does his hair look like?

Just ordinary.

You're lying, I said, you've never seen him at all!

The back view of him, standing in the street, wasn't anything much, practically nothing at all. We leaned against the corner of the room, picturing him to ourselves. Then we went into a different corner, and wondered what Mother saw in him. Even if she didn't like Father any more, she still had us! As Herr Herkenrath hadn't spoken to us yet, we wondered what he would say, and how he would express it. We wondered if it would be in short sentences like with Mother, or long ones like Father. Then we wondered whether he would have inky fingers or bite his nails.

You mean like me, don't you? said my sister. Go on, say it, you mean like me?

I looked out of the window. But I couldn't see Herr Herkenrath.

Mother didn't love Father any more, it had just gradually happened like that. You could tell by looking at them both. With Father you could tell from the front, with Mother it was easier from the side. You could see the way she wrinkled up her nose when he asked her for something. One time we were standing in the nursery, but we weren't playing. Father and Mother were standing in the corridor, our door was half-open. Then Mother said it to his face. She didn't say it very loud, but I heard it. I understood it too. If my sister happened to hear it, then she didn't understand it. What did she say? she asked, Tell me what she said? Father, who had understood it, collapsed. He

pulled on his beret and *ran out for a walk.* I expect he
needed to rethink his life. Because he didn't come up with any
answers, he came back and hung his stick and his beret on their
hook. Then he went into his work room, and didn't do any work.
He spread his hands in front of him, now on his knees, now on
the table. He had stretched out his legs, to help the
circulation. Then he reached into his trouser pocket where he
kept his clasp knife, which was good for *more than sharpening
pencils.* He sighed. When he had found it, he took it out. He
checked if it was the same knife as he had put in. Yes, it was
the same! He opened it. It had a narrow blade, and a sharp point.
I'll use it to spear flies with, he said, when I next need any.

Do you need any today? my sister would always ask, and
Father replied: You never know in the morning what you might
need in the evening! Ah me, he sighed, and leaned back. Then he
undid his shirt and put the knife-point against his heart. Instead
of packing, Father was now thinking about death. First he
thought about death in general, and then of the deaths of some
people he had known. Finally, and most reluctantly, he thought
about his own. Yes, there was plenty to think about there, it was
never enough time! Then he heard Mother laughing next door,
first intermittently, then without any interruption. With that
going on, he couldn't think about his death any more. He took
the knife off his chest and began trimming his nails. He dropped
the bits on the floor, and forgot about them. When my sister
found one, she yanked at Father's sleeve. There's something of
yours on the floor, she said, it's disgusting!

Father pushed her hand away, and said: It'll get walked into
the carpet! Then he reached for his pencil, and wrote something
down on a piece of paper. There, he said, putting it down again,
there's one that didn't get away!

Is it going to be part of a larger work this time? asked my sister.

That remains to be seen.

And what time is that man coming?

A man like that? said Father, My guess is he'll come when he comes.

What did you write just now?

Something trivial, which, by virtue of its existence will need to be pampered and made much of, he said. Then we were sitting around again, and the day continued. Or so people say, said Father, even though it's obviously stopped.

Only the birds and the flies moved back and forth.

Are you moving out now? I want to know! asked my sister, and Father said: Move out? Today? Why?

Because Mother's going to divorce you.

Ah, right, he said. Yes, perhaps I am!

Won't you put on a nice jacket then?

If I remember I will.

And nice trousers?

That would be going too far!

And what are you thinking about now? asked my sister, and Father said: About my crooked lifeline, what else? Then he thought some more, and said: And the way it gradually got to be like that!

The line, you mean, asked my sister.

No, said Father, the crookedness.

Oh, that's what you mean!

Then it was almost noon, and I was sitting and thinking. For instance about the things I would leave behind and never see again. For the moment I could still see them. The bed with the pink cover I could see and would leave behind, the wallpaper with the monkey stickers on it I could see and would leave behind, the bedside light, all that I could see, and all that I would leave behind! I nudged my sister to say: I'm not taking the blanket, you can have it if you like! but just then Father walked in again. My God, he said, how the time's running away!

The sun crept through the net curtains. It kept getting hotter. We drew the curtain as well, to keep the sun out. But no one else appeared either. Because everyone had forgotten about us, we sat around on our own. Nobody at all, said Father sadly, and went back into his room. We weren't at all eager to go to Mother, but what else could we do?

Come along, I said, but my sister said: No, I don't want to!

You've got to, I said, and pulled her after me.

Mother was sitting at her dressing-table. Where else would she be sitting? She was asking herself what time Father was finally going. Maybe she was thinking: And what time is the other fellow going to come? She didn't even look up to speak to us. She knew who we were.

Don't you knock when you walk into someone's room? she asked.

We did knock, we said.

I'd hardly call that a knock, said Mother, still not looking at us. We looked round her room. She had her curtains open, the sun was shining in. It made the room seem somehow bigger. My sister said: Five times as big! but that was an exaggeration. Mother had a bottle of perfume in her hand. It was small and round, and it had cost a ton. When I walked up to Mother, she smelled of the perfume.

I'd hardly call that a knock, she repeated, and my sister said: We're back!

And what are you after this time?

Nothing, said my sister, this time we're not after anything!

Pah, said Mother, I know better than that! You're always after something! She had moved out of the bedroom she had shared with Father, and left him all alone in the huge double-bed. At night he rolled around in it, and called out: I'm so cold! Funny that he got so cold in bed, in the middle of summer, and with the cover on! My sister, who was never cold, could hardly believe it. Why don't you take an extra blanket? she asked. Shall I find one for you? but Father said: That won't help either! I'll still be cold!

Mother knew Father was cold, but she didn't feel sorry for him. She didn't feel sorry for anyone, not even us. She pencilled in her eyebrows and said: Everyone makes their own luck in this life! I should have moved out of his bedroom a long time ago, and we wouldn't be having this fuss now. But she hadn't thought of it. She had kept holding her head and asking: Wasn't there something else? but we didn't know either. After she had stopped thinking for a time, it came to her, and she said: Ah, that's right. I'd meant to move out of the bedroom! Now Father and Mother each slept in their own bed in their own room. Each had their own pillow and their own cover. Each had their own window with their own view, and could say: This is my window, my door, my view! Their windows and doors faced different ways. When we asked Mother one time: Why did you move out of Father's bedroom? she replied: The bed wasn't big enough for two grown-ups! Another time she said: Your Father makes too much racket at night! No woman could endure it! or else: I just want to try out the other bed!

Of course, my sister wanted Father and Mother to be sleeping in the same bed again, but Mother shook her head and called:

89

Too noisy, too rackety! He imagines he's a quiet sleeper, but he's wrong about that as well. Now she was sleeping in her room, in her *boudoir*, Father called it. She didn't have a proper bed in there, she slept on the sofa. In the evening she pulled a sheet over it, then the sofa looked like a bed again. In the morning, before leaving home, she drank her coffee in there, and ate a "little crumb so the little machine doesn't break down". Father had slept badly in the half-empty double-bed, and had a little lie-in. He said: Maybe I'll manage to go to sleep again, then maybe my powers will return to me that I need to help me write! Or, even better, I won't wake up at all! We were standing in Mother's room. I was still in my pajamas, my sister in her long nightie. I could sense that Mother was thinking about Herr Herkenrath, my sister couldn't sense anything. I wanted to divert Mother from him, so I asked her: Isn't your sofa hard? but Mother replied: Years of marriage have given me a thick skin. That reminded my sister of Herr Herkenrath. To keep Mother from thinking about him the whole time, she took Mother's hand and laid it across her brow. She asked: Am I cold, or am I hot? and Mother said: Stop that nonsense! and snatched her hand away. Later on, she forgot to close the curtains in her room, and she finished getting dressed. You could see everything from outside. When my sister noticed, she ran to Mother and said: They can see everything from outside!

Oh, said Mother, who would want to see that on such an old woman! and my sister said: But you're not that old at all!

Well, I'm not so sure, said Mother, drawing the curtain. Certainly, it smelled much nicer in her room than in the room where Father now slept so badly. What it smelled of in his room no one quite knew to say, not even him. Sometimes my sister tugged at his sleeve and asked: Tell me what it smells of! Then

Father thought for a moment, and said: It smells of something perfectly ridiculous! Of unhappy human being! Mother's room didn't smell of human being at all, just of perfume.

Father sniffed the air and said: Ah me! Happiness!

When he had gone out again, Mother said: The sad truth of the matter is I can't stand to smell him! and she squirted some more perfume around. Then she thought of her marriage, and of how she'd *slithered* into it. How, she asked herself, could I have fallen for such a man, who treats me so?

How does he treat you? asked my sister, and Mother replied: Quite intolerably! What's he doing now? she asked, and my sister said: Thinking, maybe!

Mother laughed and said: I've heard that one before! Has he done his packing? and my sister said: He's pondering! and Mother said: Well, it's a bit late for that! I don't want his old junk left behind in my apartment!

I'm sure he'll pack when the time comes, said my sister, and Mother said: Well, the time is now, he's just forgotten! He imagines the day will go on for ever. In which he's absolutely mistaken. Most of all at his time of life, when time simply flies. So stop standing around, go in and tell him to pack. But don't tell him I sent you! Pretend it was your idea. And now leave me in peace. I need to get my thoughts straight!

That's just what he says!

That he needs to get his thoughts straight?

That we should leave him in peace, said my sister, and Mother said: Well then, you understand what I want!

So now she had Herr Herkenrath, Father said, "on the side".

On which side? asked my sister. Tell me which one.

Herr Herkenrath's shoes were polished to mirrors, and he

treated Mother better. Unfortunately, he lacked a sense of humour. He has had a difficult life, without much to laugh about, and it's a wonder he's come through it in one piece, Mother said to us. When he passed her in the street, he bowed and greeted her. If he was wearing his green hat, he would whisk it off and wave it in a great arc. But if he was wearing his cap, he just touched his finger to it and added: Caps like this are hard to put back on properly, so if you don't mind, I'll just touch it! They were now meeting quite often, little Herr Herkenrath and rather portly Mother. But I'm seeing to that, she said, and stopped eating chocolate. Admit it, children, there's less of me now, she said, smoothing her hands down over her hips. Generally she was standing in front of the mirror. After work, she hurried home to wash her hands and change her blouse. The new one was freshly laundered, and smelled of soap and perfume. The old one was all sweaty, because Mother had had so much to do, and thought so much about Herr Herkenrath while she was doing it. She never had any time for us.

And when you come back, will you then? asked my sister.

I hardly think so, said Mother. For then, slave that I am, I'll be standing in front of the cooker, and getting your tea for you.

What about tomorrow?

Possibly.

Or would you prefer the day after?

Yes, said Mother, I think I'd prefer the day after. She was changed now, blouse, stockings and hat. She took one more look in the mirror to see if she'd lost weight. She hadn't. She looked at her watch and exclaimed: Lord, how time flies! Then she hummed something to herself, she alone knew what it was! There, she said, that's life! And that's the way it'll always be!

How will it always be? asked my sister, but Mother was already out of the door. We stood at the kitchen window and watched her go. How will life always be? my sister called after her, Tell me!

On our last day, Mother was just the same as ever, only a little bit more agitated. My sister cried a lot. Father was in his room, letting the time go by. Was it really noon already? Did Mother have to think about lunch? My sister leaned in her corner, chewing on something again. Because he had to pack, Father said: I feel a paralysis upon me! Then he strolled through his work room and, wanting to leave it in a good state for Mother's new husband, he straightened a painting, he could be "a martyr to his sense of order". Everything we didn't pack now would have to be left behind. Will you give me a hand? he asked me.

Yes.

Good boy, he said.

Because he had to write so much, he had no time to deal with his room on top of everything else. Mother said: He's turning it into a dump! For instance, the carpet was worn. Father straightened it. So that whoever walks on it after we're gone doesn't break his neck, he said. On second thoughts . . . ? He carried the desk lamp over to the door, so that was coming with him. Probably the cane rocker as well, he said, but how am I going to move it? Then he thought of Herr Herkenrath once more, this time he could even hear him. He was slowly creeping up the stairs, gasping quietly. Then it wasn't him at all, it was . . . Suddenly, Father said: You wait here! and he went into the bathroom to freshen up quickly. As usual when he went to the bathroom, he forgot to shut the door after him. Then Mother would always exclaim: Ee, the monster! and she slammed it shut on him. Even when he was in the bathroom and doing *his little man's doings*, he didn't lock the door, he claimed to have more important things on his mind. Mother didn't believe him for a moment. Nothing in the world, she said, is more important than bolting the door when you go to the toilet. She was terrified she might encounter him sitting on the john, so before going in herself, she always called out: Is there someone in there already? Of course she particularly meant Father. She would only go in if there was a long silence, if not, she ran off shrieking. Then Father would do his low, satisfied belly laugh, and call out: The lady vanishes! In the bathroom, he went up to the mirror and scrutinized himself for a long time. He wasn't laughing then. When he saw himself in the mirror, it tended to make him sad. When we asked him why he looked at himself so much if it only made him sad, he replied: I want to see who I'm up against today!

Don't you know then? asked my sister, and Father replied: Not always!

Now my sister and I were standing outside the bathroom door, listening to Father panting. We hoped he would call us in. But for a long time, he didn't call us, he just stood around. He was looking for the last time at the bathtub and the shower and the towels that Mother always hung up on the wall for each of us. We each had our own towel. Only Father said: Well, that's just the way I am! and used them all indiscriminately. When Mother held her wet towel under his nose and asked: What happened to this then? he furrowed his brow and said: Am I supposed to have done that? Now he wanted to go on the scales. With one hand he propped himself against the bathroom wall, then he clambered up. Even though he always said he weighed half what he used to weigh, he always sent the scales spinning. Father shook his head and said: Such a lot still! Then he remembered his predicament. Children, he called out, this is the last time! Do you want to see me weigh myself? The second we heard his voice, we ran in to him.

Last time for what? asked my sister.

The last time I'm standing on your scales, said Father. You see, there's getting to be less of me all the time! It's not a good sign. Then we had to hold out our hands to him to help him get down. He said: Now then! and he pushed us out of the bathroom and made us shut the door after us so he could finally have his bath. Then we stood around some more. On one side of the corridor there was Father sighing, on the other, Mother was laughing. Then we heard Father running the bath, and doing a bit of splashing. Had he undressed yet, or not? Was he still standing up in the bath, or was he already lying down in it? Suddenly Father started muttering and banging about. He even stamped his foot. So he wasn't in the water, he was still getting ready to go in. No, he cried, I refuse to have a bath for that man! Then we heard Father pull out the plug, and the water rush away. He seemed to be getting back into his clothes, one after the other. I'm so overdressed, he cried, what's it all in aid of? And in summer too, when everything's flowering and burgeoning away! Then he probably tossed his scarf round his neck, and he came out of the bathroom.

We're striking camp, he cried, chop chop!

And what's that supposed to mean? asked my sister.

We're packing, said Father, but before that, I just quickly have to . . .

By now, the summer had spread itself evenly over the Jakobsstrasse, the Steingasse, the Finkenweg, the Königsstrasse, the Herderplatz and the rest of them. Father said: Everything is so early this year, and it'll all be dead so quickly! There weren't many people on the streets. A lot were wearing hats, to protect themselves from the sun. A few had already suffered at the hands of the summer, they had sunstroke.

Watch them go, said Father, creeping along!

What now? asked my sister.

We were still sitting around. Father hadn't had a bath. But I feel cleaner anyway just from thinking about it, he said. He went up to his desk. He had laid his pencil down on it, on the front left edge of it. But now that he had thought of a sentence—*and such a sentence too*—it wasn't there any more. He wasn't surprised. Nothing surprised him any more, his room looked in a terrible state, even worse than it had that morning. Even though Father had aimed to be ready long ago, *for this voyage to distant shores.* The bookshelves were a long way from being cleared, though they did at least show a few gaps here and there. Father pointed to them, and said: Can you see the wall peeking out? Then he knocked against it, it made a hollow, empty sound. It might take me years to find another wall I can spread out my things in front of! If I ever do, he added.

I stood by the window with my sister. Look! I said, and pointed to Malz, who was just walking past. He had his satchel on his back, school was finished. My sister had seen Malz lots of times, she just said: So what? Malz walked past quietly, without bothering to look up at us. There was some crumbled putty on the floor of the nursery, just where my sister was standing. It came from the window frame that she was forever picking at. When I asked her: What do you do that for? she replied: How do I know! and when I asked: Are you going to go on doing it? she said: I expect so! I thought about the walk to school, my fort and Father's bookshelves. Then I thought of everything together: the fort, the walk, the shelves. When we were gone, Mother would clear them, and scrub them with soapy water. To disinfect them, she would say. They would smell of it for days. We would be long gone, Father and I. Another man would be in the apartment, in Father's place. To begin with, he would stand around all perplexed in Father's study, sniffing and staring at everything. He too would have slippers on, to reduce the wear on the carpet. He would go and lean in one corner, and then another, and see which he preferred. Then he would *get a grip*, and spread himself out. His intrusive stare would pollute every nook and cranny of Father's study. Then he would go up to the books Father hadn't been able to rescue, and breathe all over them. And he would breathe on the wall and the light-switch and the windowsill. The neighbours, having heard nothing about Herr Herkenrath, would be surprised at the new face that was hanging out of Father's window. They would rush home and tell each other all about the shape of Herr Herkenrath's nose, what a funny name he had, where he'd lived previously, and how he earned his crust. (In Father's case, no one had ever understood how he earned his crust.) In time, they would get used to his face. If he happened to own a book or two, he would put them out on Father's shelves and drive out Father's books. From time to time he might even look at one of them. Mother would organise them for him, and put them in order of size, if Herr Herkenrath permitted. Father hadn't, which was why his room looked the way it did.

Because he wouldn't be able to look out of the window for much longer—Herr Herkenrath would be looking out of it instead—Father had dragged his cane rocker over to the light. That way he could better inspect *the slice of the world that had been served to him for those particular years.* He pointed and said: I used to live here! Then he corrected himself and said: I shall have lived here! Collapsed in himself, with his mighty belly, his hands on his knees, he squatted down, *as if on the thunderbox,* and invigilated the Jakobsstrasse for the last time. But there was no one coming. Everyone knew we were leaving, word had got round. When a truck lost its way and ended up in our street, and didn't know where to go, Father went into our room and called: Children, look, quickly! We raced to his window and looked out. The truck was wheezing and creaking and trying to turn around, but the street was too narrow. Well, said Father proudly, what do you say to that? I stood there, not saying anything, I couldn't think of anything to say. Even my sister didn't say anything for a long time. When she said: It's just a truck, isn't it? Father replied: Yes, but even so! and he pointed to the exhaust fumes it was belching out. Then we noticed his finger, which we'd forgotten about.

Let's see, said my sister, and Father said: See what?

Your finger!

What for?

I want to see the tip of it!

Father groaned and exclaimed: Not again! Then he said: Well, all right! and he held out his right middle finger. There you are, he said.

Not that one, silly, said my sister, the other one!

But the other one doesn't have a tip.

Exactly.

On his last day, before he turned to packing, Father showed us quite a few other things besides. He showed us an old report-card he'd found while packing, which proved that he hadn't been as good a pupil as he'd always claimed to be. Strange, he said. He showed us a rubber hot-water bottle which he immediately packed, *in case I catch cold*, a pile of greaseproof paper for wrapping sandwiches in, and his old hairnet. That, he said, I had better throw away, it won't be any great loss! Then he groaned again, and said: Well, all right! and he showed us his *actual* finger. I'm taking it with me, he said, maybe someone in Russdorf will want to see it. We pulled the finger closer, and studied it for a long time. Then Father took it away again, and stuck it in his *trouser-pouch*. Now, where were we? he asked.

About the truck.

Ah, said Father, and began to ponder again. When Thomas Mann was researching one of his books, he once took a ride on a truck . . . and my sister said: You've told us that before!

Well, let's skip that then, said Father. A truck reversing like that, he said, creates a huge impression. You want to open your eyes and ears to that, oh yes!

Don't you get to see many lorries then? asked my sister.

Not while I'm sitting at my desk, cudgelling my brains over a word, much less an entire sentence, said Father. And then I have to busy myself with things that are even more recalcitrant, because they don't exist.

Then why do you busy yourself with them?

That's what I build my life around: things that don't exist, he said. Then I'm happy if something like a truck comes along from time to time, and makes a bit of a stink. At least it's real! Apart from the truck, there was nothing to be seen from his window on our last day. No one wanted to see Father. Only if someone loses his way and has to reverse out, he said, and that's an unexpected bonus.

Because Father and Mother argued so much, the window was

hardly opened any more, so that people outside wouldn't be able to hear the argument. Mother hadn't washed the curtains for ages, she just didn't care any more. I'm fed up with scrubbing your curtains and your tablecloths and your underpants the minute I get back from the office, and ruining my fingernails, she said, fourteen years of slavery is enough! Then she held out her hands, so we could look at her nails. The poor nails! Only because, instead of following some regular occupation, Father wanted to sit at home and write the whole time! So Mother couldn't afford any help, and had to do everything herself. But that was about to change now! No wonder she was humming to herself!

Can you hear her humming? said Father, cupping a hand to his ear.

Of course I can, said my sister, but why is she humming?

She's imagining what her life will be like with Herr Herkenrath, and that, mistakenly, is making her happy. But then again, said Father, if it all goes well . . .

What if it all goes well?

Then she can wash his socks, beginning Monday.

And his underpants? asked my sister.

Them as well, said Father, and laughed. He was being very malicious. And all the plates and spoons and coffeepots that we had always used, and that Mother would now use with Herr Herkenrath, I thought. But enough of that, said Father, I need to think! There, have another look out of the window, soon we won't be able to do that any more!

10

Then it was later, and I went into town without my sister. Her breathing got on my nerves. Father's head was full of the move, and he was pushing it back and forth. Sometimes he tapped his brow, and said: Here it is, exactly here! He wanted to take leave of his work room, where he had sat so many times and not worked, and alone. My sister was in our room, and didn't know what was going on. She could see and hear and smell everything, but she couldn't understand it. What's going on? she asked, Will you tell me what's going on? Then she chewed some more paper. Sometimes she forgot that they were going to *rip us apart,* and she behaved the same as always. She even hummed. Then she remembered, and she said: Oh, of course! When I said: I'm just going out for a bit! she said: I'll come along too! and when I said: No, I've got something I want to do, *alone!* she said: You're not allowed to do that!

Since when am I not allowed to do that! I said, and she said: Because I'll tell Father!

I said: He knows anyway! and she said: Then I'll tell Mother! She doesn't know yet!

So I just took the key off the hook and said: Well, I'm going! and before she could say another thing, I was gone.

It was half past eleven, warm air, sunshine, birds yelling, not a cloud anywhere. I was tired because I hadn't slept, I think, for the past three nights. I'd crept into my pajamas at night as usual, got into bed, turned out the light, pulled the covers up over my face, closed my eyes and so on and so forth. But then I'd done something I really shouldn't have done for anything in the world: I'd started thinking. I'd stared at the ceiling and thought. In the course of the next few hours, the ceiling had been light, then dark, then light again, and all that put together added up to a night. The more I'd thought, the less I'd been able to sleep, only no one would have believed me. If I'd gone in to Mother in the morning, and asked her: What shall I do? I can't sleep any more! she would just have laughed. She would have looked in her mirror and said: You, not sleep? A squirt like you says that to a woman who has real difficulty sleeping? You're a child, she would have said, and a child just needs to close its eyes in order to go to sleep. So close your eyes and go to sleep! Or she would have said: Oh dear, you as well? and she would have rushed off to Herr Herkenrath, and asked him if *he* could sleep. And if I'd gone to Father and told him I couldn't sleep, he would have looked at me sorrowfully, and said: It's the worries that come and perch on the side of our beds that get in the way of our sleeping! But I don't have any worries, I'd have said, I just can't sleep! and Father would have shaken his head and said: Oh yes, you have worries, you just don't know it, because they've settled in one particular spot at the back of your head where you can't see them. If I'd gone on to ask: Are they really at the back of your head? he would have said: With me they are! Then he'd have called out: Well, enough of that! and: It's worry, and there's an end! All right, I would have said, and then I would have gone to my sister. If I'd told her I couldn't sleep, she would have pulled out whichever her favourite doll was at the moment, and said: Look, she's only got one eye! I would have asked her: What are you telling me that for? and she would have replied: Because she can't sleep, just like you! Then she would have held her doll up to my mouth and said: You've got to give her a kiss! and I would have asked: Why should I? and she would have said: Because she's only got one eye! When I'd given her a kiss, and said: That's not the point! The point is that I can't sleep! she would have cried, and shouted: But I can't sleep either! The best thing is not to mention it to her at all. The best thing is not to mention it to anyone, I thought, and I went off into town.

Ever since I'd known they were separating, and that I was staying with Father, I'd been thinking things over. I asked myself what would happen next. Because something always has to come along next, because life can't just be full of holes like a Swiss cheese, as Father sometimes said. So I stood there, thinking who I should say goodbye to. I could think of dozens of people, but I didn't feel like saying goodbye to all of them. In fact, I didn't feel like saying goodbye to a single one of them. It's not worth it, I thought, goodbyes are just embarrassing. Anyway, it was nobody's business that I was clearing out. But even so, I thought about what I would say to them. Or should I surprise them all by just not showing up one day? I stood there with my hands in my pockets, and imagined half my class standing in front of our house, calling for me. I wouldn't be there any more, I would already be on the way to Russdorf. Wherever I had been so far, there was now a hole, and the biggest hole was at home. Only Mother and my sister and Herr Herkenrath would be there now. They would be standing at the window, looking down, and shouting that I wasn't around any more. My class would be standing down there, shouting: And when's he coming back? and Mother and Herr Herkenrath and my sister would answer that I wasn't coming back, that I was gone for good. My class, especially Rösler and Malz, would look up and ask: For good? and Herr Herkenrath would nod and call down: Yes, for good! Then my class would call out: That's a pity! but no one would miss me, everyone would just be thinking of themselves. Well, they could all look out for themselves too, none of them needed me to be thinking about them. If I said they'd never see me again, they would all shout: Really? Never again? especially Malz.

Yes, I would reply, toying with my key: Never again!

Why not?

Because I'm clearing off, I would say. And I would take a deep breath, and shake them all by the hand, one after the other. My own hand would be clammy. I would walk back with them as far as Hilser's corner, and then they would walk me back to the house, then I would walk them back to Hilser's corner, and they would walk me back to the house again. No one would want it to end, no one was brave enough to face it alone. Finally, we would go our separate ways. And I wanted to spare myself all that, especially the shaking hands bit. That's why I preferred not to be home when they called. I wanted to leave it up to them whether they remembered me or not. I didn't want to remember any of them. That's why I resolved not to see any of them, ring their bells, or shout up to them that I was leaving— all except Hutsche. I simply wouldn't be sitting on my bench any more, wouldn't unpack my satchel, wouldn't sharpen my pencil before the lesson, and so on and so forth. I simply wouldn't be there any more, I would be . . . I saw a man coming up to me.

The man, was his name Meier—how can you be expected to know the names of everyone?—was old and frail. He wanted to stretch his legs, and he'd gone for a potter around the block. He was a bit shrivelled up, his legs, his head, the lot. His wife had already gone on, he was waiting for it to be his turn. His children had moved away, the dog he used to own that I knew quite well hadn't been able to stand it any more, and had taken itself off and drowned in the Big Pond. My source for this was Mother, who'd told us all about him. The man was bald, and he asked himself every morning why he was still alive. He had no idea. But he wasn't able to die either, maybe he didn't want to badly enough. Instead he went for walks. He still had his vanity, though. For instance, he didn't want you to see the full extent of his baldness. He had grown his remaining seven hairs really long, to make the most of them: he had trained them from one ear to the other. I had more hair in one nostril than he did on the whole of his head. When he reached me, he stopped, and he wanted me to stop as well. So he knocked his stick into the ground and called: Whoah, sonny! He'd forgotten my name, or never known it.

Hello, sonny, he called, and as I still didn't respond, he said: You're so-and-so, aren't you, and you live at such-and-such in such-and-such street.

Could be.

And isn't your father, he said, such-and-such?

Could be.

Who, he said, doesn't have a job, but just runs around with a notebook, collecting bons mots?

At present, I said, that's all he does.

Did he used to have something regular then?

Yes, I said, off and on.

Well, said Herr Meier, let's leave that! What I wanted to ask you, he said, and acted as though he'd been having a long conversation that had got sidetracked, and he was now picking up the thread of it again, you're going on your travels soon, aren't you?

Not really, I said, just going around the block.

Herr Meier stopped. He thought awhile, and concluded I'd misunderstood him. No, that's not what I meant, son, he said. I mean the thing ahead of you. He paused again. Or are you not leaving the area, you and your father? he asked.

I shook my head. No one's leaving the area, I said. And actually at that moment, I couldn't imagine I would ever leave.

Now why not? asked Herr Meier sternly. He was getting quite agitated.

Why should I leave?

Well, aren't your parents getting separated?

Not a bit of it.

Why not?

Why should they?

Because they're not happy together.

But of course they're happy together, I said. You should see them!

Curious, said Herr Meier. He didn't get it. Hasn't your mother got a close friend who's keen to move in with her?

But how could he? I said. Father and I are there.

So you're not moving away at all? asked Herr Meier.

Absolutely not, I said. And Mother and my sister aren't either. We're all staying put. For ever and ever.

Really?

Yes, for ever and ever!

So where is he now, your father?

At home.

So he's not apartment-hunting in Russdorf, because your mother's throwing him out?

Not at all, I said. He's in the kitchen.

The kitchen? said Herr Meier. And what's he doing there?

Frying himself a green herring.

Why's he doing that?

Because he likes them. He hasn't had breakfast yet.

Curious, said Herr Meier. I was convinced your parents had grown apart.

Why should they?

These things happen.

Oh, there's so much talk, I said. The fact is they're married to each other, I said, for ever and ever. Even when they're dead, they'll be together. They've bought themselves a plot in the cemetery, and that's where they'll both end up, first one, then the other. That's how it is! Now I've got to dash, goodbye, I said, and I left Herr Meier standing there with his funny bit of hair and his walking stick—in those days all our old people used to go around with sticks.

Hey sonny! Herr Meier shouted after me, he still wanted to hear more, but I ran on. And where was I running to on my last day? To my favourite teacher, Friedrich Wilhelm Förster, who else? I had had him for three years, and now I wouldn't have him any more. I think he liked me. He often put his hand on my shoulder and said: You're not as thick as you look, standing around like that. Can't you take your hands out of your pockets while I'm talking to you?

Sure.

Then why don't you take them out?

Sometimes I don't think of it.

Well, said Herr Förster, you need to think, at least once in a while!

In his class, I had to sit in the front row, to make sure I paid attention. I was allowed to get the chalk and gather up the exercise books when we wrote essays, because I could be trusted not to drop them. When he asked a question, I never put my hand up, and if he asked me anyway, I always had some kind of answer. Then Herr Förster would shake his head and say: Ask that boy anything you like, and he's always got an answer, even if it's never the right one! If there was time left over before the bell, he told us stories. To make us listen more, he said they had *happened to him*, but he was lying, because they often involved witches and warlocks that you don't have in real life. We still acted as though we believed him. I knew where he lived, and often used to go by his house. I hoped he'd be standing in the garden or by the window, and call out something to me, like: Ah, there he is, our little beacon! or: Did you know I always thought you were an outstanding pupil? I wish there were more like you! Unfortunately, Herr Förster was never standing by the window, and never called out to me. He preferred being round the back of his house. He was an *incorrigible rose breeder* and said: My house may be just a rickety little box, but at least the roses prop it up! Now I was on my way to see him. So that he wouldn't have to ask any questions, I thought I'd call out from the doorway that I was just packing up to leave. Then I would thank him for having taught me. I wanted to tell him how much I'd learned in his class—*profited* from it, Mother said—and that I would always remember him. Then I would take a deep breath, look him in the eye and say: You are the best teacher I've ever had! Then he would always remember me. Only I didn't want to tell him so in school where there were hundreds and thousands of other people standing round, listening to every word, but at his house, just the two of us, now. He lived in the Fichtenstrasse in a little house of the kind that childless schoolteachers with dogs and cats and piles of exercise books might be expected to live in. Herr Förster didn't have a dog, but he had a cat. We were very fond of it. We had wanted to tie a tin can to her tail one evening, but she didn't want us to. I knew the cat very well, but would shortly forget her. Then I would no longer know what she looked like when I wanted to think about her and picture her to myself. But that's always how it is with cats that you know.

I didn't ring, I preferred to knock, that was less disruptive. Somebody shuffled up to the door. It was Herr Förster's wife. She seemed even older than Herr Förster, maybe as much as twenty years older. She had her apron on. I took a step back so she could see I wasn't a robber. Even so, she didn't know who I was. I explained I was in Herr Förster's class. I didn't tell her what a fantastic teacher he was, she probably knew it already. I was sure I had come at some inconvenient time for her and her husband, probably in the middle of lunch. Three times she said: Yes, well? before it occurred to her to let me in. I didn't want to tell her it was my last day. In the end I did anyway. That's why I want to say goodbye to Herr Förster, because he was my German teacher, I said. I could have said: My favourite teacher! but that was none of her beeswax. Maybe I would say it to Herr Förster's face. I was rather sorry I'd knocked. I should have stayed at home, but Father and Mother would be quarrelling or not talking to each other. Maybe Herr Herkenrath would have arrived already, and would be making himself comfortable in Mother's best chair. Maybe he had taken off his jacket and rolled up his shirtsleeves, so everyone would see the hairs on his arms, if he had any. It would smell of him everywhere. So I couldn't go home, but nor could I go into town, because then everyone would ask me why I hadn't been to school. The only place I could still have gone to was the Hoher Hain. Tomorrow Herr Herkenrath and Mother would take over the Hoher Hain as well. All the places where Mother had been with Father and my sister and me, she would now go

to with Herr Herkenrath. There was nowhere left for me to go.
Then along came Herr Förster. He had a sticking plaster on
his cheek and was clean-shaven. He was in his shirtsleeves and
he saw right away that it was only me. He had got up from his
lunch, and had a napkin in his hand. He swiped his thigh with it
from time to time. On his ring finger he had a fat wedding ring
that he sometimes showed us. He would always explain the story
behind it. In Africa, he said, do you know what Africa is? Yes, we
cried out, a country! Not so, said Herr Förster, it's a
continent. In that continent, he said, the slaves . . . Do you know
what slaves are? Yes, we cried out, the negroes! Not so, said Herr
Förster, the blacks! In Africa, he said, they wear their rings
through their noses. We here wear them on our right hand. And
then, to check whether we'd understood, he asked us: Where do
the slaves in Africa wear their rings? and we cried out: Through
their noses! And where, he asked, do slaves here wear their rings?
and we cried out: On their right hands! Correct, said Herr
Forster. And the lesson carried on. I had interrupted not just his
wife, but Herr Förster as well. He still had something in his
mouth that he was bravely chewing on. I didn't know what it
was, but it was putting up quite a struggle. If it had been Father,
he would have said: A piece of a dead animal! The dead animal
wasn't so tender that he could swallow it, nor so tough that he
had to spit it out. It was somewhere in the middle. Herr Förster,
like his wife, wasted no words. He said: As you see, we're eating!
    I apologized like crazy. Ideally, I would have kissed his feet.
I said I would never have gone and disturbed him and his
wife, if I'd known . . . Ideally, I would have chopped off the hand
with which I'd knocked on their door, only I didn't have
an axe with me. Herr Förster adjusted his mouthful. It smelled of
meat and gravy. I thought: It'll fall out of his mouth any

moment! but gradually he swallowed it. I could tell by his eyes that he wanted to speak, and I said: Sir? and Herr Förster asked: Is something amiss at home?

I scratched my head, even though it wasn't itching. I wanted to indicate to Herr Förster how awkward I felt. Then I scratched a different place, to indicate that I was thinking. I deeply regretted having come to say goodbye to Herr Förster. I should have written him a postcard and speedily forgotten him. I should have gone up to be with the deer in the Hoher Hain. Herr Förster bravely swallowed. Now he could speak again. All right, he said, but I haven't got long! I've other things to see to, by which he meant his lunch.

Herr Förster was wearing a waistcoat. The waistcoat was undone at the bottom. In the waistcoat pocket was the book where he kept our marks. Herr Förster always carried it about his person. He led the way to his little study. A picture of Goethe was hanging crookedly above his desk. A pile of exercise books lay on the desk. He had to correct them. Well, sit down, as you're here, he said, pointing to a chair. But the chair wasn't empty. Herr Förster groaned and had to move all the exercise books off the chair. A couple fell on the floor. Dammit! he swore, and I picked them up for him. All the trouble I was putting him to! I'm sorry, Herr Förster, I said. Then I handed him the exercise books that he'd overlooked. I hadn't wanted to sit on them. I'm so sorry, Herr Förster, I said. Herr Förster was in his slippers, he couldn't have been out yet that day. His eyesight wasn't good, and he wore glasses. Have you got the window open? he asked.

It's shut, Herr Förster.

Then open it, boy, open it! Then we were sitting there again, on our respective chairs, and he spoke. So you propose to abandon us just like that, he asked, in the middle of the summer term? I sat up straight, chest out, belly in, the way Herr Förster liked us to sit. He always said: Sit up straight, the lot of you! Chest out, belly in! Now he repeated: Abandon us!

Unfortunately yes, I said, I have to!

Are you moving?

Yes.

When?

Tonight.

I have had no written notification to that effect.

It might not have arrived yet.

That had better be the case, said Herr Förster. A school isn't a place you can breeze in and out of when you feel like it. Where would that get us?

That's true, I said, and Herr Förster asked: And how's your father getting on?

Very well, thanks.

Has he found a suitable occupation for himself yet? he asked, and I said: No, unfortunately not yet.

So he's sitting around at home?

Unfortunately.

Well, they don't grow on trees, suitable occupations, Herr Förster remarked smugly. You need to take steps! Look through the situations vacant columns, and write letters of application, and go knocking on doors until one day one might open. You need to grit your teeth for months, and go looking from door to door, if need be. Is he looking, your father?

I don't know, I said. I sighed.

Not one of life's great seekers, eh?

Maybe not terribly great.

He'd sooner wait for something to fall in his lap?

Yes, I suppose so.

Is he in fact looking, or has he given up? Has he ever looked?

He has looked, and I think he's still looking, at least a bit. He used to look more.

That was probably a while ago, said Herr Förster, and I said: Maybe. But yes, I said, he has looked, he just never had any luck. Now he's lost heart and says to himself: I won't find anything any more! That's why, of late, he might not have looked *quite* as much as he should have done.

And what does he do instead?

He stands by the window and shakes his head.

And why does he shake his head?

Because he hasn't found anything. Then he sits down and makes up something.

I see, said Herr Förster, meaning what?

Something he can write down and maybe sell. A story or something.

And I take it no one's interested?

Generally not.

Instead of showing sympathy for Father, Herr Förster laughed. A story or something, eh? he cried.

Yes, I said stoutly, a story!

And what else is he doing with his life besides that?

Oh, nothing much. He says he works too hard as it is.

Herr Förster laughed again. He had brown teeth. That was from smoking, same as with Father. Even though, compared to Father, Herr Förster didn't even smoke all that much. Now he had swallowed everything and felt better able to laugh. And what is this occupation in which he apparently so over-exerts himself? he asked.

Oh, I said, he's a writer I suppose. I tilted my head doubtfully and shrugged my shoulders.

Does he still say that?

Sometimes.

An artist, then?

Yes.

And what does your mother say to the fact that she's got herself an artist, all of a sudden?

She's got used to it.

A writer, eh? said Herr Förster chirpily. There's a thing! Just lately someone was telling me—who was it again?—they'd seen your father standing in the tobacconist's, volunteering the information that he was a writer. There was a somewhat grim silence in the place, so I heard.

Yes, I said, but sometimes he doesn't talk. Sometimes he doesn't say anything.

And he doesn't want to go and look for anything else?

He looks, I said, but maybe not hard enough. He ought to look harder, much harder.

Quite so, said Herr Förster, quite so!

But then, I said, he has some pupils he has to look after as well.

Really? said Herr Förster, Explain!

Private lessons, I said.

So he still gets a few pupils?

Yes.

How many does he have?

Not very many, I said, the odd one comes from time to time. Only Father expresses it differently.

What does he say?

He says it's better than doing it in your pants. I'm sorry, I said, but it's what he says.

And what does he teach them?

Various things, I said, English for instance.

Does he know English?

Probably more than anything else.

I asked you: Does he know English?

I suppose not very well, I said. He began studying it once, but never finished.

Why was that?

It wasn't logical enough for him. So he lost interest in it.

But now he teaches it?

He needs the money, sometimes.

I see, Herr Förster exclaimed sarcastically, he needs the money?

Yes, I said, unfortunately.

And that's all he does to try and make money?

No, I said, there's authorship as well.

There always is, said Herr Förster, and once more it sounded very sarcastic. Well, he's a lucky man! When I think of other people, myself for example, and the kind of working day I routinely put in! The sheer quantity of teaching, the innumerable extra-curricular activities that aren't even remunerated!

Yes, I sighed, it must be difficult!

Let's leave this rather sterile topic and go on to something else, said my teacher Förster. So you want to bid us adieu?

Don't want to, I said, I've got to.

And why so suddenly?

Father's taking me away.

What about your mother? Is he leaving her here all alone?

No, my sister's staying with her.

Whatever for?

It just panned out that way, I said, and paused. Father and Mother are getting separated, I said.

A family tragedy then? observed Herr Förster sternly. A divorce?

Could be.

Has your father got someone else in mind?

Not so far.

He's still looking?

Maybe.

So your mother's found someone else?

I think so.

Haven't you met him?

I saw him on the street once, but only from the back.

And?

He's quite short.

Where's your father taking you to?

To Russdorf, I said, he's taking me to Russdorf.

My God!

Yes, to Russdorf!

Herr Förster expelled some air through his nose. Whatever made him decide on Russdorf of all places?

It was pure chance, I said. It was pure chance that he decided on Russdorf. There were a couple of rooms to let.

Well, said Herr Förster, at least it's not a million miles away! Russdorf, he said, and shuddered. Have you ever been there?

I cycled through it one time.

A dump that you wouldn't send your worst enemy to, said Herr Förster, ghastly place! So that's where your father wants to take you to, and settle to his various avocations?

Yes, I said, as a writer! In Russdorf!

Well, I suppose he knows what he's doing! He's old enough! How old is he, by the way?

He never says.

Whyever not? asked Herr Förster. Is he coy about his age? He must be as old as I am, if not a couple of years older. Only

I'm still in possession of my own hair and my own teeth. Even though, compared to some other people, I've led a hardworking life and taught manners to hundreds of young louts. Made them fit for human society, or at least I tried to, whereas some other people . . . Herr Förster went on ranting for a while until he forgot what he wanted to say. He cleaned his teacher's glasses. Then he remembered, and he said: Now then! and he reached into his waistcoat pocket. These things being so, he said, it seems we won't be seeing each other much in future.

If at all, I said.

Well, we might bump into each other on the street.

Yes, I said, possibly.

Herr Förster had now said everything he'd wanted to say, and he was silent for a while. If we're not going to see each other any more, he said, I imagine you will want to know how I've evaluated your work for me in this last term. In fact, that's probably what you've come for. Be truthful, boy!

Yes.

And don't be so sluggish in your speech! Leave grunting to the pigs! You're a human being, or at least you're aspiring to become one. And as such, your speech should be in the form of complete sentences, consisting of main clauses and subclauses. Therefore I should like you to say: I have come because I was dying to know how you assessed my schoolwork this term!

I have come because I was dying to know how you assessed my schoolwork this term, I said.

There, said Herr Förster, now at least I know what's going on in your head. You want to know what mark you're getting from me for your overall performance in this current term. The record of your overall performance is in here, said Herr Förster, patting his waistcoat pocket. There was the bound notebook that he always carried around with him. When he went to buy rolls he took it with him, and when he drank the occasional beer. Sometimes it was in his teacher's waistcoat, at other times in his jacket pocket. It had all our names in it, Jassing's, Hirschberg's, mine. Well now! exclaimed Herr Förster, Do you want to know the mark you're getting from me for your current term's schoolwork, or don't you? You don't seem to be that excited!

I do. Thank you. I do want to hear. I am excited.

Perhaps you should hear the mark before thanking me.

Yes, perhaps I should.

Then say: I should like to hear how I've done, irrespective of the final mark, I want the truth!

I want the truth, I said.

Well all right, if you absolutely have to know, said Herr Förster. Well, he said, it shouldn't have escaped you that you are not among the intellectual heavyweights of your year.

No.

Say: I'm afraid I am not among the intellectual heavyweights of my year.

I'm afraid I am not among the intellectual heavyweights of my year!

More spurning than learning!

Yes.

Well, let's see where Fate has hit hardest in the current term, said Herr Förster. He had two fingers in his waistcoat pocket, and flicked through the notes he kept on all of us. The marks I give my pupils don't just drop out of the sky, he said. Each one is based on actual academic performance. Or non-performance, he said. On, as unfortunately is often the case, profound and chronic lack of interest that is an expression of idleness. Now tell me, said Herr Förster, what you think will meet my eyes when I open my little book, so that I'm not completely unprepared? I shrugged my shoulders. I didn't care. I could have yawned. The scales dropped from my eyes. Herr Förster was nothing like the man I'd taken him for! I'd got him utterly wrong. He was a creep.

Well, I don't want to keep you on tenterhooks any longer, said Herr Förster. Let's see the full and ghastly picture!

I nodded and thought, now he'll get his little notebook out at last, but he still didn't get it out. Instead, he pulled out his handkerchief, and wiped his hands. Maybe they had some crumbs on them. He was determined to tell me what sort of pupil I'd been. But I wasn't interested any more. I wasn't even looking any more, certainly not at his face. I looked at the purple slippers he was wearing to make his feet nice and sweaty. There was no stopping him. He pulled out the notebook with our names in it, and laid it across his knees. They were knobbly old man's knees. The notebook was a thick red one. It had a rubber band around it. With the notebook in his hand, Herr Förster had always prowled round the classroom, leafing around in it and then calling out: Now I'm looking for someone who will be able to tell me . . . A terrible silence had followed. Then Herr Förster said the name, very quietly, but four or five times in rapid succession. Of course everyone would have loved to know what marks had been entered beside their names, but Herr Förster was always careful to hold the notebook so that no one could see.

Right, said Herr Förster. He had long since stopped chewing, he was digesting now. He had his reading glasses on, the ones with the thick rims. Right, he said, and started leafing in the notebook. He was looking for my name. Now he just had to . . .

I sat up straighter. He said: Aha, there's the blighter! I didn't listen.

11

With Mother there was no untidiness, with her everything was light and bright. With her everything was *tidy*, with not a speck of dust to be seen anywhere. No one would have dreamed that we were going our separate ways today. It looked as though everything would go on as it always had done, as though Father would go on hanging his stick and his beret on the wall, as though he would go on helping himself to a piece of bread and liver sausage between mealtimes, would go on putting his slippers on in his work room, and go on and on writing. In the garden, the birds would be yelling.

Mother's room had a large bright window without a tree in front of it. She wouldn't have a tree in front of her window, they took away the light. The window had net curtains that we weren't allowed to tug. Mother liked standing there, not tugging at the net curtains. She pointed to the garden and said: My garden! In spring she said: My green! Oh, she said, if only I had the time . . .

Unfortunately, she didn't! Father would have had the time, but he didn't care for the garden, and he didn't lift a finger. He looked at it and yawned, he wouldn't bestir himself. Earlier, when there was something flowering and he stood in front of it with Mother, and she said: Well, what do you say? he replied: Your garden! Mother liked to talk about it. Anyone who wanted to please her just had to ask her what was *growing* or *blooming* there. Then Mother would say: Come and see! and take them by the hand. She would drag him—or her—over to the window, or to the fence, and explain what was coming up now, and what the name of it was. It didn't matter when you looked, something was always flowering. Her room didn't smell of smoke and cigarettes, the way Father's did. When he had been smoking in her room, she tore open the window and flapped her handkerchief about. Then it smelled of lavender.

Mother was sitting at her sewing-table, but she wasn't sewing. The table was tidy. The sewing-machine had *got its head down,* and was packed away under the table. Mother was wearing the red blouse she had *quickly and ruthlessly* bought for Herr Herkenrath. She wasn't satisfied, though. You can pull at it where you like, it just doesn't sit properly, she said. Ah, she said, there you are again! Well, she asked, and what's he doing now?

What do you think he's doing? said my sister, Nothing!

But a grown man with such large hands and such a large head must be doing something when he's moving out in three hours' time, said Mother. He can't just sit there and yawn!

But he doesn't want to move out!

He's got to!

He's unhappy.

Did he have a bath?

He was going to.

Then why didn't he? Was the water too wet for him?

He felt too sad.

No wonder, if he washes so infrequently, said Mother. She could be catty like that. Then she tugged at her blouse again. What else? she asked, What else is he doing, apart from not having a bath?

That's all he's doing really.

But he can't just spend all that time sitting around like a fish and not talking! He has to say something occasionally, exclaimed Mother. I can hear him through the wall! Who's he talking to?

He's talking to himself.

And what does he say when he talks to himself?

He says: Go on, you'd better pack now!

And then what does he say?

Let's give it another moment or two! Let's think it all through again!

How far has he got?

Not very far yet.

Mother laughed again, and then she turned to me. What about you? she asked, What have you been up to?

I went to see Herr Förster, I said.

What for?

I said goodbye to him.

And what did he say?

Goodbye back to me.

Nothing else?

He couldn't, I said. He had a bit of gristle in his mouth.

Why didn't he spit it out?

He did, I said, but only later, and my sister asked: What time is that man coming?

Soon.

Is he on his way? asked my sister, and Mother said: Not impossible, but unlikely!

What if he doesn't come? asked my sister, but Mother just laughed and said: Never you worry, he's like any other man! He's coming, never you worry! And she tugged at her blouse again. Then my sister picked up Mother's perfume bottle to open it and sniff it, but Mother cried: Oh for goodness' sake, you and your clumsy fingers! When my sister still tried to open it, she got a rap on the knuckles. Then she put the bottle down again and cried: You've hurt me now, and I've had enough! Each time I want to do something interesting, you hurt me! I'm going, she said, and we wandered off to see Father.

He had his silk scarf wrapped round his neck, so that it covered everything from his chin to his chest. That's so you can't tell that he hasn't washed, Mother always said. When we walked into his room, he was lying stretched out on his cane rocker. One of his eyes was completely red, maybe he'd been lying on it. Or perhaps he might have been crying? The other one was just the same as always. Perhaps he'd cried with one eye, and not with the other? Where have you been? he asked, Why have you left me sitting here all alone?

But you're not even sitting, said my sister, you're lying down!

Only briefly, said Father, I'll pull myself up in a moment, I just didn't have the strength. Where have you been? he asked, Don't you want to tell me?

She was in her room, guzzling paper, and I went out to say goodbye, I said.

Who did you go to say goodbye to?

Herr Förster.

And what did he say? asked Father, and I said: He wasn't there.

You could try him again later, said Father, but I said: No, I won't try him again!

And what's your Mother doing? asked Father. He looked at the tip of his finger. He hoped it might have grown back, but it hadn't yet.

What's she going to be doing? asked my sister. She's still not doing anything.

But she's got to be doing something! Did she ask if I was packing?

Not so far, said my sister. Perhaps she will later.

Father examined his hand, and then the individual fingers. Finally he got on to the fingernails, and that was about as far as he could go. She's still waiting to see if she means it, he said, and then . . .

Yes?

And then she'll mean it, he said.

He stood up. He felt like having a cigarette, but he couldn't find any in his pockets. He looked around hungrily, but he couldn't find any. Well, I'll have to go looking for them, he said, God knows where they've run off to this time!

And that man, is he going to come now? asked my sister.

I'm afraid so, said Father, and he drew the curtain. How much light there was outside! With the curtain out of the way, we could see the garden.

I can't see the man coming, said my sister, and Father said: Go and ask your Mother! He was her idea!

Perhaps he can't come, said my sister. Maybe he's broken his leg?

I'd rather it was his neck, said Father. Then he thought about it and said: But a leg wouldn't be bad either! There are said to be certain fractures, so I've been informed . . .

Fractures? said my sister, Like what?

Fractures, said Father, that . . . Ach, forget it, he said.

In the time when Mother still used to love him and talk to him, she had sometimes knocked on the wall. Then Father would know that she had something to tell him, and he'd always gone to see her straightaway. If he'd just had an idea, or was stuck in the middle of a difficult sentence, he would knock back. That meant: I'm just stuck over a difficult sentence. Why don't you come here? There had been no knocking now, on either side, for a long time. Father was still waiting for it. He folded his hands behind his back, and trotted back and forth. He was probably thinking about the time when Mother had used to knock, or had simply turned up in his room. He no longer hoped for that to happen. But he was still waiting all the time, instead of getting on and writing something. Have you noticed? he asked one time. She's stopped knocking. She's a—

A what? asked my sister.

— abandoned me, said Father, dropping into his cane rocker. It always creaked, especially when Father perched on the front of it. It had a broken spring, which should have been repaired really, only once he was sitting in it . . . So, when it was creaking, he preferred to go and sit on the little chair in the opposite corner of the room. That was where he *thought about his oeuvre*. Unfortunately, nothing was to come of it. I have too many worries to be able to charm stories out of thin air, he said. A couple of books lay in his trunk. He pointed at them, and said: They're coming with me, in case I have to go.

Don't you have to go?

Why are you asking me that, said Father, when I don't know myself?

Later on, we were in our room, listening, Mother was next door. She wasn't alone. When there was silence, it was a different sort of silence, there had to be somebody there with her. The voice we heard then talked quietly and fast, as though it would never stop. It was a woman's voice. Mother didn't have many visitors. Those she might have had were afraid of getting in the way of her marital dispute, and so they stopped coming. All of them were women anyway. Mother didn't want anything more to do with men, two were enough for her. In the evening, when Father was sitting at his desk and she was getting bored, she slipped into her yellow cardigan and went to the *Capitol.* First she walked up and down outside it, looking at the pictures. Then she thought: Oh, what has life given you? Why don't you go in? and in she went. Then she would watch whatever was showing, but only if there was a man she liked in the leading role. It might be that there was more than one such man in a film. Then she would enthuse about it for weeks afterwards. If she liked it *very much*, she would go to Frau Schädlich at the box office, and ask her if she had a programme.

As luck would have it, I do have one left over, said Frau Schädlich. I could let you have it cheaply.

Then Mother would buy it for herself, *without any regard to the expense involved,* as Father would always say. The little booklet would have pictures of the man she had liked so much, in various poses. Thank you very much, Frau Schädlich, Mother said, put down her two bits, rolled up the programme and bore it away home. Then she would put it in her linen closet, between a couple of corsets (she said: corselets). And then she would forget all about it. When Father once said over supper: I've heard there's a film in which Clark Gable appears in his underpants! Mother said: I know. He's in the linen closet, on the third shelf. And sometimes she would go and get him out.

On my last day, when we went into Mother's room, she wasn't alone. We weren't surprised. We'd sniffed the unfamiliar perfume and heard the unfamiliar voice. The different smell was Mariechen, her very oldest friend. Mother had clung on to her from childhood, and *was keeping her going for unknown reasons*. Often Mariechen wouldn't turn up for months at a time, so Mother would already be shaking her head and saying: I wonder what the matter is with her? Do you suppose she broke something? She has these terribly thin ankles! Once Mother had quite stopped thinking about Fräulein Mariechen and had no more use for her, she would suddenly reappear. No wonder she had come today! So that Mother couldn't send her away immediately, she had quickly sat down. She was sitting next to the window, in Mother's green armchair that overlooked the garden, and that we weren't allowed to sit in because it was fragile. Not even Mother would sit in that chair, so as not to set us a bad example. When we walked in, Mariechen was just telling what was happening in her life. Then she'd heard us coming, had broken off her story in mid-sentence—put it on ice, she said—and looked up at us. If I'd known it was her with Mother, I wouldn't have gone in. But it was too late now, and we had to say hello. I gave Mariechen my hand and said good afternoon. Because my sister always copied everything, she said good afternoon as well. When Mariechen saw me, she completely flipped.

My goodness! she exclaimed, Is this the same boy who not too long ago barely reached up to my belly button? It's not possible!

Mother sat back in her chair. She was blushing with pride. Oh yes, she said, it's quite possible!

He was standing in the corner over there, exclaimed Mariechen, and he wouldn't come out, because he was too timid to let us look at him.

Oh yes, said Mother, it's perfectly possible!

But Mariechen couldn't believe it. Come here, she said, and took my hand. Then she went and took both of them. She had loads of rings on her fingers. She had some in her ears as well, none in her nose though. Each one was bigger than the one before. She could hardly lift her hand for rings. Some were broad and some were narrow, with stones and without. Mother would always say: Fools' gold! There's nothing genuine about that woman! Mariechen wouldn't let go of my hands, and kept pulling me in to her. She was trying to get me to sit in the armchair with her, and kept saying: Oh, come on, come on. But I wouldn't sit down with her, I preferred to stand.

Doesn't he like me any more then? Mariechen asked Mother. He used to like me.

He's shy, said Mother. It's the age.

And why won't he sit down with me? asked Mariechen. He won't even look at me.

Really, said Mother, he's not looking at you, and Mariechen said: No, he keeps looking down in the corner over there.

Then Mother clapped her hands and cried: Quick, no more looking in corners. Look at Mariechen!

I looked at Mariechen, but only briefly and from below.

Fräulein Mariechen couldn't get enough of me. Now she looked at my eyes, now she looked at my mouth. You must be terribly proud to have such a good-looking big boy for a son, she said to Mother. You see, she didn't have any children, she didn't even have a husband. She had a little hunchback. See how he's grown, she said, so straight and tall! And look at his eyes! A woman daren't look at those eyes, she'll simply melt on the spot! Mariechen held on to my hand for a long time, I could hardly move. I would have liked to free myself, but she wouldn't let go. A lace collar frothed up out of her suit, as though it was boiling over. Unfortunately, it's got a bit tight for her, Mother would say every time when Mariechen came round in her suit, she's putting on weight. Don't you think so too? she asked Father.

Don't ask me, said Father, who had just embarked on a new book. Things like that are wasted on me! If you say so.

Especially round her hips and her derriere, said Mother pitilessly, that's where her problems are concentrated! She's had to let out another inch or so, didn't you notice? And you don't have to have a crystal ball to know it won't end there!

Really, said Father, as much as that?

She can't let it out as much as she would need to, said Mother, it's physically not there. She'll have to think about what to do with that suit. She can't carry on like that much longer.

Father had a book in front of him that he wouldn't have minded having written. That's why he always carted it around with him. At night he put it under his pillow, perhaps that would help. When he got to a good bit, he would either exclaim: Yes, that's the way to do it! or else: Yes, that's how I'll do it too! For now he was drumming on the table with his shortened finger. I have nothing to say on the matter of Fräulein Mariechen, he said, she doesn't inspire me!

You don't need inspiration, said Mother, you just need to open your eyes for a minute and look.

I can't open my eyes too far, said Father, I'm just in the middle of my new novel.

Did you at least notice her hunchback, asked Mother, or did you miss that as well?

Her what?

Her hunchback!

Has she got a hunchback then? asked Father.

Well if you want to go through life dumb and blind and you don't even know she's got a hunchback, then I really don't need to talk to you, said Mother. Then she quickly explained to us how important it was that a tailored suit *fitted*. Otherwise you might as well put it in the bin, she said, and Father said something vague like: Good point! or: You could well be right about that! and he went off into his work room, God knows what to do.

On our last day, Mariechen sat in Mother's room for a long time. She wore black shoes, which always look smart. She was still gripping my hand. She tinkled with her jewellery and shook her head. And you want to leave him with your husband! she exclaimed, pointing at me. No man deserves something like that! No man! Then she went right up to Mother's ear with her mouth. She spoke a little more quietly too. Is the matter resolved then? she asked.

Plenty of things in the world could do with resolving, said Mother. Instead, they just drag on.

I mean, about your separation?

How do you know we're separating?

From various quarters, said Mariechen. In town, they're already talking about it.

Not in front of me they're not, said Mother. In front of me, they hold their tongues.

They're too scared.

Well, said Mother, I've not talked to anyone about it. *He* must have been bruiting it about.

So there's some truth in it?

Mother took a deep breath. She looked quite inflated, even more than usual. It's a fait accompli, and there's nothing left to be decided, she said. If there was anyone who gave the matter any thought, and who showed any patience, then it was me! And now it's over. Now I can breathe again.

And how did he respond? asked Mariechen.

Apathetically, said Mother. He's sitting in his so-called work room, tugging at his so-called beard, calling out: Hold it, hold it! I'm about to have an idea! That's what he's been saying for twenty years now.

So he's really moving out? asked Mariechen, and Mother said: Hopefully.

And when?

Very soon. Although . . .

Yes?

. . . although he hasn't packed yet.

And you want him to . . .

Yes, I do!

Good Lord, exclaimed Mariechen, after so many years! I can hardly believe it! And the boy?

He's taking him, and she's staying, said Mother, pointing first to me and then at my sister. Just as long as he goes!

You're very strict with him!

I've grown a thick skin over the years.

And when's it going to happen?

As luck would have it, very soon, said Mother. Today.

Your husband's moving out today? exclaimed Mariechen.

Unless he pulls some stunt at the last minute, and I have to turn to the authorities to have him removed.

Would you do that?

It's my happiness that's at stake. I would kill for it!

Mariechen was now sitting in such a way that I could see her hunchback. It was small and neat and perfectly unmistakable. We all looked at it. Mother, who was quite familiar with it already, quickly dropped her eyes. My sister wasn't yet acquainted with it, and she couldn't take her eyes off it. Of course, I looked as well. When Mariechen noticed we were looking at her hunchback, she turned away. Then she looked almost normal, with hardly any hunchback at all. But I don't see any signs of moving. Where is he? Packing?

He's sitting in his room, hoping his boxes will pack themselves. It's time that man woke up and did something on his own behalf. He's not a child any more!

I want you to leave this one with me, said Mariechen, pulling me closer to her. She knocked my arms out of the way, so I couldn't touch her hunchback. There were two metal plates under her blouse. Everything was packed up between them. What, she exclaimed, is a single man going to do with such a treasure? They will both go to the dogs. And the boy deserves better than that. No, said Mariechen, if I were you, I wouldn't give him up.

Mother sighed. That's a sore point you're touching on, she said. She ran her slender fingers across her throat, as though looking for the sore point. It wasn't there. It will take a long time to heal, she said. In spite of that, it's my duty to think of myself too, once in a while. God knows, I've lived for so many years at the side of a man who doesn't love me. When I think of how I compromised myself in the hope that he'd *understand*. And he understood nothing. But now that's over! Now we'll draw a line between us and split up, even if an innocent party suffers from it . . .

Who's this then? Mariechen suddenly exclaimed. She let go of me at last. She had caught sight of my sister.

Good afternoon, my sister said once more, and held out her hand.

Who on earth is this ravishing young creature? exclaimed Mariechen, and pretended she'd never seen my sister before in her life. She pushed me away, and pulled her nearer. My sister was completely shameless, completely without scruple. She beamed. I looked for the door. Mariechen put one hand on my sister's head, right on her parting. With the other she petted her cheek. It was revolting! Slowly, very, very slowly, I backed towards the door, and out of the room. No one paid any attention to me. It was my sister's turn now.

12

Back then, the days were longer, and more fitted into them. In the evening, we drew the curtains and fell asleep right away. And in the morning, we carried on exactly where we'd left off the evening before. Even the weather . . . If it rained, it was *nice rain*, warm and refreshing. Father slipped into his loden coat, he was always in a good mood. When he wanted to say something, he raised his finger—*that* finger—in the air, and cleared his throat. And then he would say it quietly; back then he wasn't shouting yet. Unfortunately, he didn't speak very clearly, and he never explained what he meant. He just threw it out. Then he would go on to the next question, and the one after, and so on. We nodded and didn't listen. When we asked: What did you mean by that? he said: It's gone, it's gone! When we said: But didn't you just . . . ? he said: It's an idiosyncracy of mine, it comes from thinking so quickly.

Faster than Mother? asked my sister.

Faster!

Faster than me?

Faster!

Faster than God?

Faster, faster! Father exclaimed impatiently, and leafed around in a book. Now he was leafing around in a different book, which he wanted to take with him to Russdorf. He could have packed it away really, but he was still sitting around. When I work, I work, he said, and when I sit, I sit. Then he closed the book again. How thick they make them these days, especially if you're expected to move house with them, he said.

Do they make them thicker these days?

Afraid so!

What for?

Because the authors refuse to get to the point, said Father, and laid the book on top of some other books. If he hadn't done any leafing for a while, he missed it. Leafing reminded him of the time he'd read a lot, and then his eyes would start to shine. He always hoped he'd stumble across something that his writing had been missing all along. He referred to that as *the real find*. That's the best thing that can happen to you, he said. Generally, the find was pretty small, often just a word or two that he could use in a story. If we were talking about something together, or thinking about various things, separately, he some-times leapt up, put his arm in the air and cried: Ssh! Quiet! and when my sister cried: What is it? he repeated: Quiet!

But why quiet? we cried, and he said: I think I'm on to something.

What? asked my sister, and Father exclaimed: A find! A find! A find, he said, is when you run into something in the course of your thinking, that you weren't expecting, and you pick it up and put it in your sack.

What sack will you put it in? asked my sister, and Father replied: In the one I keep for my ideas!

Because he was a writer, finds with him tended to be a word or a sentence that *wanted to be written down*. Often he had to wait a long time for one to come along. Then he just stuffed it into whatever he was writing.

What if it doesn't fit? asked my sister.

I'll stuff it in anyway, because then no one will understand, and that's never bad, said Father. It stimulates the thought processes, and what more can you hope to do! His writing hand shook, but so did his cigarette hand, so that he scattered lots of ash about the place. That too, he said, and he brushed it off the table on to the floor. Then he moved his chair across, so no one would see it.

You make such a mess, said my sister, and Father said: Ash gets trodden in! The whole world is nothing but dust and ashes that have been trodden in. The issue is a different one.

And what's the issue?

The issue is: What will we do with Herkenrath, when he comes? Do we ply him with food and drink, or . . .

Or?

. . . or do we beat his brains out?

Would you really beat his brains out, or are you just saying that?

We should wait and see what type of person he turns out to be, said Father. Then he held his half-finger in front of his eyes, and said something we didn't understand. He was leaning against the wall again now, which left such nice chalk marks on his clothes, and he was talking to Mother *in his heart of hearts*. In reality, Mother had gone for a turn around the block. She had her light summer coat on, which made her look younger. You play something, she said, I'll be back before you know it!

Where are you going to? asked my sister, but Mother left without giving an answer. My sister ran after her to the front door and tore it open. Are you going to see someone whose name begins with H? she asked.

I'm not sure yet, Mother called back.

And what shall we play? asked my sister.

Something that whiles away the time, called Mother. Downstairs, the door closed.

We knew where she was going, even if she didn't tell us. We stood by the window, with Father in the middle. We watched her for a long time. Father gritted his brown teeth, and breathed even more noisily than usual. When Mother heard him, she said: Listen to him panting! Spittle was running out of his mouth from sadness, not much, but even so.

You've got something on your face, said my sister, there's something trickling!

What is it now?

From your mouth.

Ach, said Father, that's no big deal! and he wiped it away. If you think about all the trickling and dribbling that goes on in this world, it's really nothing!

Because Mother had gone out *for a turn*, the family was smaller. There was an empty chair. When Father and I were gone, it would be even smaller. That's why Herr Herkenrath was coming along, to provide reinforcements. Father stood by the window, breathing in more than out. God knows what happened to the air that stayed inside him. He was thinking about the conversation he would have to have with Mother, my sister was thinking about her dolls, she wanted to kill them all, and I was thinking about my bicycle. Sometimes, unwillingly, I thought about Herr Herkenrath as well. When he turned up, there would be more of us again, though not as many as before. Father tossed a book into the box, and said: You're coming! Then he shook his head and said: Running off without a word like that! As though I'd offended her. When it's the other way round. She offends me!

I don't offend anyone, said my sister, or do I? and Father said: What? and my sister repeated: I don't offend anyone! and Father said: What are you blathering on about now? He went up to the curtain and pulled it back a little. That way we could look down on the street without being seen. For a long time we looked down, and thought, maybe Mother will come back and be different! Maybe she'll wave up at us like she used to. But Mother didn't come back, and even if she had, she wouldn't have waved. Oh well, at least we know where she is, said Father. She's with Herkenrath, where else? he said sadly. We'd come to the same conclusion, but it was a shock to hear it all the same. We looked down at the floor and stood around for a long time.

Why won't you talk? my sister blurted out suddenly, Why are you like that? She was going to cry again. Father was upset by her crying, and he turned his back on her. Oh God, he said, and he wished my sister wouldn't cry so much. Then he tugged at his ear and said: We're not like that! Listen, any minute we'll all be talking again!

What will we be talking about? asked my sister, and Father said: No man knows what he's going to talk about in advance. He waits for the moment, then he grits his teeth, and he starts talking.

But if he grits his teeth, he can't talk.

Oh he can, said Father, he can! And he yawned again. Ever since he'd known that Mother was going to leave him—give him *the old heave-ho*, Father said—he felt like sleeping all the time. The yawning began the moment he went to his desk in the morning. God, he said, how good it would be to shut my eyes and sleep! The yawning continued in the afternoon. In the evening, when we sat around the kitchen table without Mother, *playing a little game*, he often dropped off. My sister jabbed him in the side, she didn't like to say ribs because that made everybody laugh. It's your turn, she said, wake up! and Father gave a start and cried: Eh? Then he opened his eyes and said: Haven't I moved my piece?

It's not that kind of game, said my sister, we're asking each other what cards we've got.

That's what I said, or did I just mean to say it? asked Father, We're playing Happy Families, aren't we? Sometimes we play board games, and sometimes we play Happy Families! How can a man keep up!

But lately we've always played Happy Families!

That's what I was saying, said Father. Doesn't matter, he said, and he dozed off again. When he yawned, he didn't hold his hand in front of his mouth, he just forgot himself completely. If you were looking in his direction, you could see inside his mouth. It was all black. You couldn't help seeing the stumps. Mother said: Some people have no manners! Then Father hurriedly put his hand over his mouth, and said: Forgive me, Your Worship! or: I forgot I had an audience! He had spread his artist's neckerchief, to cover *an old man's turkey wattles—not to mention the dirt!* Mother said—as much as possible. When she came upon it in the morning, she said: That won't help him either! According to her, he was too old and fat to go around in a silk scarf. He was still wearing the same sorry jacket over the same dark shirt. In his right jacket pocket he had his notepad, so that, if he should have an idea after all, he could . . . None came. He only used his pencils to gnaw on. When Mother came across one while tidying his room, and said: This one's had it! and threw an ancient pencil in the bin, he cried: For God's sake don't throw any pencils away while my work's not selling! Then he laboriously bent down, fished out

138

the pencil and put it in his pocket. There, he said, now stay there! If Mother had missed the wastepaper bin with her throw, he got down on all fours to look for it under the desk, to *save it from the abyss.* I'll write three more long novels with this if I have to, he said, and smiled at us. He had saved some money.

Have you written one yet? asked my sister.

What a question!

Well, have you? asked my sister.

Never you worry, said Father, it'll come!

On the last day of my childhood, I stood by the door muttering: Out of here! My sister was standing next to me and asked: Why don't we both go? I wanted to say goodbye to Hutsche, in my imagination I was already on my way to his *den.* First of all we'd talk about football, then we'd stand around in an obstinate silence. By the way, I would say, we're moving, the old man and me, for good! I won't tell you where we're going, the place has got such a ridiculous sounding name. But we won't be seeing each other any more! Hutsche would give a start and blink his eyes. He'd heard about it, but hadn't believed it. Never again? he would ask, and I would say: Never again! That's how I imagined our goodbye, like that or a bit different. Now I went into Father's room and plucked at Father's sleeve and asked: Can I go and say goodbye now?

I thought you'd been already, said Father.

I've got to go again!

To whom?

To Hutsche, I said, and Father said: To him? and furrowed his brow. Well, if he's your friend and you have to go, then I suppose you have to go, said Father. Don't ask so many questions! Too much hot air gets blown into the sky as it is, it's unnecessary.

Better do something, he said, and lowered his head, and did nothing.

My sister was already standing by the door. She wanted to cry again, but Father said: Not now! and she didn't cry. Mother had got back some time ago, without Herr Herkenrath. She had taken off her coat and hung up her bag. Now she was sitting in her room, forgetting about us. Father was in his room, thinking about the conversation with her that he was about to have. He was grinding his teeth. He had put on black socks, because he was in mourning for his life. For all of life, he said, not just mine! Mother would laugh if she heard that. What's there to giggle over now? he asked. Then he talked about the new life we would have, starting tomorrow, he and I. We would live in Russdorf, in a *hole with two rooms* that Mother had found for us. The larger hole was for Father, the smaller one for me. If I shut my eyes, he said, I can picture the holes that she will stuff us inside. I have, may I say, the gravest fears regarding them. Finding a proper apartment for us would have been the least thing she could do for us, seeing as she's walking out on us.

But she's not walking out on you, you're walking out on her! exclaimed my sister, and Father shook his head and said: It's mutual, it's mutual.

If it had been left to Father to look for a apartment for us, he surely wouldn't have found one. And so Mother had had to use her influence.

He sat around at home, drumming his fingers on the dining table and saying: I hope she doesn't find anything! Perhaps he even prayed she wouldn't find anything. But it didn't help anyway. The apartment that Mother had *unearthed*—is it underground? asked my sister—was some distance away. That was intentional, of course. Mother had chosen it so that Father couldn't turn up at any moment and interrupt her *wild marital bliss*. But it was unnecessary. He had sworn to himself never to see her, her and *that other fellow*. I had sworn it to myself as well.

Will you promise that you won't chase after her? Father often asked me, and I said: Yes.

Good boy, he said.

We hadn't seen our new apartment yet, we didn't want to see it. We didn't even want to hear about it, not even at bedtime. When Mother started describing it to us, Father ran out of the kitchen and slammed the door behind him. I hung around with her for a little while, then I ran off after him. I wouldn't have minded seeing the apartment, but he couldn't bring himself to look at it. When I see a apartment that I'm supposed to move into without your Mother, it breaks my heart, he said. Doesn't it break yours too?

Mine too, I said, and my sister said: I'm the same, I'm the same!

Then Father would calm down again, and say what he always tended to say in these cases: There's still time! The first time we wanted to talk about our new apartment together, after we'd both separately thought about it for a long time, we couldn't think of much to say. When I brought it up, Father said: Quiet, this is our apartment! and he knocked on the wall. When he had been knocking for long enough and thinking about the new apartment, he brought the conversation round to it himself. It was, as it always was, a beautiful day, *at least there's no raining going on*, said Father. We had *got our skates on* and were stumping round the block. When we were back outside the door and I was already thinking that once again he hadn't thought of anything to say about life in our new apartment, he suddenly started talking about it.

Unless I'm mistaken, he said, there's change on the way!

For better or worse? asked my sister, and Father said: It appears that your Mother no longer loves me!

Is that right? I said.

It appears that we're going to get a divorce, he said. At any rate, there is a growing risk of that happening. As ever, there are various permutations that we need to take in.

What are they? I asked, and Father said: It's as follows. If, Heaven forfend, your Father and Mother do end up getting divorced, certain changes will follow. For instance, we'll have to leave. You your little room, and I my . . . well, my study, said Father. (He was always afraid to say the word because Mother would always butt in: You mean your bedroom! and laugh sarcastically.) She will insist, he said, that we make way for her new helpmate, you and I. Then it'll be his turn, he said.

And then? asked my sister, but Father had fallen silent. Go on, she said, what then?

We walked round the block a lot. We looked at everything again. We even looked at the sky, which was pretty much the same all over. Sometimes my sister came with us, otherwise she would have *moaned*. Father had his beret on his head and his stick in his hand. Sometimes he tried to be cheerful, that was especially depressing. There now, he said, I've got my stick on my head and my beret in my hand, right?

No, cried my sister, that's wrong!

Oh?

It's the other way round! she said, and Father said: Clever girl! The apartment she wants to transplant us to isn't really so bad, I've thought about it, he said. Then he slowed down, stopped and began to describe our new apartment. Apparently, it was on the small side, but it offered *a garden to catch a breath of air*, if we needed any. To begin with, he didn't want to describe the garden to us, he hadn't seen it himself after all. But by and by, the more he thought about it, it finally loomed in front of him. Yes! exclaimed Father, I can see it exactly, it's spreading its pinions.

Its what? asked my sister.

It's an expression, he said. More and more he talked about the garden, and pictured it to himself. Another time he went around the block with us, he wanted to *get away from the misery*. The more Father talked about the new apartment, the more extensive and magnificent it and its gardens became. My sister and I had been picturing it to ourselves for a long time, and the garden had kept getting more splendid. One day Father suddenly stopped in mid-flow. Then he took a deep breath, and proclaimed: A park!

How come? asked my sister.

A park, I tell you, it's a park!

I thought it was a little garden, said my sister.

Not a bit of it! exclaimed Father. Who says a park's only little? A park is never little! Afterwards we stood around some more. Another day was drawing to a close, one of the old sort, he said. There wouldn't be many more of them. So, pay attention! cried Father. Then he took his stick and sketched the park on the pavement. Of course we couldn't follow it, because its iron tip didn't leave any marks, but even so, even so!

You understand what I'm telling you now, asked Father. When I say it's a park, then I mean it's a park!

But you've never seen it!

Don't contradict me when I'm stating a fact? said Father. I don't need to see it, it's all in here, all right? he said, tapping his brow.

Yes.

Well then, said Father. And what enables me to picture it to myself?

Your whatdoyoucallit!

She means imagination, I said.

Well then, said Father contentedly. He was even smiling. But then he collapsed again. We couldn't leave Father like that, we had to help him.

What will the inside be like? I asked.

What are you rabbiting on about? he said.

What the apartment will be like on the inside? I asked, but Father's enthusiasm had been quenched. Ach, all these questions, he said, all that nonsense, he said. What do you think it will be like? Just like any other, he said, a apartment!

And what are apartments like? asked my sister.

Poky! cried Father, They're poky!

The more our separation—our *dissolution*, Father said— approached, and the more he talked to us about the new apartment, the more detailed his picture of it grew. He would close his eyes. He put his hand across his forehead and said: Now, our apartment! Then another pause. Maybe it's not much to look at, you know, at first blush, he said, but we'll get it to look like something. In the new, still unknown apartment, we would fend for ourselves, Father and I. On even-numbered days he would do the cooking, and on odd-numbered days, I would. Together, he said, we'll hack it!

What about me? asked my sister, What do I do?

You wait till we get you to join us, said Father, Possibly. Then we'll all be together again.

What about Mother, though? asked my sister, Hey, what about Mother? but Father turned chill and curt. His cigarette hand started to shake. Mother won't want to, he said, she's betrayed us, now she's getting her comeuppance! and when my sister said: But Mother . . . Father cut her off: That's enough!

There's been enough talk about her, I don't want to hear another word! Anyway, we wouldn't make too much fuss over meals. I'm approaching an age where the inner man requires less in the way of sustenance, he said. There are more important things in life than sitting at a table stuffing yourself.

Such as? asked my sister.

Not so many questions, please, instead keep your eyes and ears open and, with the help of observation and thought, find some answers for yourself, said Father, who was unable just then to come up with anything more important. And now go and stretch your legs, but not too long!

Where do you want us to go and stretch our legs? asked my sister, and Father, with his most magnificent gesture: Wherever they take you this sunny day!

13

Because it never rained then. I didn't like being at home. I stood in front of my window a lot and scratched the pane. Then Mother came in and asked what I was doing. Are you waiting for something? she asked, and I replied: I don't know if I'm waiting for anything or not.

Funny boy, she said, and she went out. In winter—the flakes, the solid-fuel stove—it was hot and dry, and in summer there wasn't much air. So I went up to the Hoher Hain. Put your cap on if you're going outside again, Mother called after me.

Not that cap, I replied.

I knew a secret path up to the Hoher Hain, through people's gardens. I often went that way. I'd shown it to my sister, so she could meet me on it. I'd made her kneel down and swear to me never to betray the secret of the path to anyone. Then I took her by the hand and showed it to her. So that you know it if you need to find me quickly, I said, or for that other thing.

For what other thing? she asked.

In case I leave here.

But where will I be if you leave?

Where do you think you'll be? I said, Here!

Then where's the path?

You're standing on it, I said.

Oh, she said, I know this path!

Anyway, this is our secret path, got it?

All right, it's our secret path, she said, and we walked on. In the evening she started again, by now she was in her nightie. She hadn't cleaned her teeth, only pretended to. The sun had already *plummeted*, but it would probably be back in the morning. You and your stupid secret path, she said, tell me what can I not do with it?

Not show it to anyone!

Why not?

I explained it to you.

But I think I've forgotten.

Oh, I said, just do what you want! It was useless trying to forbid her to do anything, she just forgot what it was right away. That's why I would rather have gone into town on my own, but I wasn't allowed to. She needed to be *dragged along*. Then Father and Mother would be alone at home, with the curtains drawn and the door bolted. They used to sit in the same room, but now each of them locked themselves up in their own room. Mother because she wanted to *dream*, whereas Father wanted to *doze*. But he didn't say: I'm going to lock myself in, so I can doze more effectively! He said: I'm going to lock myself in, so I can work better! or: Think about what's preying on my mind! That's how it was on the last day too. Because my sister was soon going to be on her own with Herr Herkenrath, she stuck to me like a burr.

What's that? she asked.

A type of man-eating thistle that attaches itself to you.

I see what you mean!

When I stopped in front of a shop window, she stopped in front of the shop window too, when I helped myself to a roll at lunch, she helped herself to a roll too, when I was reading something, she picked up a book and pretended she was reading too, and so on. All right, because today's the last time, I'll let you come too, I said. We went to get our shoes.

And where are we going? she asked.

I wanted to save air, so I just replied: Town!

Why?

Do something! Under one condition, I said. You have to promise . . .

I promise!

. . . not to ask any questions.

Why not?

Because I need to think!

What about quietly? What if I asked them quietly?

No, not even quietly!

Well, then I'll just have to think as well, she said.

Before I got out, I wanted to think about everything one last time: How long I'd lived here, what room and what storey, what the pollution smelled like that came out of Scharschmidt's factory chimney, what friends always used to come and see me here, the rattle of the looms at Liebeneiner's, and so on and so forth. That's what I wanted to think about once more, so that some of it might stick later: my street, my sky, my way to school. So I could remember later where I'd grown up, and could tell my children—Father: They're still securely in the womb of the earth!—what the district used to look like, if they happened to ask. I went over to the window, and looked up the street. Frau Rammler was just crossing the road, wearing an apron. This is the last time you'll see Frau Rammler crossing the road in her apron, I thought, but I didn't feel anything. Then I pulled the window up, stuck my head out and looked the other way, but I didn't feel anything either. To get in a sort of goodbye mood, I looked at the opposite roof and said farewell. I was only able to say it softly, though, because my sister was standing behind me, looking at me strangely.

Who's that you're talking to? she asked.

I'm not talking, I replied, I'm thinking!

But I heard you talking!

That still doesn't mean I was talking, I said, and from now on I *thought* farewell, but the goodbye mood still wouldn't come. Instead I started to shiver. Was that the goodbye mood? No, I was getting ill! Tomorrow, I'd have to lie down in a bed I didn't know. Maybe the day after tomorrow, I'd die in that bed, and be buried the day after. Even though time kept passing—what else is it supposed to do? Father always said—it was still early, but the sun was moving on. Now it was falling on our patch of garden. I'd used to dig stuff there, and Father had mown the lawn. Lately he had called out: No, I'm not going to do it any more! From now on Herr Herkenrath would mow the lawn, the grass was already pretty high. I looked at everything, because I wanted to take in as much of it as possible and carry it away with me, as Father said. I didn't manage it, though. It all looked so dead standing around, I couldn't carry it away. Just as well you're leaving, I thought, and: Let's get out of here! I was thinking all that while my sister stood around, not thinking anything at all. She was just yawning.

I went out into the passage and put on my street shoes. I said: For the last time! My shoes weren't clean, but then I had clean fingernails, and my sister didn't. She'd splashed water on her face, I've no idea why. Mother probably didn't know either. She came out of her room. When she saw we were going, she wasn't best pleased. But she didn't like us sticking around in her room either. She suddenly felt sorry for us, especially my sister. The poor girl is so mixed up, she said. She's started biting her nails again! That's never a good sign!

I know, I said.

Do you bite your nails? she asked.

No, I said, not yet.

Wonder what the matter is with her this time, said Mother, and went into her room, and we stood around. When I asked my sister: Why do you bite your nails, *really*? she said: I don't know why I bite them *really*! and when I asked her: Do you eat them too? she said: I think so!

But why, I asked, why? and she said: They're my nails, aren't they! I can do what I like with them!

Where do you spit them out when you don't eat them? I asked, and she said: Wherever there's room for them!

But that was a lie, she did eat them! When I said: Admit it, everyone knows! she started crying again. Then I said: Oh, eat them if you want! I'm leaving anyway.

And when are you leaving? she asked, and I said: In three hours, when do you think?

She had her Sunday dress on. Her hair was carefully parted.

She had her dolls under her arm, they were all sad too. We stood by the door of the apartment, and Father called out: What are you still doing here? And then we left. I wanted to imagine what it might be like, going down a different lot of stairs, on my own, without my sister. But because I didn't know them yet, I couldn't imagine it either. We stepped out of the front door.

It's no easy matter saying goodbye. Father was by the window. He pressed his nose against the glass, the tip of it was completely flattened. He mopped his brow with his handkerchief, and then he waved to us. His hair was uncombed again and he looked ugly. Saying goodbye, he always said, is never easy, especially when you're supposed to be saying goodbye to the known world! Then he wanted to say something else, but thought better of it.

Whenever we set off somewhere, Mother always put her arms round our shoulders and said: Let's all stay together! She didn't mean in life though, she meant on the pavement. Not each one off on his own, she said. And don't look so stony if you can help it! Nothing's happened, or at least not yet!

Is something going to? asked my sister, and Mother said: You never know!

When Father and my sister and I walked into town of a fine afternoon, behind or next to Mother, she didn't want people to think we were quarrelling. She wants everybody to think that something has broken out that I once called the *great big peace*, said Father.

And then? asked my sister.

I crossed it out again, he said.

When we asked Mother: Why should people think we're not quarrelling? she said: The truth about our family is nobody's business! or: It creates a bad impression! or: Because people like to be deceived! Father always brought up the rear and *often found himself left behind.* He would have preferred to stay at home, but that wasn't allowed, he was needed for carrying things. So far, he was only carrying his stick and his hat, muttering to himself. Everybody knows what's going on anyway, he was muttering, the sparrows are shouting it from the rooftops!

And what is going on? asked my sister, and Father said: Not rotten, but Danish!

And what rooftops are they shouting it from?

The rooftops of Proverbia, said Father, and we went on walking. Mother and Father and sister and I were an unhappy family, but no one was supposed to know that. We had to talk and smile and look as though we were a happy one. When we ran into someone and they talked to us, Mother always pretended she was in a good mood and that we never argued. When Father then caught up with us, she was very nice to him and smiled at him. That forced him to be nice back to her, and to smile, and ask her, for instance, if her foot was better yet. Often Mother wouldn't know what he was talking about, and asked: What foot?

You remember, the one you sprained, Father would say, and wink at her.

Oh, that one, Mother would reply. Yes, darling, she said, it's much better! or again: No, honeypie, still no improvement, maybe tomorrow!

When the people had said goodbye again and walked off, and we were once again on our own, Father and Mother didn't say a word to each other. Nor did they walk side by side either, they walked apart. Sometimes Father now went on ahead, but usually it was Mother. She had more energy. My sister couldn't understand why they weren't walking side by side any more. Once again, she took Father and Mother by the hand and said: Stop a minute! I need to tell you something important! and Mother said: What's this nonsense? and took her hand back, and Father said: Stop it!

But wait! cried my sister and took Mother's hand again. Then she put Mother's and Father's hands together, and she said: Now you're to stay like that!

But unfortunately Mother didn't keep Father's hand in hers, and before long we were walking along separately again.

We were walking to the end of the Moritzstrasse, for the last time. Unfortunately, there was nothing to see except the heartily familiar gardens and streets and houses that were always there, whether a person was leaving or not. That's what I said too. There's nothing to see, I said.

Because she always had to contradict, my sister said: Yes there is! Then she looked about her and said: Houses and trees and sky and street and a socking great pavement.

They don't count. They're always there!

We walked into town, where we had seen everything before. There was nothing new there either. They must be out, said my sister.

No, they're at home all right, I said, they're just not looking!

Except for Frau Jahn, and she was looking! She was leaning on the windowsill, and she saw us. She was no spring chicken, and she had stuck her head right out. And she was a widow too. So she only had to cook for herself and had nothing else to do. Of course she wanted to talk to us, especially me. She had doubled up her pillow on the windowsill, that was more comfortable. She had a double chin, and we came nearer, and I said: I'm leaving!

So I've heard, said Frau Jahn. What about your little sister, what's she going to do?

I don't know what she's going to do, I said, but I think she's staying.

What about your mother, Frau Jahn called down to us, doesn't she mind at all? She was pretty excited. Are you leaving her on her own?

I didn't feel like talking about Mother very much, especially not to Frau Jahn. You only had to say one word to her, and she would go digging around for more. So I gave my sister a nudge and said: You tell her! Then I pushed her in front of me.

Oh, said my sister, Mother's not being left on her own. She's going to marry this man. Then she turned to me: What's that stupid man called again? and I told her. That's right, she said, Herkenrath.

But surely she's already married, said Frau Jahn.

She's going to get a divorce first, said my sister. And when she's divorced, she can marry the other man.

So you two are going to get a new father?

I'm not, but she is, I said, pointing at my sister. I'm keeping the old one.

Well, if that's not news! said Frau Jahn. She was beside herself with excitement. And what's she doing with your father? Is she going to throw him out?

She doesn't need to do that, I said, he's going anyway.

And he's probably going to remarry?

I expect he'd like to, I said, but he needs to find someone first.

And when are you leaving?

Tonight.

What! she exclaimed, So soon? Have you met your new father yet?

Not yet, I said, but we're meeting him quite soon. In three or four hours' time.

Well, you have got your work cut out for you then, cried Frau Jahn. Where will you be moving to?

We're not allowed to say, I said.

It begins with Ru, said my sister.

Yes, I said, with an R.

Like Russdorf, said my sister, no?

You weren't supposed to say it, I said.

I didn't say it, she said, I was just saying how it begins.

They're bound to want to take everything with them, your menfolk, said Frau Jahn to my sister. The place will be stripped bare!

Not completely bare, said my sister, they will leave a bit behind! They're taking ten books and three saucepans and the desk lamp and their shoes and shirts and socks, but the rest is staying. With some things we haven't worked out who's going to get them.

And what about your new father, asked Frau Jahn, where's he come from?

Mother picked him up somewhere, said my sister.

And when's he coming?

He's already on his way, but he can't walk very fast. He's only got one leg, said my sister, the other one came off. Then she went on to talk in some detail about our new father, most of it was lies. Everyone will hear him coming, she said, because of his wooden leg.

No, I said, it's made of ivory!

Anyway, it makes a terrible racket, said my sister, and I said: It's his right! and my sister: No, his left! When he arrives, she said, he'll first crawl down into the cellar, and then he'll go up in the loft. Then he'll poke around a bit to see if he likes it. If he doesn't like it, he'll leave. If he does, he'll take off his jacket and marry Mother. Before that he'll have to discuss money with Father. Then he'll go over to the window, and have everything explained to him, the other houses and who they belong to, the trees and what type they are. That's why they're moving out now. Tomorrow the other man is moving in, and then we'll be full up again.

Well, all I can say is good luck to you, Frau Jahn called down from her pillow, and my sister said: I'm sure it'll be fine. How else could it be? Father's thought about it all long and hard. If we ever missed each other, we could see each other. We'd just get on the train, we don't mind that.

So the moving van's coming tonight?

Yes, said my sister, after dark, so no one will see. Before that we need to pack.

And what about your father? What will happen to him?

Oh, he's a writer, he'll be fine, said my sister. Once he's moved and got his new desk, he'll write a novel, a really really long one!

I pinched my sister in the leg, but so that Frau Jahn didn't see. My sister went ouch. I said: She's getting impatient to leave! Then I said goodbye.

Wait! cried Frau Jahn on her pillow. She leaned out a little further. I hope she doesn't fall out, Father always said, because that'd leave a nasty grease spot! Wait! she cried, I've got something else I must ask you! but I just walked off. My sister had to walk off too, because I pulled her by the sleeve up the Bismarckstrasse for the last time, which made it a very sad street. We looked up at the sky. Then there was the garden with the dogs.

Come on, I said to my sister. I dragged her.

The dogs were lying in wait for us, but they were chained up so they couldn't bite us. They barked and snapped in our direction, but only in the air. Come on, I said and made a little detour. My sister made a large one. She was more afraid than I was, I was almost not afraid at all. For the last time we went over the bridge, past the rubber goods shop, for the last time a pigeon followed me. My sister wanted to talk and talk, and I knew what about.

I've told you everything, I said.

Tell it to me again!

I stopped, and my sister stopped too. I leaned against a tree, because one happened to be there. For the first time, I was without a stick, I didn't want one any more. I scraped at the ground with the tip of my shoe and started talking. I told my sister about the new father she was getting. I won't be around any more, I said.

Why not?

Only you'll still be here, I said.

No, she said, I'm going to be gone as well!

No, I said, you're staying with him! You're going to be staying with him for ever and ever. With Mother and the Herkenschwein, I said. Then she started crying again, and I said: Crying won't help either! Then, because I couldn't stand the noise of her crying any more, I said: Well, I won't be that far away, at least not to begin with! In case I forget to take something, you can bring it to me.

So can I come and see you sometimes? she asked, and I wanted to torment her a bit more and said: Maybe! and then, just as she was beginning to think she could come and see me, I said: Maybe not! My sister wasn't crying, though, she had a *crying intermission.* She couldn't hear enough about her new father.

Why won't he be yours too? she asked.

Because I'll be gone!

And what then? she asked. What will be then?

I had already told her everything, but she wasn't content. She wanted to hear it over and over again. So I said: All right, listen! and I told her once more. I told her what he would look like, and walk like and talk like and what his voice would sound like. Then I imitated his walk and his voice.

She asked: Does it really sound like that? and I said: Yes, pretty much!

As squeaky as that?

Yes, as squeaky as that!

What about his smell? she asked. What does he smell like?

I'd had enough by now. I gesticulated. I said: Like all of them!

Like all of the whats?

Like all fathers, all fake fathers! Then I still had to tell her what kind of fingers and eyes and teeth he had, so she could picture them for herself as well. At last I drew a deep breath, and began about his claws.

Does he have claws then? she asked.

Yes.

And pointy teeth?

That as well.

My sister stopped again. She looked at me long and hard. How do you know all that? she asked. You haven't seen him either.

Yes, I said, from the window!

Then why didn't I see him?

You weren't paying attention. Anyway, I'm just imagining him.

So he might be different?

As far as I'm concerned, he might, I said, I'm out of here anyway! and we walked on a bit. She wanted to talk and talk, even if there was nothing to be said. All right, she said, that man! She couldn't keep the name in her head, she didn't *want* to keep the name in her head. It was Herkenrath, of course.

What was that stupid man's name again?

I laid my hand over her mouth. I couldn't bear to hear it once more. I said: Quiet!

Why?

Quiet, I said, and we drifted on on our last day.

Why do I have to be quiet? she asked. Tell me! and I said: Because I need to think!

And so we drifted through our town. The women were in blouses, and the men in shortsleeved shirts. When we passed someone we knew, we said hello. If someone had long sleeves, they would be rolled up. Some were even not wearing socks. Others didn't seem to notice the weather, because there's more than weather in this world, as Father always said.

Like what? asked my sister.

Like cares, he said, they come before the weather. The weather only comes afterwards.

I don't understand that, said my sister.

I don't either, he said.

No one can say goodbye to all the people he knows, there would simply be too many of them. So you need to think about the people you *really* want to say goodbye to. You need to know who deserves it. Then, once you've disappeared somewhere and haven't thought of them for years, you might think of them again. And then you think: Oh yes, you really should have said goodbye to so-and-so! but by then it's too late. They might be living abroad, or even be dead. Never, if you live to be a hundred, will you get a chance to say goodbye to them! They're lost to you. That's why, when you say your goodbyes, you need to think carefully to be sure you don't leave anyone out. So I thought carefully, and I thought of one person after another that I knew. Most of them were in my class. You'd better tell him you're going, I thought, you have to say goodbye to him! or again: No, there's no need to say goodbye to him, him you just leave standing there! In the end there weren't all that many people that I had to say goodbye to. Had I left some out perhaps? I slowed down. I said to my sister: I've got to ask you something!

I'm not allowed to talk, she replied, and when I asked: Why not? she said: Because I'd be disturbing you!

You have my permission, I said. Then I asked: Who, in your opinion, do I have to say goodbye to?

My sister scratched her doll. There's something wrong with her, she said, maybe it's smallpox! Then she thought for a time, but she didn't come up with anyone. How am I supposed to know who you should say goodbye to? she asked, and I said: Think about it, think about it!

My sister allowed a lot of time to go by, then she said one name. Maybe, she said, you should say goodbye to him.

To him? I asked.

Yes, to him!

We were standing on the Bismarckstrasse. For a long time we didn't speak. Then I asked her why I had to say goodbye to him of all people, and she said: How do I know!

Then why did you say him? I asked, and she said: Because I just happened to think of him! And who do you want to say goodbye to? she asked, and I said: I don't know either!

Just like me, she said, just exactly like me!

I shouldn't have asked her, she didn't have a clue. She didn't even know what saying goodbye really meant, never having done it. I hadn't really said goodbye to anyone either, at least not for good. Not even to my grandfather and grandmother. They just suddenly weren't there any more, never to be seen again, as Father said. But at least I'd heard of saying goodbye. And I had more imagination, and I could *imagine* it to myself.

And now, she asked, when we were on the opposite side of the road, what are we doing now? and once again I said: Quiet!

Why do I have to be quiet again?

Because I have to think, I said, and I pretended to be thinking. In fact though, I wasn't thinking, too many things were happening to me all at once. I had to try to limit myself. I only wanted to say goodbye to those people who had meant something to me. How can you say goodbye to someone you're glad to see the back of? My sister didn't give up, though. She kept looking for someone I could say goodbye to. How about Hirschberg, Gottfried, she asked. Don't you want to say goodbye to Hirschberg, Gottfried?

There is no Hirschberg, Gottfried!

There is so a Hirschberg, Gottfried!

His name is Hirschberg, Gerhard, I said, and my sister said: But that's what I've been saying all along! What about saying goodbye to Hirschberg, Gerhard?

No, I said, not to Hirschberg, Gerhard!

How about Jässing, Rainer, she asked.

No, I said, nor to Jässing, Rainer either! Certainly not to Jässing, Rainer, I said, him least of all! and we drifted on. I was sorry I'd asked my sister, she didn't have a clue. She kept coming up with more names, but they were all the wrong ones. To him? she asked, and I said: No, not to him, and she asked: What about him then?

Please be quiet if you don't know either, I said. Let me think!

For a certain reason, we went to the park on our last day. The Faulerbach flowed through the park—Father called it *our pathetic dribble*. When the weather was humid, it stank. For God's sake don't take it into your heads to go in there, Mother would say, and we said: No! and went to the Faulerbach. We took off our socks and shoes and waded into it. My sister went in up to her ankles, I went in up to my knees. We stood around in the water. Are you only going in up to your ankles? I asked my sister.

Yes, she said, what about you?

Up to my knees, I said. At home, we didn't say we'd been in the water. In the evening, Mother remarked on the fact that we smelled so bad and sneezed so much. That was all in the past. There wasn't much time now.

Come on then, I said to her.

There were lots of tall trees in the park that we drifted past. I had my penknife in my pocket, like Father had his. Mine was a bit smaller. When my sister asked me: Why have you got it with you? I said: I have to take care of something.

What do you have to take care of? she asked, and I said: Something important!

Because today is your last time?

Could be.

Then we were under the trees. There was a little breeze blowing. Apart from us and the trees and the breeze, there was no one around. People were all hunched in their gardens or their kitchens or in front of their houses, and they had no idea that today was my last day. We drifted in and out of the trees.

Father called the ground the forest *floor*. The floor was very soft here. Then we got to the tallest tree. At least it was one of the tallest, a beech. I had carved my initials in it back in May. So you'll know later that you were once in this area, I had told myself then. I went up to the tree. My sister trailed after me.

What are we going to do now? she asked. Tell me, what are we going to do now?

I was very short with her again, and just said: Take care of something!

What? Tell me! Take care of what?

We had been walking pretty fast. We rested under the beech. I didn't need to rest, but my sister did. Then we walked round the tree. I brushed the bark with my hand. When my sister saw me doing that, she started doing it too. I was touching the tree quite a long way up, she was touching it somewhere down by the roots. I pulled out my penknife and went right up to it.

What are you doing now, asked my sister, and I said: Now I'm looking for something!

What are you looking for? she asked.

I stood right next to the beech that I had carved my initials in, three hundred some years ago. They were still there. My sister couldn't make out the letters until I went over them with my finger and asked: Now can you see them?

Of course I can see them, she said. I'm not blind!

First I just went over my name, then I went over the bark beside it. Then with my knife, I scratched out my name, first my Christian name, then my surname.

Why did you carve that? asked my sister.

So everyone will know I was once here.

And what if no one comes this way?

Then no one will know.

And why do you want everyone to know?

Just so.

And why are you scratching it out now? Tell me: Why are you scratching it out?

I used to play here. I used to know every bit of root. Once I lost a shoe here, the right one, I think. I took it off to play, then it wasn't there any more.

It will have leapt into the Faulerbach, said Father, laughing. He put his arm around me to comfort me.

Mother shook her head, and said: I don't know how you can make a joke about it! Shoes don't grow on trees. They cost money!

That's enough of that, said Father, and drew a line under the conversation with his hand. I've got other things on my mind.

When I had scratched out my name, the tree had a wound. I brushed it with my fingers, but the tree wasn't bleeding. I put my knife away.

Can we go now? asked my sister, and I said: Let's go!

The park had two entrances, the "nice" one and the "grotty" one. I don't know who lived near the "nice" one, my friends and me all lived near the "grotty" one. Sometimes I would run into one or other of them on my way back, Malz or Koller.

Hello, I said.

Hello, they said.

They were in shorts and down-at-the-heels shoes. I don't know what would become of you if I didn't keep an eye on you, Mother liked to say.

Yes, I said, I know!

Look, she said, the way you . . .

Yes, I said, I know!

They had scabs on their knees, and they didn't know that I was clearing off. They would get to hear about it tomorrow or the next day. They wouldn't believe it to begin with. For a while they would miss me, then not.

What are you saying? asked my sister, and I said: Then not!

What's that supposed to mean? she asked, and I said: Let's go, because I . . . I explained to her that I would have to leave her on her own for a bit now, because, before I left, I had to take care of something. Of course she didn't want me to take care of anything without her, and I had to take her by the hand and drag her, otherwise she would have put down roots. Mother dragged her like that too. You wilful creature, she said, you can be just like a snail at times. Come on, snail, I said, and dragged her along. That made her cry again. And so we finally got to Hutsche's house, I pulled her all the way there. I told her she'd have to wait until I was finished.

When will you be finished? she asked, and I said: Soon!

And where do I have to wait? she asked, and I said: Here! and stood her outside Hutsche's house. You can play with your dolls, there are enough of them, I said.

But I don't want to play with my dolls!

You can play with whatever you like.

I don't want to play with anything.

Fine, don't play with anything!

But I don't know what I want to play with, said my sister and she started wailing again. I suddenly felt sorry for her. My God, I thought, what's going to happen to her when I'm not there and she can't ask anyone what she should play with? But I didn't say that. I stayed quite calm and told her she was an ungrateful creature, because up until now I'd taken her everywhere with me, but in this case there was a particular reason why I couldn't take her.

Why?

Because I'm having important discussions with Hutsche, I said. He doesn't allow girls in his room.

Why not?

He can't stand the smell of them.

And what are you talking about in your discussions?

I'll tell you that when I'm back, I said, maybe! and with that I went off and left her standing.

14

Sometimes, when I wanted to go out, Mother would come out on the stairs with me and say: That Hutsche! I stood right next to her and said: I've got to go!

He's too old to be your friend, she said.

I'm just on my way to see him now, I said.

Mother had put on weight, especially in the chin area. My chinnychinchins! she said. She watched me go. She thought: That peculiar boy is too old for my son! And too poor! Then she went into the kitchen to do some ironing. I leapt down the stairs and thought about my friend. For a while he didn't have a satchel, that's how poor he was! He carried his books under his arm. Sometimes he had a rubber band holding them together till the rubber band broke. Sometimes they would get rained on. The next day would be fine, and they dried out. Once, when I'd been talking to Mother about Hutsche in our room, and she then talked to Father about him in his study, Father took his stick and went up into the attic.

There, said Mother, after Father had spent a long time puffing and swearing and had found my old satchel for Hutsche, now he's got one!

It'll be a miracle if I don't break something, Father shouted down.

What might you break? asked my sister, and Father said: Well, my neck for example.

When I held out the satchel to Hutsche, he didn't want it and said: What am I going to do with that piece of junk? The next time he was around to our places, I simply put it on him, and said: There! He still didn't want it, though, and flung it in a corner. Finally he beckoned me over to him, and I had to *beg* him to accept my satchel. All right, he said, if I'm doing you such a huge favour! Then he left with it. Father stood by the window, eating a little sandwich. Your friend Hutsche, as he likes to call himself and perhaps that really is his name, is the biggest eccentric in these parts, wouldn't you agree? he asked. Does he never say goodbye?

I don't know, I said, sometimes he does, sometimes he doesn't.

And today, because we've made him a present of a satchel, he doesn't, said Father.

I'm just on my way to see him now, I said. I got my stick and looked up at the sky. The weather was, as always, beautiful. First I walked slowly, then I speeded up. Then I was with him. Hutsche was in his room, thinking or reading. Anything he'd particularly enjoyed or detested, he would set aside for me. Then I would have to sit down with him, and he would read it to me aloud. Fantastic passage, he would say, so expressionlessly, that I didn't know whether he was being ironic or whether he really meant it.

On my last day, Hutsche had been waiting for me. He always had time. He never needed to do any work for school, he hadn't set himself any particular goals, and he always got by. No wonder, because he didn't have a sister, nor even a father. He wouldn't have wanted them either, certainly not the sister. When I mentioned mine, he shuddered. You couldn't have given him a sister. Of all the people I knew, I had the best conversations with Hutsche, even though he didn't say much. He always looked at me in such a way that I knew he was listening. I had to go on talking, even if I had nothing left to say. Later we just sat hunkered down or stood leaning against the wall, letting our arms hang down, and not saying anything. We could have said a lot more, but we didn't feel like it. It was almost as good as if we had said it, no, maybe even better. And so the afternoons went by, his and mine. Often he thought the same thoughts as I did, only in a different order. He would close his eyes when he was thinking. When we noticed that we had thought or said the same things, we would shake hands, and he would say: Schiller! and I would say: Goethe! He would have his eyes closed then as well, or be looking up at the ceiling. Then he would say: Stupid, isn't it? or: Load of crap! That was generally in front of our house, or at school, or, if it was raining, up in his room. If there was a wall handy, we'd lean against it. It makes talking easier, he said, and then didn't speak.

Yes, I said and didn't speak either. A lot of time went, as he would say, downstream in this way. You're not saying anything, I said, when he had been silent a long time.

Yes, it's good for silence too, he said.

How do you mean? I asked, and Hutsche said: Here, in this room! or: Outside the house here! And if I did happen to say something, he blinked and looked at me. Ah, so that's what you mean, he said, and I said: Yes, more or less!

Even if he didn't say anything, he always understood me. If

something came out wrong, he always knew what I meant. That's not what you meant to say, is it? he would say, and I would say: No, not really!

If he ever didn't understand what I said, I knew it was badly thought out, or I'd said it wrong. He tipped his head to the side, and asked: Is that *really* what you wanted to say?

I thought about it and said: No, I suppose not!

Then what did you want to say? he asked, and I said: Oh, it was just a joke!

Yes, said Hutsche, closing his eyes again, that happens to me too! Then he would talk about something else, like the book he was reading. He had long fingers that were good for flicking through pages. He had long hair too, which his mother cut for him. It saves money, he said, and he grinned. You know she's obsessed with money. Because the poor woman hasn't got any!

None at all?

Pretty much.

Then what do you live off? I asked, and he said: Fresh air and cheerfulness! His mother was a small embittered woman who didn't need much. Her husband was Hutsche's father. Though you wouldn't think so to look at us, he sometimes said. Since he'd left her, she'd crumpled. Funny thing, he said.

I know someone who's crumpling as well, I said.

Man or woman? he asked, and I said: Man.

Is he getting hunched over or is he more collapsing? he asked, and I said: Both!

For the same reason? asked Hutsche, and I said: I think so! and of course I was thinking of Father.

Have you seen my mother lately? he asked, and when I said: Yes, he said: Well? Did you notice?

Notice what?

She's got smaller again. Quite a bit this time. Once a month, to save a few pennies, she tied an old tablecloth round his shoulders, sat him on a stool and cut his hair.

Does she know how to do it? I asked.

'Course not, said Hutsche, can't you tell! But she keeps trying.

Each time she cut his hair, you could tell from a long way off. That's why he put his hands to his head as he approached me, and called out: She's had a go at me again! Then he took my hand, and pressed it against his head. He moved it around, so I could feel how short his hair was. His mother cut awful holes in it, especially behind the ears. Hutsche looked pretty weird. Don't look at me, he said, first let it grow back! and he covered his head with his hands. He had fine slender fingers with marbled nails that we sometimes *examined.* I compared them to mine. We sat together, held out our arms, and put our hands next to each other. A long time we looked at them. Finally, he said: Well, that'll have to do! and he pulled his hand away again. So that I didn't see his hands any more, he shoved them in his pockets. First he just put the tips of his fingers in them, then his whole hands up to the wrist. Because I didn't want to do anything to order, I left my hands out a while. Then I put them away as well, and we stood around.

What'll we do now? he asked.

I don't know. Any ideas?

Nope!

He never bit his nails either, he didn't even chew them. They were regular and even and I liked them. What I liked best were the tight shorts that Hutsche wore all year round, even in winter. He didn't have any others, but he didn't admit it. He behaved as though he had thousands of other pairs. When he was up in his house and saw me coming, he pulled the window open and called out: You coming to see me?

Shall I? I called back, and he said: Can if you like.

We could go up to the Hoher Hain, I said.

OK, he said. And what trousers should I put on? The dark ones or the light ones or the shorts? But he only had the one pair. I looked up. I saw his smile. Your shorts of course, I called up. Are you sure? he asked.

Quite sure. When he asked: Isn't it a bit chilly for them? I called out: Not a bit of it! It's perfect shorts weather! The fact of the matter was: I liked him best in them. Mother shook her head and said: A shame to put him in trousers he's long since grown out of!

Do you think? I said, and I looked at my nails and thought about his.

That was when we used to go up to the Hoher Hain all the time, he in his old shorts. They smelled of tough canvas and of him. Sometimes he tweaked at them and said: These have been with me for about a hundred years now! I can hardly squeeze my thighs into them! I stood next to him, and I liked it when he said *my thighs*. He couldn't say it enough for me. I pretended I hadn't heard, and asked: What is it you can't squeeze in?

My thighs, said Hutsche, what do you think? These, he said, and patted them. He had squeezed them in with difficulty. That was why he kept pulling at his shorts and saying: They're so tight! They rub so! The shorts were of black drill, washed out and fraying. Sometimes I would go up to him, and pluck at them. Hutsche let me pluck a while, then he said: Ooh, it tickles! Careful, they'll burst! and he pushed my hand away. Sometimes I felt like putting my hand inside them, of course only for a little while. I said: Hey, Hutsche! and stood in front of him.

What is it? he asked, and I said: I want to ask you something. Ask, said Hutsche, ask away! but I didn't dare. Then, when he said: What is it you want to know? You can tell me! I said: I've forgotten!

But you knew it a minute ago.

Yes, but now I've forgotten it.

When I went up close to him, I could smell his skin. Sometimes he held out his arm to me, and said: My skin! I don't know if it's true, he said, I haven't tested it, but apparently it breathes. Curious, isn't it? When we stood close together, he breathed more rapidly. Sometimes I thought I could hear his skin breathing, but I must have been imagining that. It didn't smell sour or acrid, it smelled like mine. When we had stood around for long enough, he said: Let's go! and he didn't move.

Hutsche lived up under the eaves. He said: Halfway up to the sky. The window bars were close together and rusting away. One pane was cracked, maybe "new stuff" would get put in one day. But that would have to be after my time, it wouldn't be something I'd experience. The last time I went to Hutsche's, I stood at his door a long time. There used to be a bell. Now you had to walk up the stairs and knock. So I walked up the stairs and knocked. For a long time I didn't hear anything. Then I heard Hutsche's footfall. It was a very particular footfall that only he had. He opened. He blinked at me.

Oh, it's you, he said and yawned. Maybe he was just play-acting. I'd run up the stairs and I was out of breath. Yes, I said, it's me!

You're panting, he said. Were you so desperate to see me? Come on, it's just a joke! Are you on your own at least, or has someone attached themselves to you?

She's standing downstairs.

Did you drag her along with you?

I had to.

Hutsche was disappointed. I could see it in his eyes. I could hear it in his breathing as well. Why do you always have to drag her along with you, even today, he said, on this day of all days! Couldn't you have parked her somewhere? He shut the door behind us. Because the passage was so narrow and we were walking so close together, and our elbows, legs, fingers, and so on, were all touching, we had the same thoughts as well. If you hadn't dragged her along with you, he said, we might have been able to go up to the Hoher Hain together once more.

Couldn't we take her with us? I asked.

Is that your idea of a joke? I couldn't do it with her there.

No, nor could I, I said.

Hutsche lived in a tiny room that he called his den, his domicile, his dump, his midden, his refuge, and so on. It was on the third floor. Sometimes we leaned against the wall, looking for different words for the same thing.

Now do you see that there are more words than things? he would say.

Nonsense, I said, a word is rarer than a thing. There are lots of things for each word.

You're wrong, he said, you can get a table for instance in lots of different languages, I don't even know how many. The word "table" exists as many times as there are different people using it.

No, I said, there are always more actual tables!

When you went into Hutsche's room, it was always dark. He said: The mystery! He went ahead, so I didn't "bark my nose" on something. He took his chances. His room he referred to as small, but mine own! I'd known it now for three years. In spite of that, I was always astonished by how cramped it was.

Then I would remember how it was, and I would say: Oh yes, it was always cramped up here!

So? You knew that!

Yes, but as cramped as this!

It concentrates your ideas, I find, said Hutsche, and was proud of his cramped room. I'm surprised he can even turn around, I thought and was about to say it. If you wanted to put another chair in here, I said, as well as yours . . .

I know, said Hutsche, it's a mousetrap! Would you rather talk on the street?

No, I said, *she's* there! Anyway it's cozy up here.

What are you being a hypocrite for? he asked. Why don't you say this place is a dump? His room smelled of him. I was always happy there. He'd been reading a book by the window when I came. If I want to read I have to be near the window, otherwise there isn't enough light.

I see.

Do you go over to your window too?

I don't read much, I replied.

On that day, it took me a long time to get used to the dark and the smell of his room. I looked at it all again: Hutsche's table, his chair, the darkened walls. Then I looked at Hutsche. He'd been leaning against the darkest part of the wall. He had shot up and was quite a bit bigger than me. He would probably have to start shaving soon. He was getting a pair of glasses too, next week. But I'd already be gone by then. When I said: Over the hills and far away! he said: Where the elves come out to play! and when I said: To pastures new! he said: Yeah, Russdorf!

Now we were leaning against the wall, and I asked him if he sometimes thought about it.

What are you talking about, for Christ's sake?

First I'd wanted to say: Our separation! or: My leaving! but I ended up saying: Your new glasses!

Why should I think about it? he asked. It'll come and that'll be that.

What kind would you like? I asked. Some with metal frames or celluloid? Then I made a little joke, a little play on words. If you get thick black rims, you'll look like a represser.

A what?

A professor?

And if I have thin ones?

The same.

He had pressed his back against the wall. It left me more room. As ever, he was speaking quietly. I'm a poor rat who has to hang off my ears whatever my mother sees fit.

And what will she see fit?

The cheapest kind, of course, he said, what else? Then we were silent again, each of us staring at the floor. I reached out for the book that was lying on his desk, I put out my hand to pick it up. No, don't touch that, it's rubbish, he said, and smacked the back of my hand. Sorry, but I don't want you to dirty your hands on it. The stuff would wreck whatever image of me you might have.

I see.

Or then again perhaps not.

Perhaps not, I said.

Hutsche had gone red. He jerked the book away from me so fast that I couldn't see the title. Then he tossed it on to the wardrobe. Now I can rest easy, he said.

Will you stop reading it now?

I expect I will again, he said, once you're gone and I feel weak.

He leaned against the wardrobe. The wardrobe contained his clothes, an old pipe he sometimes stuck in his mouth, a family photograph that he studied, *to see how I mustn't ever become*, a couple of dirty magazines. I need them, he said, I couldn't live without a bit of filth and squalor.

What about you?

I'm not sure yet, I said.

Hutsche's parents had got divorced, after long reciprocal torment, as he put it. Since they've started living apart and I don't get involved in their squabbles, I've more time for myself. And for you too, he said. Maybe he would have had more time for me earlier as well, but we hadn't known each other then. The Hoher Hain had stood there without us, and it hadn't missed us really. Then people sundered what God, in a moment of thoughtlessness, had unwisely attempted to glue together, Hutsche said. Now he lived with his mother in the aforementioned dump on the Kanalstrasse. To show me what he meant, he ripped a piece of wallpaper off the wall.

Hutsche! I exclaimed, What are you doing?

I'm getting down to fundamentals, he said. The wallpaper was grey and hung down uselessly. There, he said, and flapped it about.

I shook my head. I always tried to arrange it so that his mother was out when I came round. Then I didn't need to greet her. Standing at the door, I asked: Are you alone?

He usually replied: All alone!

Good, I said, then we can talk.

What shall we talk about?

Everything under the sun, I said, making an expansive gesture. Sometimes when I asked: Are you alone? *he pulled a face* and said: Unfortunately not! His mother was in the kitchen, *scraping away.* Can you hear the poor creature? he asked.

I cupped my hand to my ear. Yes, I said, I can hear her!

Have you ever seen her scraping?

No.

Then you've missed something, he said. Come on, I'll show you! We went to the kitchen door. You really must see her beavering away. You don't have to say anything. You can go and stand in the corner and see what a woman does in a kitchen. Watch her fighting against the most natural things in the world, decay and dirt. Have you ever seen her hands?

No.

They're awful, said Hutsche, sad! We went in the kitchen. I said hello. His mother was scrubbing and polishing. I don't think she said anything at all. Because I wasn't able to talk to him, I wanted to go home. Just say something nice to her, he said, it doesn't have to be much. Then we walked round the other side of her, and I watched. After I'd seen it, I said goodbye and we went out. Hutsche walked me back, just to get out of the house. I'll suffocate if I stay, he said.

In the bright sunshine one thing was clear: Hutsche was losing his hair! What he did have was thin and fine. He said that was because of intellectual labour, "something you don't know much about". He had his *summer and winter cap on, which keeps the brain nice and warm.* When we passed someone who knew us, he quickly whipped it off. There seemed to be a huge detachment in the way he talked about everything, his cap, his parents, school. He called his father *that man* or *the poor bastard who has no idea what happened to his life,* his mother was the woman who *had drawn a blank in the marriage lottery,* the teachers merely *passed on their own ignorance* and so on and so forth. About the situation in my home he said: I know how that feels! His parents hadn't talked to each other much at the end either. Hutsche's mother didn't talk a lot now. She's said all the words that were given to her to say, he once put it.

We hung around in front of his house. We couldn't go inside, she was cleaning.

How do you mean: *given to her?* I asked.

By the world spirit or whatever you want to call him, said Hutsche, and he said: At birth, everyone is allotted a certain number of words to say in the course of their life.

What if he says more than that?

They're all included in advance, he said. Once you've said them all, that's it.

Why? There could be more! I could say them too.

You don't understand, said Hutsche. Everything that you're allowed to say has been said.

But there must be more to come!

The great silence, said Hutsche.

I didn't understand him, and so I said: I see, that's what you mean! And then we were both silent too.

Now, said Hutsche, she's got to the point where there's not much to come. It used to pour out of her, but now there's just a trickle. That's why she's getting so peculiar. She thinks of me as a prop, and hasn't realized that I'll be gone soon. I'm just waiting for the right moment. Then I'll break it to her.

And where will you go? I asked.

Africa or beyond.

Beyond Africa?

Why not? We were standing around again.

Will you really go to Africa?

Come along, he said, we'll go together! What do people always say then. Oh yes, *choking back her sobs*, he said. When I asked what had befallen his mother, he said: What do you think? Life in all its splendour, what else? Then he apologized for the way *she was either screaming or silent.* She can't communicate any other way, he said, poor woman. She doesn't mean badly, you have to look the other way. Apparently she's kind-hearted, though I've no idea what people base that on. She's just got a lot on her plate. That terrible divorce from that awful man . . .

Do you mean your father?

Who else! After all, it was him who put us out on the street. So she has to scrimp and save, he said, and it seemed he wouldn't stop talking. As much as he had been silent earlier, now he was talking. Usually it was while we were walking somewhere. I always stayed at his side, so he didn't run off without me. He had his cap—*my lid*—on, and pushed it this way and that. He said how every so often he had to crawl into his Sunday shirt and visit his *so-called progenitor, to remind him of my existence.* I didn't know his father, he was always at work, in some foundry or other. He sings the song of the good working man, pouring and pouring metal. They're happy to let him slave away till the day he throws up his arms and collapses. And then he'll be dead, said Hutsche, isn't that strange? Sometimes he would wave a bar of chocolate, and say: Come on, we're going up to the Hoher Hain. I've got something for us. He put his cap on, and rammed the chocolate into his tight trousers, and took it up to the Hoher Hain. There we crept into the underbrush, where the little streamlet flowed. There were fish in it, but only very little ones. We often saw them lying on the bank of the stream, with their bellies all swollen. They had been washed up by the stream. We bent over them and studied them. Hutsche took his cap off, and shook his head.

Shame about them, he said, just like everything else.

What else?

Everything, said Hutsche, and gazed into the distance with his shortsighted eyes. God knows what he saw there. He picked up a stone to hurl it against a tree trunk, but he missed. Shame about the whole shebang, he said, putting his cap back on.

D'you think it'll rain today? I asked.

How do I know? he replied.

In the summer—we didn't have many of them—we would hunker down by the widest part of the stream. Sometimes we stood up and skimmed stones over the water. Sometimes it worked. Then we would cry out: Look! or: Six times! But usually we just sat around. It's almost time, he said.

Time for what?

Time to get out of here!

Of course what I should have asked was: What then? But I said: And then?

Then, said Hutsche, we'll do something, yes, he said, something will be undertaken!

Unfortunately, he never said what he wanted to do. When I asked him, he said: Ssh, top secret! Later he had forgotten all about it, and once again, we hadn't *done* anything. Sometimes he really did think about something, like building a fort, or digging a trench. But then he forgot that too, he kept having new ideas, whereas I never had any at all. I couldn't go from one thing to the next the way he could, I didn't have the imagination. We should join forces, he said, and do something about it.

Who?

Everyone.

About what?

What do you think? he said, Against the whole thing of course.

Sure, I said, but what whole thing?

Oh, he said, you know! or: Just forget it! You don't understand.

One time, a little before Father and I were going to leave—only I didn't know it at the time—we were going to bury the dead fishes, but with all due ceremony, he said. I had my anorak on, Hutsche was freshly scalped. We had brought our sticks along and scratched a hole on the bank of the stream. But there were too many fishes, they wouldn't all go in the hole. Anyway, said Hutsche, they're just fishes, they don't deserve it! He had his stick in his hand. Then he decided just to toss them all in the water, and not to bury any of them. He prodded around in the stream. Let the poor buggers float off, he said, then at least they'll be in their element.

A little way downstream was a large flat stone. It's standing with its foot in the water, said Hutsche.

A stone hasn't got a foot, I said.

This one does, if you look at it closely.

We sat down on the stone and clasped our knees to our chests. If it was warm, we took off our shoes and stuck our feet in the water. Then we went and sat in the grass, which was softer. We looked out for more fishes. Sometimes we looked up and watched the clouds go overhead. Mostly there weren't any fishes. There are getting to be less of them, said Hutsche.

Yeah?

Shame, said Hutsche.

On one particular day or other, we rolled up our sleeves and stretched out side by side on the grass that grew in between the rocks. We looked up at the sky. There was the faintest breeze.

I didn't know yet that Father and Mother were separating, I didn't want to know. When a fish came along—so rarely, so rarely!—we watched him go.

There he goes, alive or dead, leaving us behind, said Hutsche.

What else is he going to do? I asked.

Take us with him, said Hutsche, blinking in its direction. He couldn't stand sunshine, it didn't bother me. Sometimes our arms brushed against each other. Then Hutsche would move his away, I left mine where it was. Then we closed our eyes again, and didn't say anything for a long time. Sometimes he would say: How quiet we are!

What is there to say?

A few words, said Hutsche, doesn't matter what they are! Not that fish-like silence! When he brushed against me with his hand or his bare arm, he jumped and said: Sorry! Sometimes, to make a joke of it, he would say: Excuse me for being so forward!

I would reply: That's quite all right! and he said: You never can tell!

I had closed my eyes, and was thinking about his hands. I was picturing them to myself. I didn't know what went through his mind when we touched. We lay there in the warm part of the year, side by side in the grass by the stream, taking quiet, shallow breaths. From time to time, a bird circled above us. Sometimes it was a bird of prey, like a buzzard. Look at that, Hutsche would say. I would already have seen it, and had stopped looking. I said: I know. Finally, he made an effort and sat up. He leaned on one hip, pulled the chocolate bar out of his opposite pocket, and held it aloft. See what I've got, he said. He waved it around. From my old man, because he doesn't give a shit about me and feels guilty. Then he broke the bar in half and said: Close your eyes and open your beak!

I opened my mouth.

Wider!

I opened my mouth as wide as I could, and Hutsche stuck a piece of chocolate between my lips. Little fledglings gotta eat or die, he said. Then he took the other piece. Ain't life sweet, he said and smiled. Often I wouldn't know what he was getting at, or why it amused him. I grinned anyway. Then we lay down on the ground again, close together. We sucked at our chocolate, he right beside me, till it was all melted. He cracked another one of his jokes. He said: That's all, love, dad.

There's no smoke after the horse is gone, I said.

That day, we brushed against each other many times. He stopped saying: Excuse me! Nor did he say what was on his mind, and I didn't ask him. I sweated against his arm, and he against mine. Our knees were touching, our thighs as well. We made as though we didn't notice anything. On that and other days, we lay there silently. Then, as if on a word of command from somewhere, the air grew colder, a wind got up, and the sun disappeared. Hutsche stretched and said: Well, that'll have to do!

In other words?

Let's creep off to our respective abodes!

OK, I said. I quickly stood up.

The time I came to say goodbye, everything was different. We couldn't go up to the Hoher Hain any more. Hutsche said: From today forth, it's closed! My sister was leaning in the doorway downstairs. I stood by the window with Hutsche. He had bolted the door of his room, which would otherwise have opened by itself. And he didn't feel safe behind a door that opened by itself. He was pressed right back against the wall and said: I'm waiting for my glasses.

So the whole time you've been waiting for your glasses, and not for me!

No, not for you, he said, for my glasses!

Did you think I'd come and see you again?

No.

You thought I'd just disappear?

Yes.

Hutsche—Saturday, poverty, sunny—was in his shorts. His mother had gone out cleaning.

Does she clean on Saturdays as well? I asked.

She has to take whatever she's offered, he said. It can only be a matter of weeks before she runs out of steam.

The summer had arrived. Hutsche smelled of it. He was a bit excited. I'd hoped it was because of me, but it was because of his glasses. Can you imagine, he cried, my first pair of glasses! He had pressed his chin against the windowpane, and was breathing over it. I stood behind him, far inside his room. I hoped he would talk about our parting, but he talked about himself.

Just imagine, he cried, I'm getting a pair of glasses! He shut his eyes. They were tired. Often they were red. Then he said: Just a second! and he went into the kitchen to cool them. Then he rubbed them again. Now he laid his hand across his brow and said: Can you imagine me with glasses? I can't! And he was looking over his shoulder, at himself in the mirror.

Tomorrow, isn't it? I asked.

No, he said, the day after! Tomorrow's Sunday, no glasses on Sundays! Monday's the day of the glasses! Then he suddenly said very quietly: You're gone tomorrow, aren't you?

Yes, I said, I'll be gone then.

When you've always been here before.

No, I said, I'll be gone then.

There was another pause. Then he said: If there's another war, I've got my excuse. They won't take anyone with glasses. Then he meant to say: Because they will come, the glasses! but he misspoke and said: Because it will come, the war!

Eh?

The glasses, he said, I mean the glasses!

We leaned against the wall, close together. His den was full of our breathing. The window was hard to open, he would suffocate in here one day. The sky was still bright. Outside the house was my sister. She looked up at us and called my name. We looked at one another. We didn't pay any attention. Soon I wouldn't see him any more.

Then you'll be . . . a memory, faint and getting fainter, said Hutsche. One day you'll be so faint, I won't be able to see you any more. Then I'll say to myself: There was something there! And that will have been you.

Maybe I'll come and see you some time.

You're never going to come and see me!

Why not?

Because you're going to forget me immediately, said Hutsche, and he laughed.

He was the only friend I had, then or later, only he didn't know it. He thought I had others. He had only one pair of shoes, and they were brown. In the right one, there was a hole.

Look, he said, and he put his foot down on the chair. Then he pushed his finger in, and I nodded and said: A hole!

The very word I was going to use, said Hutsche, and we laughed. We stood like that for a long time. You will often think of him standing like that, I thought, unbespectacled for all time. He had no idea how attached I was to him. He had loads of friends, I knew them all. Often he would be walking up the street with one of them, with Malz or with Alwin. I always saw them first. When he finally saw me, he would call out something to me which I could never understand. I nodded all the same. Then I made a little sign, often just with one index finger, usually the right. One time he was coming out of the Hoher Hain with Koller. They were suddenly standing in front of me. Hutsche carried the length of beechwood he always carried when he was with me. They were walking close together, with their arms touching. They swung their sticks, and walked in step.

Hi, called Hutsche. He was startled.

Hi, I said, and we carried on our separate ways. Sometimes they trailed their sticks behind them and dragged them in the dirt. You could hear them from a long way off. I turned round when I heard them, and ran off. Or, quite unexpectedly, he would have one of them at home with him. That was the worst. Even as I stood at the door, I could hear something. When I knocked, there was a sudden silence, and I thought: No, you were mistaken. But then it was *too quiet*, and I knew he was at home, and not alone. Then the other voice spoke up again, Koller's or Malz's as it might be. I gritted my teeth, and pushed the door open anyway. I wanted to know for certain. Was it Koller? Was it Malz? Was it Schuster, Manfred, or someone else who had never been at his house before and whom I didn't even know? I immediately hated whoever it was, who would be squatting legs apart on my chair, as though he would be there for ever. A blushing Hutsche would be standing right next to him. He might have his hand resting on the other fellow's shoulder. He had told him something or maybe shown him something that he had once told or shown me, on the same stool. Certainly he would have an open book in his hand too. I walked in, and they fell silent, pushed the book away.

Hi.

Hi.

Hi.

Of course they couldn't fail to notice my disappointment, my shock. Hutsche had moved back against the wall, far away from the other guy. I didn't say anything to either of them. I looked at the floor and said I'd been in the area and had just wanted to *pop by*. But now I have to go again, I said, I've seen you anyway.

No, no, said Hutsche, stay!

Afraid I've got to dash, I said, see you! and I ran out of the *ghastly hole*, his room. I plunged down the stairs. I didn't want to be with Hutsche *and the other guy* for a second. Once on the street—the light, the air—I took a deep breath. For a long time I didn't look round. Then finally I did, and I saw that Hutsche and his new friend had stepped up to the window. They were a couple of silhouettes, standing close together. They had inclined their heads together, and were looking down at me. Sometimes one of them laughed. Sometimes they both laughed together, which was particularly horrible. Sometimes, when Hutsche had someone with him, and I wanted to run off, he wouldn't let me and said: No, wait! I would already be on the stairs, and he would be after me. He caught up with me quickly, I wanted to be caught! He seized my arm. He smiled and said: Not so fast! Not like that! Don't! Then he put his arm around my shoulder, and said: We were just talking! Talk to us a bit! Sometimes I actually would go back up to his room again, but I wouldn't talk. I just stood around. I couldn't think of anything to say, and anyway I wanted him to see that I was hurt. The other guy, the guy that Hutsche was deceiving me with—

Schuster, Manfred or Dreeser or that Malz again—would stand up the instant he saw my face. He sensed he was in the way, and he wanted to get to the door, but I wouldn't let him. Then he wanted to put me down on Hutsche's stool, but I wouldn't submit to that either. Finally I looked at my watch and said I had to go. Hutsche leaned stiffly against the wall, the other guy next to him. I saw how their shoulders touched. Then I ran off.

Hutsche thought I had other people besides him as well. But I didn't. If I ever missed him at lunchtime, I spent the afternoon on my own. Sometimes, when I said someone's name—like Jassing's or Bender's—he would look at me oddly. You know him, don't you? he asked.

Sure.

Well?

No, just casually.

Does he often go round to yours?

No. Never.

Has he never been at yours then?

No.

Hutsche laughed. He expelled air through his nose, as he always did when he didn't believe something. I don't believe that, he said. But he never asked me whether I had anyone else except him. He was too proud for that, too cool, too lazy, didn't want to force himself, didn't want to have embarrassing conversations that didn't get anywhere, didn't want to create a bad atmosphere, and so on and so forth.

On our last day there wasn't much time. It was shorter than the others. (My sister claimed later that it was *longer.*) She leaned against the garden fence, calling out my name.

She's wailing for me, I said.

Yeah, said Hutsche, I can hear it. When I wanted to look down again, he dragged me away from the window, and said: She only wants to bother us. Then he said: Stay, I've got something to tell you! He was wearing his shorts, his down-at-heel shoes, no socks, nothing on his eccentrically beautiful skull. His freshly laundered shirt smelled of soap. Before we went our separate ways, he wanted to talk to me. So that was it then, he said. He corrected himself, and said: That will have been it! There was something else he wanted to add, but he let it go. Strange, he said.

What is?

The fact that you're going. I mean: just like that.

Yes, I said, it is strange.

How are they going to move you?

In a moving van.

And when is that coming? Next month?

Tonight, I said. Now.

What! So soon?

Yes, so soon.

And then you're going to creep into that, you and your suitcase?

Two of them, I said, two suitcases!

And your old man?

Yeah, him too.

And the little thing downstairs?

She's staying here.

Right, I remember, said Hutsche. He'd been properly scalped again, and was scratching his head. No fleas, he said, just nervous! He was thinking again. There's this line that people like to say in these kind of situations. In these cases of farewell and such sweet sorrow. When one takes the high road, and the other takes the low road. Let me think! Something about a noise that gets made, or not made.

A noise?

A noise that goes over the landscape and finally . . . Ah now it's come back to me! Funny, he said, wonder where it went, now that it's back? Then he paused and said: There's no smoke after the horse is gone.

What?

There's no smoke after the horse . . .

What do you mean by that?

Hutsche shrugged his shoulders. That's just how it goes, he said. Then he tipped his chair back against the wall. It was all scraped there. So often I'd leaned there when I'd been with him, either me or somebody else.

Do you remember, I said, when I . . .

Hutsche waved to me to stop. He didn't want any more talk about us. He kept me waiting a bit. Finally he straightened himself up and said: Everything's going to be different from now on.

I see.

Well, maybe not everything, but quite a bit, said Hutsche. I've got something planned, but don't breathe a word of it to anyone!

What is it?

Promise?

I promise!

OK, said Hutsche. Then he started to talk. I thought he would talk about me, or at least about us. But he talked about something completely different. He said he wanted to build something. Yes, he said, that's for sure.

Build?

Yes, build.

Build what?

Oh, said Hutsche, just something. Then he pointed to the darkest corner of his lair and said: There it is! At the moment he didn't quite know what it was.

Don't you know what's over there?

What will be there, he said. That's why I said *something*. But that doesn't matter really. He had recently been collecting, *picking stuff up from the carpenter in the Albertstrasse*. That's what he would use.

And what have you been collecting?

Oh, he said, what do you think I've been collecting? The kind of things I need, pieces of timber for instance.

And what do you need pieces of timber for?

Hold on, said Hutsche, I'm telling you! For weeks these bits of wood and board had been lying in his room, in the corner behind his bed. I don't know if you noticed, he said, I guess not. He pointed to the dark corner behind us. It took a while before I saw that there was something lying there. Wait, he said, I'll show you. You do want to see, don't you?

Yes.

Really?

Yes, very much.

He took me by the sleeve and pulled me into the corner. When he knelt down, he was able to reach the boards. At night, he said, when the cats are grey, I can picture it to myself.

You mean you . . .

I can picture it to myself, he said. He saw something, but not clearly, more in a kind of haze. That's the way it was with the imagination. He saw what he wanted to build, unfortunately not very distinctly. Then he stooped down and pulled out the boards and the pieces of wood. There, he said, and held them out to me.

He shrugged his shoulders. He didn't really know what to do. He held two little planks together, now this way, now that. He rattled them together. If you, he said, and then he thought. No, he said, it wouldn't work. If I had proper tools, he said, and a proper workshop, a real little . . .

Yes?

He clenched his fist and said: Then I'd show them all right!

Show whom?

All of them.

Show them what?

Ha, yes what, said Hutsche. He put the little pieces of timber together in different combinations, and with his shortsighted eyes looked up at the ceiling. That could have done with a coat of paint too. Just there was no one who thought of it, or they didn't have any paint. Finally, he stacked his little boards in the corner again, the way they'd been when he got them out. He passed his hand through the air as though to dispel something. That meant: Can we talk about something else now!

I moved away from his planks. What about? I asked.

So you're getting out of here.

Afraid so.

And you won't be back any time soon either?

No.

And when are you off? Exactly!

I had told him already three times. Tonight, I said.

So soon?

Yes, tonight.

Ah well, said Hutsche and he clicked his tongue, I don't know why. The wooden blocks he wanted to make something out of, they were lying on the floor again. Maybe he really would make something out of them, long after I was gone. One of them he still held in his hand, a short, solid piece that would be good for scratching. Hutsche first scratched his armpit, then the back of his head. Then he rapped his knee with it. Are you packed? he asked.

No.

Have you got to pack?

Yes.

Will it all go in one suitcase?

Yes, in two.

And you'll carry them yourself?

Yes, one in each hand.

And what's the dump called where they're dragging you off to?

Russdorf.

Sounds hideous!

It will be.

And your little sister?

She's the lucky one, I said, she gets to stay here!

Russdorf, said Hutsche. Factories?

Yes.

Where they'll put you to work in a couple of years' time and where you'll probably stay?

I suppose.

Hutsche sighed. Then the pause returned. It came through the window and the door and crept up the walls. I knew it already. And what kind of prospects do you have, he asked, in general?

None really.

Any plans?

None either.

And what are your feelings about the whole thing, if I may be permitted to ask? Have you got any feelings, or do you just let it all bounce off you? That would be the best, I suppose.

How about you?

We're not talking about me.

Oh, I said, sure, I have feelings, but I try not to think about them. I think about them so little that maybe I don't have any. When I think about Father for instance . . .

Yes?

I mean, when I try and put myself in his shoes . . .

Yes?

Poor fucker, I said.

Why?

I mean look at him. Look at his slippers. He wanted to be a writer at one time. And now this other father who's slowly sliding up to me, as if one wasn't enough. He's probably even now slipping into . . .

Yes?

. . . his jacket.

What's it like?

I don't know, I said, I've not seen him yet. We're drinking coffee with him, Father, Mother and I. And then we hit the road! Someone needs to buy cake first.

What sort?

With crumble, I think.

Nice big bits, with butter and sugar?

Yes, nice and big like that!

Oh well, said Hutsche, maybe you'll be in luck and he'll choke on one. There are still signs and wonders.

I'll be gone when he settles into our place. I won't be there to see it.

You'll be in . . .

In Russdorf, I said, in Russdorf!

Hutsche still had the lump of wood in his hand. He was about to give it a lick. But then he just sniffed at it instead. Finally, he got a grip on himself and tossed it down on the floor. So we won't be seeing each other much any more, he said.

Not at all really.

Only so little!

Really not at all.

We stood on his tatting rug. It had once had tassels. Then Hutsche had taken out his scissors and cut them off. He was too spartan for tassels. I had watched him, and never forgot it.

Strange, he said, when you think . . .

Yes?

If you tell yourself what a long . . . what a short . . .

A long or short what?

Nothing, said Hutsche, nothing at all!

Yes, I said, that's right!

My sister was outside, shouting. When I looked past Hutsche I could see her. I could see her hair and her throat and her hands in which she was clasping her dolls. Sometimes she looked up, not knowing quite where to look. If she looked up to our window, we quickly moved back out of sight. Suddenly Hutsche had an idea, I could see it in his eyes. I could hear it in his breathing too. I asked him: What do you want to do?

We were standing around for the last time, and Hutsche was saying something. He was saying: Before you push off and leave my sight for ever . . . He corrected himself: Before you leave and abandon me to fate in this dump . . . No, no, he said, that's just what it is! I'd like to . . . I mean there was one thing! But we don't have to.

What is it?

Oh crumbs, said Hutsche. He was embarrassed. He had moved away from me, into the corner past the window, where no light fell on him. If I hadn't known that he was standing there, it might just as well have been someone else, Malz or Koller or Jässing. He said something peculiar. He said: Those trousers you've got on . . .

Yes?

It's not important, if you don't want to.

No?

I quite fancy trying them on.

My trousers?

Or do you think I'll split them?

I don't know.

Hutsche came right up to me. He plucked at my trousers. First he plucked at a belt-loop, then he plucked at a trouser-leg. You couldn't have put turn-ups on his trousers, they were much too tight. My God, it's hardly the first pair of someone else's trousers I've tried on, he said. I won't split them! But if you're scared that I'll wreck them . . .

Wreck?

That I'll ruin them.

No, no, not at all, I said. But how come . . .

I'd like to see you in my trousers. I want to see what that looks like.

Your trousers or me?

Both.

OK!

I just want to see . . .

OK!

A car drew up under Hutsche's window. Someone got out. He wore a large grey hat and a black waistcoat. My sister was calling me again. She was beating a doll against the wall and shouting along the buildings: Where are you? Where are you? She shouted my name. I turned to the wall. I unbuttoned my trousers and thought: What is it this time? Then I pulled down my trousers. They were stiff and hard. I said: You did mean this, didn't you? Then I held them out to Hutsche. He was unbuttoning his trousers. He was standing in the dark corner and he was a little bit slower. I heard my sister shouting again, the same thing over and over. She was shouting: Are you coming or not? Are you coming or not? Then Hutsche too had taken off his trousers. He was hopping on one leg. His thighs were those of a young man, they were different than mine. First he hopped on one leg, then he hopped on the other. There, he said, all right!

Outside, my sister was still calling. Are you coming, she called, or not? It sounded very far away, Hutsche slipped into my trousers. My sister kept calling and calling.

Afterwards, when we'd swapped our trousers back again, there wasn't much else. Hutsche's pad was as cramped as ever, if not more so. Everything had been said. So we won't be seeing that much more of each other, I said.

No, he said, I guess not.

Not in this life at any rate.

Nor in the other either, he said.

I was long since back in my own trousers. I was still plucking at them. Oh, I said, that's what you mean! Then my sister was calling again. She was calling uninterruptedly now. She had nothing else to do. I thought: Why does she have to call like that! And then after a while, I went.

15

Father was standing in his room, making a stack of books. He ran his hand up and down them and said: These are the ones I can't live without! (But then it turned out that he could.) His head hurt with worries, that was his *Achilles heel*. He brushed it with his fingertips and said: Ow, ow, ow! We were back from Hutsche's, from now on I would begin forgetting him.

Is that man there now? asked my sister.

You mean Herkenrath the adulterer? asked Father. Not so far as I know.

Were we gone a long time? asked my sister. Please tell me! Tell me! Tell!

Father flung open the window. He had to struggle with the bolt, but then you couldn't hope to do anything in this world without force. He sat down at his desk and let his arms hang down. He breathed the same indoor air as we did, only a little bit more of it. His lungs, his stomach and his heart, they were all bigger than ours. He had more thoughts in his head too, only he often couldn't track them down. Then he said: What was it I was going to say? He had a question. It's in there, and it'll come back to me, he said, knocking on his forehead. In any case, he said, you are back in one piece, or two pieces, and we should be thankful for that! Then he asked whether Mother had come *floating out of her boudoir* yet, or if she was still *rootling around in her hair*.

But she doesn't rootle, said my sister.

I know, he said, she just tweaks! What I meant to say was: Is she still in her room, or has she . . . Well, and now you're back, he said. Did you manage to gasp a little fresh air? Taking deep breaths! Like Thomas Mann in the days when he used to walk through the Bayerischer Wald, taking nice deep breaths, as he never tires of informing us, whereas you are incapable of giving me an answer to the most elementary question. So, packing, he said. He was nervous, because any moment now Herr Herkenrath would come *steaming round the corner, making straight for us*. He reached for his handkerchief to check if it was sodden. He didn't tell us though, he just shook his head. Then, as if he *didn't have enough on his plate anyway* there were people coming, visitors, at last, at last! Because my sister was standing at the window, she was the first to see him.

Here comes someone, she called.

Male or female? asked Father.

Male.

Young or old?

Sort of in between.

And what makes you think he's coming to see us? asked Father, still not getting to his feet.

Because he's heading straight for our house.

Do you know him?

I think so.

Good, said Father, excellent! Then he sat still for another long spell, breathing and thinking. And what's he doing now, he asked, is he in the building yet?

Almost.

Very well, said Father, let's not be impatient and not pressurize him! Let's wait and find out if it's really us he wants to see, and if we want him to see us. Otherwise we can send him straight home again. We waited some more. What was I saying all along, and no one believed me? said Father. He was pleased that someone was coming to visit *so soon before the final hooter*, he just didn't want to let on. Not even in the grave will I get a moment's peace, there'll always be people talking at me, and thinking at me, he said, that's how fanatical people are about me, and merely because I have a few ideas from time to time, and cover a page or two with my writing! In spite of which one would dearly like to know who this is!

We all had a think. I know who, said my sister. It's that man.

It wouldn't surprise me if it were a man, rather than say, a mouse, said Father. The question remains: which man?

The one you're always talking to on the street, who you're then rude to and leave standing, said my sister.

You mean the man from the tobacconist's, who comes chasing after me waving his bill?

No, not him!

The man who always comes on Sundays to discuss the future with me?

No, nor him either!

Is he coming to see me, or does he want a word with your Mother?

I think he's coming to see you, said my sister. He wants to say goodbye.

How does he know I'm leaving?

Perhaps he heard about it?

Nonsense, said Father. Anyway, it's far from certain. Well, he said, it's possible he's come to plead with me to stay, but there's no point in pleading with me, everything has its limits! But it could be! The whole town's buzzing with the news. The best thing is you tell him I've already left.

And where shall we tell him you've gone?

Just left.

Yes, but where to?

Father thought for a long time. Tell him anything you like, if you have to tell him something, he said. Tell him I've made an end.

But where?

In the Big Pond.

So should we let him in after all?

No, on no account!

But then how can we tell him?

True, said Father. All right then, he said, I can see I won't get any peace otherwise! Then he got up—*struggled to a vertical position*—pulled his little comb out of his back pocket, and ran it through the remains of his hair, combing it first one way than the other, to make sure it was evenly distributed. There weren't allowed to be any strings in it either. Then he put the comb away, and the bell rang. We could hear Mother in her room getting up and going over to her door. She was hoping that it was for her, but she wasn't going to open the door yet. She wanted us to. You go before she does, and let the man in, in case it's the one I'm thinking of, said Father.

And how will we know whether it is or not?

I'll tell you when I see him, said Father. Tell him to wipe his feet, and make him do it so that Mother hears it. I want her to appreciate how much I always did her bidding and supported her in everything. She will remember that when I'm gone.

Where will you be?

In Russdorf, said Father, where else? All right, he said, clapping his hands, and we went to the front door. And tell him to be quiet, he shouted after us. She doesn't have to know who's coming to see me.

And who is?

One of my admirers, someone who knows every line of my writing.

I thought you hadn't written all that much, said my sister.

It'll come, said Father, it'll come!

The bell rang again. We opened the door wide. There stood Herr Kappus, lanky and lean. He was wearing a dark jacket and light trousers. He must have been hot in the jacket. And there was something on his head too. He had Brylcreem in his hair, his narrow skull was gleaming with it. If you went right up to him, his skull smelled too. Herr Kappus said: Is . . . ? but my sister put a finger to her lips and went shh. Is the maitre at home? whispered Herr Kappus, and my sister went shh again.

Father's in his room, packing, I said.

So it's true, said Herr Kappus bleakly.

We went into Father's study—*alleged* study, Mother always called it—first Herr Kappus, then my sister, then me. I shut the door quietly behind me. Herr Kappus was very quiet as well, going along on tiptoe. He was a teacher, but at the Pestalozzi, not the Hindenburg School. He was a friend whom Father had kept from his *wild period*. The others had either moved or married or had in some other way been *punished and tamed* by life, as Father said. Now they were just *shadows of their former selves*. With the word *shadows*, Father rubbed his forehead to get *the blood flowing to his brain*. Then he laid his hand on the table, and drummed with his fingertips. When he spoke about his old friends, it always sounded as if they were all dead. My sister and I hadn't known any of them, they were all before our time. Because we didn't have any imagination, we were unable to picture them to ourselves, just as we couldn't picture Father at our age. Also, we got all of their names muddled up, or maybe Father had made them up anyway. When my sister heard one of them, she said: I know, he was a friend of yours once! But who was he *really*? When Father had just been in a reverie, he would smile a little. Yes, he said, he was wonderful, he was excellent! Then he said another name that we hadn't heard before. Urbanek, Willi, he said.

Did you used to know him too? asked my sister.

Oh yes, cried Father, oh yes!

And who was he again?

He was another one of them, said Father.

And is he dead as well?

Father rubbed his forehead again. I really don't know, he said, but it's a possibility! There's not much I'd put past Urbanek, Willi! If I remember correctly, he was always a bit of an invalid. Then he made some concluding gesture with his hand in the air, and said something mournful, like: So long ago now! or: All gone, all gone!

So he is dead? asked my sister.

No no, said Father, I wouldn't go so far as to say that. It's perfectly possible that he's still among the living. And how!

How?

You shouldn't ask!

But how? Tell me! How?

Well, quietly then, said Father, quietly. There's a word for it, it's slipped my mind just now, but maybe if I rub this spot here it'll come back to me, he said and rubbed his forehead. Then he cried: I've got it! *Vegetating*, that's the word I was after! Urbanek, Willi, is vegetating. He's vegetating in the bosom of some family somewhere, and nobody knows about it, that's how much he's withdrawn. Perhaps in some two-room hole of the kind that we're looking at too now, you and I, he said to me. But back then . . .

Yes?

Back then he was . . . different!

Have you seen him since those days? I asked.

Oh no, said Father, I wouldn't have risked it!

So he's not your friend any more? asked my sister, and Father said: Don't be absurd! We haven't seen each other in decades, and have completely lost touch with each other.

You mean that if he were to pass you in the street . . .

I wouldn't know him!

And if he says his name?

Then I wouldn't believe him, said Father, and went on pondering. Herr Kappus had been standing with us in the room for some time. He had never married, and was always asking: Does it show?

Let's have a look, Father would say. He took Herr Kappus by the shoulder, steered him into the light, looked at him narrowly, and said: I think not yet!

I hope you're right, said Herr Kappus, and Father said: I think I am! Whether Herr Kappus was talking or not talking at all, he was always a disruptive presence. He always let Father finish his sentences, though, and waited till he was done. If ever he happened to interrupt him, he gave a start and said: I'm so sorry, my mind was elsewhere! Please, pray continue! Before taking his jacket off in summer, he would ask if it were permitted to do so, and if Father didn't immediately give his permission, he said: I think I'll keep it on after all! Then Father regretted that he hadn't given his permission, and began to *badger* him, but Herr Kappus remained adamant and said: No, not in shirtsleeves, not with a polyester shirt! Father could press him any way he liked, Herr Kappus simply would not take off his jacket. Sometimes Father would go and drink a swift half with him, or even two. That would always be in the evening, when he'd written his quota for the day, and crossed it out again. Herr Kappus would stand in the gutter and shout up: Well, how about it? Shall we wet our whistles? Or is Inspiration in the way?

Father stood at the window, he had opened it wide. He replied something like: There's no such thing as inspiration, and anyone can have an idea! All that matters is what you do with it! But I agree! he cried, I've written enough for one day, and I'll slip my moorings. Wait on the corner, why don't you, there's no need for the wife to see you! Then he got into his street shoes, put on his beret and took down his stick. He disappeared swiftly and silently. Herr Kappus revered him, and paid for his beers. Often they would sit around till eleven, talking about life and art. Then, because they'd be the last, and he wanted to go home, Franz the barman brought them their bill. When he put it down on Father's side, Herr Kappus would reach across the table for it and say: Now just let me quickly and unobtrusively settle this!

You! exclaimed Father in surprise, But I could settle it as well myself! and he reached for his back pocket, but Herr Kappus said: No no! and he was faster on the draw.

Very well, said Father, if you insist! In return, he would tell Herr Kappus various things, but all of them grim. He talked about sudden fatalities, serious car accidents, suicides and divorces. Or he would talk about his new book, to be called *Death in the Home*, but which he had stopped writing. You're the only one who will have heard about it, said Father, and began to talk about his *impending disappearance*.

Are you going somewhere? asked Herr Kappus innocently.

You never know.

But not now!

What may appear to be a distant prospect often isn't!

You don't mean to say? cried Herr Kappus with open mouth and staring eyes.

My future is to be found there, said Father, pointing to the ground.

Impossible, said Herr Kappus, when I see you sitting in front of me like this!

I have received certain indications from highly qualified sources, said Father mysteriously.

Have you been to the doctor?

I don't need a doctor.

Then how do you know?

Mother Nature!

Well, if that's how it is, said Herr Kappus, shaken, and they sat around gloomily. They each drank another beer, and went home. When Father got back, he woke us all to tell us about it. That fellow Kappus worships me, he said, have you noticed? He's one of an ever-growing army from whom I will soon be unable to protect myself! These people begin by flattering one, but they soon become irritating. When I think about . . . Well, he said, one isn't able to choose one's admirers! They too are handed down to one from on high. For the time being, I'll tolerate it. I hope he profits from intercourse with me, and listens as I unfold my ideas before him.

And what about when you're not unfolding anything? asked my sister, and Father said: Then he'd better be listening as well!

Hello, Herr Kappus greeted him.

Hello, Kappus, said Father, seeming lost in thought. He had his glasses on and a book in his hand. He was leafing around in it, and did not look like someone who would be leaving in two hours. Have you done your duty for the day? he asked Herr Kappus.

I chased the rapscallions home for the Sabbath, said Herr Kappus. And have you been writing?

As ever, Father replied quietly.

What's up? asked Herr Kappus. Are you ill?

Why would I be ill?

You sound so strange.

Ha! Do I sound strange? said Father. He was almost inaudible. Well, there's a surprise. I thought I was.

Is that why you were lying down?

I suppose, said Father, I must have had some reason. I like to put my feet up, it aids the concentration. As he viewed Herr Kappus as his Boswell, he kept him abreast of everything relating to himself. It's like this, he said. First I'm sitting there like this, and he demonstrated how he was sitting to begin with. Then I close my eyes, that's how I do my best work. The pencil's always to hand. Yes, he said, exactly here! Then he put his legs down again. The springs of his cane rocker squeaked. Sometimes I prop myself on my elbow. That's how I get the clarity.

What about?

What do you think? said Father. About the whole thing, of course.

Am I interrupting then?

No, not at all, said Father, you've come at exactly the right moment! There are developments. Something has happened that I would have had to talk about with you anyway. But don't come too close!

So there is something the matter with you?

I don't know yet, said Father, it's too early to say. If I am coming down with something, it won't be anything very nice. Up till now, I've just had a little tickle, like this, he said, and he did a little cough for Herr Kappus. But that's just the beginning. I don't even want to talk about my head.

I've never heard you coughing before.

Well, you've only just arrived . . . Have you seen the state of the place?

I was just looking!

Well? Anything strike you?

It looks a bit of a mess. Are you tidying up?

If that were all! cried Father. No, I'm packing! With one foot I'm already on the street. If you'd arrived a couple of hours later, you'd have missed me. But since you've found me at the eleventh hour, I can't keep silent to you. I'm burning my bridges, I'm being forced to. But one thing at a time. The best thing is if I sit in my corner for the last time, then I'll have an overview of everything, and you can sit in the other corner and fire off questions.

What in Heaven's name is going on? What are you telling me?

One at a time please, said Father, let's sit down before we go any further! There'll be space between us, so I don't infect you. We'll be able to see and hear one another, without getting too near . . . *Too close*, Father said, in English. He pointed out the corners where he and Herr Kappus were to sit without infecting one another. Then he crept off the cane rocker. My sister and I were standing by the window, where we attracted the least attention. Then Father was talking again. What's happening now, he said, is something I've been expecting for a long time.

Is it your marriage? asked Herr Kappus.

Yes.

In crisis?

Are people talking about it yet?

In innuendo, said Herr Kappus. No one knows anything precise.

Ah well, said Father, they'll know about it tomorrow, or at the latest, the day after, when the week begins. Then he coughed a little and started telling Herr Kappus about the misfortune that had befallen him, that he hadn't yet told anyone else about. You're the first to hear about it, he lied. Herr Kappus was incredulous, or anyway seemed so. And Father in turn didn't believe him. But they know all over town that my marriage is at an end, he said. Everyone's seen it coming.

Not me, said Herr Kappus, I didn't! He kept looking round for a chair to sit on, but everything had stuff on it. Then he admitted he had heard *rumours of some such developments.*

No, said Father, no rumours, this is strictly real, facts that you might find in a book! Changes are overtaking the edifice of my life, that I worked so hard to erect, he said. A moving van is even now on its way.

And what will you do when it's here?

I will have to leap aboard it, what else can I do?

And where . . . ?

I forget the name of the place. I can't seem to keep it in my head.

You don't know where you're moving to?

Nor do I want to know.

You're not going to Russdorf, are you?

Why not? Everything's possible!

So you're going to Russdorf!

Please not to bruit the name about before the die is cast and the final discussion with my wife has taken place, said Father. After that discussion I will decide in which direction to proceed with my life. If any.

What do you mean: *Which direction?* asked Herr Kappus. What do you mean: *Proceed?*

Up or down.

Are you entertaining the possibility . . . ?

That's all I want to say at this point!

Surely you won't take it so hard as to . . . ?

Everything has its limits, said Father, that's all I'm saying! Remember the children are standing listening, he said, and pointed at us. And please not to come so close, you've been outside.

But so have you!

I was wearing a jacket.

And I've been in the sun.

That's not what it was either!

I know what you're saying, said schoolmaster Kappus. He was still looking for somewhere to put his teacher's cap, but everywhere was either dusty, or there was something else already there. Of course that was Father, with his *mindless tidying.* In the end, Herr Kappus didn't put his hat anywhere. He carried it over to his chair, sat down, and put it on his knee. That way he could fool around with it. But if you move away, we won't see each other any more, he said.

This is true, said Father.

Perhaps we could manage the occasional visit?

I shall be staying at home.

In Russdorf?

Yes, in Russdorf.

But isn't that sad?

Very sad!

Shouldn't you be thinking of getting back to your packing?

I'm thinking about it the whole time, said Father. It's not possible for someone to think any harder about packing than I am!

And what will become of the little ones?

The boy, said Father, I will stuff under my arm and haul off. But there's the other thing to be settled first.

What other thing?

Before I board the moving van, I will need to speak to my wife, said Father. This is the conversation I am now looking towards. I can't say whether it will take place or not, the deci-sion isn't mine. Naturally, I expect she would like to avoid it if she can.

She won't allow you one final conversation?

She hasn't spoken to me these past twenty days. She doesn't need me any more! She has another.

She does! I didn't like to ask.

A dwarf.

A dwarf?

A dwarf! At least he's fully a head shorter than she is, so he must look up to her, said Father grimly. That's why she wants him. But I won't tell you his name or anything about him. There's no point in your even asking.

He's called Herkenrath, isn't he?

I believe that's right.

Do you know him?

I've heard of him, said Father. Since that time, the name seems to have been etched into my brain with a steel nib, he said, tap-ping his brow. It's going *Herkenrath, Herkenrath* all the time! He's favouring us with a visit today. He wants to introduce himself to me and explain why he's depriving me of a wife and my son of a mother. He wants to survey the goods and chattels that will be his. Upon which, in the time to come, he can lay his rapacious paws and reap without ever having sown, said Father. At the most, I will exchange a word or two with him, not more. Then we will board the moving van and leave him master of the field. Such, more or less, are the prospects for the next few hours, but what else can I do? I can do nothing, nothing at all. Father and Herr Kappus sat there, blinking in the sunshine. Father had stopped coughing, he had forgotten to cough. But his eyes looked bad now. When he so much as thought about his eyes, he . . . Herr Kappus had a dodgy knee, and he knew why too.

It's from all that standing in classrooms, isn't it? asked Father. Quite possibly!

When I feel a pain coming in my knee, I lie down.

Where can I lie down in a classroom? asked Herr Kappus.

I can't really advise you on that, said Father. Now be a good fellow and draw the curtain, the sun's shining right in my eyes! Herr Kappus went over to the window and drew the curtain. Well, said Father, that's the gist of it, in broad brushstrokes.

It's all so sad, said Herr Kappus, so terribly sad! and Father said: Yes, but it's the stuff of life! They didn't really have any more to say to each other, but seeing as Herr Kappus was sitting in Father's study, he said a few more *tsk tsks*, and one or two *dearie-mes,* and Father said: Yes, that's the way of it, just as you said, and so it will always be! And he gazed at his half-finger. Then they talked about their health, and about how far it was to Russdorf. Herr Kappus claimed the maps had got it wrong, they were full of inaccuracies, and in fact Russdorf was both further and *much smaller* than it seemed from looking at the map.

My God, said Father, even smaller!

Indeed, said Herr Kappus, even smaller!

Then the teacher lit a cigarette and wanted to talk to us a bit as well, beginning with me, of course. Come here, he said, and beckoned me to him. He asked me whether I was still coughing so much, but he was mixing me up with someone else who lived on the Jakobsstrasse. Well, forget that, he said. Then he asked whether there were any complaints from the school, and I said: Sometimes! and he came over all strict and professional and asked: In which subjects? and I began by listing the three principal subjects. But Herr Kappus had stopped listening, and said: Good boy, very good! Then he asked whether I was looking forward to the move, and I said yes. Then he asked: What bit of it in particular? and I said: The driving! and he asked: Why?, and I said: Because I don't like all the standing around!

Good boy, said Herr Kappus, very good!

Then he turned to my sister and asked her whether she was pleased she *didn't* have to move and go on such a long drive, and she said yes to that. Then she thought about it, and she started crying. Father said she should go and sit on his knee, or at least look for her handkerchief and if she found it, blow her nose with it. Of course she couldn't find it, so she sucked it all back up. Then there was another pause, because neither Father nor Herr Kappus nor my sister nor I could think of anything else to say. Maybe it had all been said. Then my sister stopped crying and said: Boring! and I said: Come on! and took her by the hand, and we went into our room and shut all the doors behind us. Then Father and Herr Kappus would have to decide for themselves whether they still had anything left to talk about.

16

On that last day, I remember quite clearly, there was some washing on the line in the garden. The washing was white, and it was almost dry. Some clouds had got in front of the sun—God only knows where they had come from! Father looked up a lot, and shook his head. Before long, that sun too would go down, then it would be evening. We couldn't talk with Father about the evening, he would only shake his head. With Mother we couldn't talk at all. She was in town.

All right, said Father, then come and be in here with me until she's back and I talk to her!

And what will you say when you talk to her? asked my sister. I mean *really*?

What would I say? said Father. I'll get it all sorted out.

Everything?

Yes, everything!

Will you tell her you're not going to leave?

Would you like me to?

Yes, said my sister, and I said yes as well.

Very well, said Father, then I'll tell her that!

And everything's to be like it was before, said my sister, but Father flapped his hand. He didn't want to hear any more about it. Let's play a game of something, he said.

What game? asked my sister, putting her handkerchief away. Just then she didn't want to cry.

Some kind of game, said Father, that will while away the time! He stood up to stretch out, but then he didn't stretch at all. He looked in his desk drawer. That was already almost tidy now. Some things were in the travelling chest, other things would soon join them there. Other things again had disappeared, *the earth has swallowed them up.* Father sighed, and he pulled the Happy Families cards out of the drawer. We weren't allowed to look inside it. He would have preferred to keep it locked, but he couldn't find the key. It was where he kept his virility pills and his sock garters. Did he not need them any more? I pulled three chairs up to the table. Of the three of us, the fattest was Father, and the shortest was my sister. She sat down first. I was like all boys, I was normal. Shouldn't we pack first? I asked.

But we don't need to, said my sister, no one's going anywhere! We're all going to stay here, for all eternity.

There is no eternity, I said.

Yes there is, she said, there is so an eternity! and she wanted to cry some more, but Father clapped his hands and called out: There's an end! Let's begin!

We still need to put everything in one place, in case we really do move out, I said and dealt the cards, but Father said: There's no sense in rushing into anything, *softly softly does it*, otherwise we'll just end up breaking a limb and nothing will have been gained! Wait till Mother returns, and I can have a calm conversation with her.

But a long one, said my sister, and Father said: Whatever! and my sister asked: Like ten hours? and Father said: Till everything's been thrashed out! and she said: More like twenty then? and he said: Whatever it takes! We had the cards in our hands.

And what will you talk to her about? asked my sister, and Father made a comprehensive gesture and said: About every thing, what else? And then we began. Only I was really concentrating, the other two were looking round. Father was the worst. He kept patting his pockets for his handkerchief. When he found it, he mopped his brow. Then he left it on his lap, so he would find it right away, in case he started sweating again. But then it would fall down again, and he wouldn't be able to find it. Then he would shout: Where's my hand-kerchief? and we said: On the floor! and we had to pick it up for him and lay it on his lap, or stuff it in his pocket. Then he called out: Excuse me! got to his feet in a laboured way, and went over to the window. He pressed his brow against it. That way he could see down the whole street, and would spot Mother right away when she came back. I thought: I hope she doesn't come with Herkenrath, how would Father be able to talk to her then? But she didn't come. Maybe she had gone to collect Herr Herkenrath, and they would arrive together? Maybe he didn't have his socks on yet, and it was all taking longer than she thought? When Father had stood by the window for long enough, and had strained his eyes in vain for a sight of Mother, he said: Nothing! and he returned to the table. Then he sat down with us again.

God knows where she's got to, he said. She had something she wanted to see to, that's all I know. So presumably she'll . . .

Weren't we going to play? I said, and Father pulled out a card and said: That's how it'll be! She will have gone into town, and once there, because there's so much to see and to think about, the reason for her going there will have slipped her mind, that often happens to her. And then, just as she's thinking she won't remember it any more, it'll come to her again, and so now . . . Well, said Father, now she's seeing to it!

Yes, now she's getting it, said my sister, and we carried on with our game.

But even so, she ought to be back by now, said Father after a time, and I said: Yes, she ought!

But how could she? said my sister, There's something she has to see to!

But not for such a long time, I said, and Father called out: And what is it, what is it? What, he said, could she be seeing to on a day like today?

You mean on a Saturday? asked my sister, and I said: Most of them are already shut anyway! and Father said: Yes, you're right. There would have to be some shop that's still open for her to buy whatever it is.

It could be something for me, said my sister.

No, I said, for me!

He's quarrelling again, she said.

No, I said, I'm not quarrelling, I'm just telling the truth!

Your Mother should think of herself more, and not of us all the time, said Father. I'm always telling her she should buy something for herself, like a pretty scarf or a pair of gloves.

No, said my sister, no more gloves! She's got too many as it is!

Then some little delicacy to pop in her beak, said Father, but my sister said: No, that'll make her fat!

At least she'd be happier then, said Father, and my sister said: Maybe she's buying herself something that's making her happy, and we just don't know about it yet!

But what, cried Father, what? and he was up at the window once more.

Maybe she's buying herself a hat, said my sister.

She's already got one, I said.

Then maybe she'll buy herself another one?

That's within the bounds of possibility, if not of probability, said Father, looking up the street. You never know, he said, with women! If they have a hat, however beautiful, they immediately want another one, maybe even the opposite one.

And then?

Then they'll spend forever in the hatshop, trying on the entire stock, said Father.

And where's Mother?

She's the one I'm talking about, said Father. She's got caught up in the hatshop, he said, and we went back to our game. Father held his cards in his left hand, and called out whatever happened to cross his mind, just so it wouldn't be so quiet. Sometimes he called out: You can have her, I don't want her! or:

What a wretched life I lead! Who would have thought it! What a wretched life we all lead! and my sister asked: Me too? and Father called: Yes, you too! or: I was just waiting for that miscreant to come home! or simply: I've got another one! meaning another happy family. Well, he said, so what do you say? and he spread it out in front of us. Unfortunately, he was often mistaken, because his eyesight was poor, and he wasn't really concentrating. Then it turned out not to be a happy family at all, and he had to take back what he had just put down in triumph. I don't understand, he said, it was one a minute ago!

You just didn't look properly, said my sister.

Strange, said Father, I could have sworn . . . Well, it happens to the best of us, he said, and my sister yawned again. She wasn't concentrating either. She didn't know how to play properly, and forgot what cards went together. Sometimes she forgot the names of the ones she asked to see. Then she stamped her feet. She couldn't even hold her cards properly, she was always dropping them on the table. I shot a look at them and said: I've seen all your cards! and she yelled: You didn't at all! and Father put his half-finger to his lips and called out: Quiet, I've had another idea! or: Quiet, I can hear footsteps! and I said: I've seen every last one! Then my sister started crying again, and saying I was trying to cheat, and Father said: I can hear a noise on the staircase! and my sister stopped crying, and we listened to see who it was, perhaps even Mother. But it wasn't, and my sister started crying again, and Father called out: Quiet! and each time he thought it was something else. Then he thought of his marriage again, and he called out: Why did this misfortune have to fall on me! Then he went to have another look to see if Mother was coming, on her own or with Herr Herkenrath. It's getting later and later, he said, and this woman just won't come home! How can I talk to her about our future together, when she just won't come? And then we went back to playing. Father held his cards more skilfully than my sister, but not as skilfully as me. He just had bigger hands. He probably would have been a good player, but he wasn't concentrating at all. He even overlooked happy families he had in his hand, that's how badly he was playing.

Father, I called, please pay attention!

Am I not paying attention? he asked.

Then what's that, I said, pointing to a happy family he hadn't played. He put his hands to his head, and said: What's that doing here? It must have wandered in while my attention was briefly elsewhere, because it wasn't there a moment ago! He kept muttering: I'm going to talk to her! I'll tell her! I'll be completely honest with her! Then he went over to the window again. There was still no sign of Mother, and Herr Herkenrath wasn't coming either. I won almost every round. The next time Father stood at the window looking out, I could tell from his eyes that Mother was finally coming. He didn't say anything to us, he just breathed a little more. Silently he sat down with us again. He didn't know what to do with himself, and pushed the cards around the table. My sister said: Why won't you play? You're getting everything in a muddle! Then she threw her own cards down on the table, face up. We could see what she had in her hand. Because she was such a poor player, it wasn't much.

I think that's enough now, said Father, collecting the cards together. Then we stood up, and my sister said: That's the last time I'm playing cards with you two, I'm not going to play again! Then we all went over to the window, and watched Mother approaching.

She's not got the Herkenschwein in tow, said my sister, and

Father said: Will you watch your mouth! Haven't I told you not to be rude like that! and my sister said: But it's true! and Father said: She appears to be heavily laden! God knows where she's been! Father was pleased that Mother was returning without Herr Herkenrath, even that she was returning at all, and he said: Thanks be to God! In his relief, he made a couple of noises we'd never even heard from him before. When my sister asked: Are you trying to say something? he replied: Now I'm going to talk to her, at last, at last! Then he put the stack of cards next to the stacks of books he was going to take to our new address. Maybe he would take the cards too, if he didn't forget them. But who would we play with? There were only two of us.

Mother was carrying a package of cakes, my sister was holding her dolls. She had charged out into the corridor to meet Mother. Father had wanted to *take the weight off his legs*, and had sat down. I was hovering in the background. My sister had pulled the door wide open, and was standing in the doorway. She reached her arms out to Mother, she wanted to give her a big *squeeze*. Mother, though, wouldn't let her, she simply had too much to carry.

Gently, gently, she said, you'll push me over!

Father found a cigarette, but was now missing a match. He looked down the hallway, maybe he might come across one there. He needed to talk to Mother pretty soon now. If you don't talk to your wife regularly, she'll run away, he had once said. He kept to the background and cleared his throat, but Mother and my sister didn't look at him. Only I looked at him now and again, maybe that was a help. Mother was afraid my sister would ruin her hair, and kept saying: Gently, gently! Father plucked up courage and came a little nearer. I must have certainty, he said to Mother, I must talk to you! He couldn't understand that she didn't have to have certainty too. Then there was silence again.

Mother was half dead from lugging the cakes home. She must have lost some weight, but she was still fat. She was amazed that after seventeen days Father suddenly wanted to talk to her, and she asked us: Is he talking to me? She had bought a ton of cakes at Sanne the confectioners for Herr Herkenrath and Father and my sister and me, so that Herr Herkenrath would see what a wonderful housewife she was, and what a good life he would have at her side. She had carried the cakes home all by herself. All right then, she said.

Father tugged at his silk neckerchief. Whenever there was something important, it was always askew. He was almost brusque. Drop all that and come in the study with me, he said to Mother. We need to talk. Please, he added.

Mother set everything down on the kitchen table. I didn't try to elbow my way forward. My sister was less restrained. She wanted to be affectionate to Mother and squeeze her, but Mother didn't want that, and said: Don't touch me with your dirty fingers, but show a little respect for those of us who are saddled with all the work, and have to do all the washing.

But now you're not going to go out again, are you? asked my sister.

Come along, said Father, I'm waiting!

Mother sighed. Your Father imagines he suddenly needs to talk to me, she said to us. God knows what he wants now, so soon before the final hooter! and my sister said: It's sure to be important! Can I listen?

Father stood by the door of his study and said: Come along, come on now! He was talking to Mother. She stood there and pulled a face, as though wondering: Should I now or shouldn't I?

She said: But only if I have to! We all need to be sensible about this! You too, she said to us, wagging a finger in our direction.

Father had drawn himself up as high as he could. He thought of his troubled marriage and said: Well now, well now! We could hear every word. We stood in the corner by the window, as far in as we could get. It was still nice outside, but no longer *that* nice. The day wasn't over yet, but it soon would be. Then, after seventeen days and nights, Mother and Father began to talk to each other.

When Father and Mother talked to each other for the last time, they shut the door behind them. They were in Father's room, we weren't allowed to go in. Mother had pushed us into our room and said: You stay there! But be quiet, she said, and no fighting!

I don't fight, said my sister, I get victimized!

I want no fighting, said Mother, and she followed Father into his room. Oh, if only I had a padded double door to keep reality at bay, what wonderful books I would write then, Father was given to saying. Our room was a bit small. Because Father was round and mighty, he needed a lot of space. When he came to see us, he squeezed himself into the corner by the window and said: I can see I'm going to suffocate in here! or: This is nice and snug! Then he looked lovingly down at us and said: A couple of demi-portions you are! Sometimes he pushed us across to the door jamb, and marked a line on the wood over our heads with a pencil. Then he would say to us: You go up to here, and you go up to there! Then we could see how big I was, and how small my sister was. She asked every day: How big am I *today?* but she never got any bigger. Even so, the room seemed to shrink. There's something to be said for having a small room, Father would say sometimes. You feel secure. Do you still feel secure in your room? he asked.

Not really, replied my sister.

Oh Lord, said Father, you are growing up! That's always the way it manifests itself first!

The first and last time that Mother and Father had a proper conversation together again, they shut the door tightly behind them. We were in our room. Our door was shut too, only the window was ajar. My sister was standing next to me, breathing deeply. She wanted to try something.

All right, she said, watch me!

Then she took a deep breath, held her nose shut, and counted to see how long she could hold her breath. She only got as far as nine. I got up to forty-eight, which was a lifetime record for me! She couldn't even count that far, holding her breath or not. She wanted to have another go, but then she thought of Herr Herkenrath, and she fell into a rage. She hurled her dolls at her bed, right across the room. Of course she missed, because her aim was terrible. Two of them landed on the floor.

What will you do now? I asked.

You mean whether I'm going to pick them up? she asked.

I mean after I'm gone!

What do you think I'll do? she said.

Well, I said and we were standing around again. Father's and Mother's voices came through the wall, sometimes loud, sometimes quiet. If they wanted to fit in another quarrel, they would have to hurry. I wanted to educate my sister, it was almost too late. And what about them? I said, pointing to the dolls that had fallen down, what are you going to do with them?

What should I do with them?

Aren't you going to pick them up?

No.

What if someone treads on them?

Their problem, said my sister. That's the way she was! At least I didn't tread on her dolls, at least not on that last day. I stepped around them. Then I went to the door, and covered her mouth with my hand. I wanted to listen to them. Father was talking a lot, catching his breath in between. He was now saying what had been going through his head at night, when he hadn't been able to sleep. It was the first time in many weeks that they had stood so close together, and said long sentences to each other. As soon as one sentence was over, it was the turn of the next. God knows how long Father had been pushing these sentences around in his head! Now he was letting them all out. Sometimes he got mixed up while he was speaking, and a pretty sentence broke in half. Then he forgot how he meant to go on, and he asked: What was I going to say? Mother shrugged her shoulders, she didn't know. Maybe she nodded, or she shook her head, we couldn't see her after all! Sometimes she said something herself, but it would always just be something short. Often she sighed or she took a breath and said: I don't understand that! or: Carry on, I'm listening! Outside it was still warm, especially the walls and the air. Father's pauses got longer and longer. Because of all his cares, he wasn't able to think quickly. Often he left Mother hanging on a while till he had assembled his thoughts again, and then he said the next thing. My sister wasn't standing beside me any more, it was too boring for her. She had got herself one of her dolls, and asked: Do you understand what they're saying?

Not all of it, I said.

Like me, she said, I don't understand all of it either!

That's why we moved closer to the door. Father was talking

quite loud. He hadn't meant to speak so loud, it just came out that way. I pressed my ear to the door. It was cool, like doors usually are, unless the sun's shining on them. The varnish was flaking. My sister liked scratching it off and saying: I'm smoothing it down! Next door it was quiet again. We waited to hear if Mother or Father would say something, but for a long time they didn't speak. When there was so much they might have said to each other, God, so much, so much! Instead, Father remembered his cough. He said: It's just a nervous cough! Of course he was excited, because *his happiness or otherwise* depended on this conversation. Maybe he didn't know what he wanted. Mother knew what she wanted, and she said so quite clearly. Father never knew what he wanted to say until he had said it. Then he knew. Then Mother would ask: What do you mean by that? and Father said: But I just told you! He had one or two favourite expressions that he used a lot. Mother said: He wears them out! and smiled whenever one came up. She knew them all, and rejected them all. She had other favourite words of her own, like the word *happiness*, for instance. What's that? cried Father when she said the word, and Mother spread out her arms and cried: My happiness! My happiness! By doing that, she took it out of the ruck of other words she had said, and left it floating in midair. It was her favourite word.

My sister stood in the corridor with her dolls, and yawned. She asked: What's she talking about?

Be quiet, I said, I can't hear her!

Never mind, said my sister, but what's she talking about?

Happiness, I said, happiness!

What happiness?

Hers, I said. There was another pause. During the pause we each tried to imagine Mother's happiness to ourselves. We couldn't do it. Later we imagined other words, for instance the word *longing*. The word *longing* floated quite nicely, but not so high up. We'd known it for a long time. We had heard it from Mariechen already, and now we were hearing it a second time. Then there were two short and terrible words, the most terrible of all. They came in quick succession. They were the words *too late*. My sister had sat down on the chest, and was swinging her legs.

What did she say? she asked, What did she say? and I said: *Too late*! She said: *Too late*?

The words *too late* were said very quietly by Mother, that was the terrible thing about them. Even I, with my keen hearing, could barely make them out. Father was probably standing next to her when she said them. He only just heard them. I wanted to hear the silence better, and I put my ear to the door. Father let his heavy hand drop on the table. Then he said something that sounded like *our future*. When Mother heard those words, she shrank back, I could practically see it. Father, who now had to say something, walked up and down in front of her, that way he could think better. Unfortunately he didn't have any thoughts today. When he had been silent for a long time, Mother started up again.

Boring, said my sister. She wasn't standing by the wall any more, she was skipping back to our room. She hadn't caught much of the decisive conversation. She'd mainly been skipping and yawning. When she yawned I could see her gums. They were a sort of rosy pink like they were in medium-sized mammals. She wanted *the man* to come at last, but he wouldn't come.

*

17

When our parents had told each other the truth about their marriage, Mother said: That's it! and she walked out of the room. Since we were standing and listening at Father's door, she walked smack into us. What are you doing here? she asked, and my sister said: We're not doing anything! and Mother said: Have you been eavesdropping? I told you to stay in your room! Her face was all red from so much talking with Father. Can you not keep yourselves busy for one moment, and sit quietly in a corner and play like normal children? she asked.

My sister said: We weren't eavesdropping, we've behaved just exactly like normal children and . . . but by then Mother was back in her room. We weren't eavesdropping, my sister called after her, but Mother's door was already shut.

We stood in the corridor, wondering where next: to Mother, to Father, or out in the garden? The sun would soon be disappearing. Any other time, we would have liked to go out in the garden, but then the neighbours would have come up to the fence and asked us whether our parents still loved each other, and we would either have had to tell a lie or else: No, they're getting separated! But we didn't want to do that, we would have been ashamed on their behalf. We didn't want to go to Mother either, we would have just got on her nerves. But least of all did we want to go to Father. So we went to him, we didn't even knock. Because the decisive conversation with Mother was now over, he had taken his jacket off again. He stood surrounded by the luggage he had to move out with. He was on his feet, but he seemed to be asleep or, if not, at least dreaming. When he finally became aware of us, he picked up a book, out of old habit, as he always said. He turned his back on us. When we had walked round the side of him, we saw that he was crying. Of course we were shocked. There was no mistaking it though, his eyes were red. A tear had emerged from each, and rolled on to the cheek. One had rolled faster than the other, and was now dangling from his chin. We wondered why he didn't wipe it off, but left it to dangle. A long time Father stood there with his handkerchief in his hand, not wiping away the tear. Then he noticed his handkerchief, and said: Oh yes! and put it in his pocket. Because he didn't want to show us he had been crying, he brushed his sleeve across his eyes. My ruthless sister looked on the whole time, while I pretended I hadn't seen anything, and looked away towards the window. There were birds crouching outside. I was afraid my sister might ask Father why he had been crying, but she didn't. A long time we stood around in silence. I felt like running off to the Hoher Hain or somewhere. I asked myself if we shouldn't have gone in to Mother or out into the garden, and was on the point of saying: Come on, let's go! But then we ended up staying with Father instead.

All this stuff that collects, he said, and plucked at his silk neckerchief. Then he laid the book he had picked up back on the desk, and slid it about. Superfluous, he said, quite superfluous!

What is? asked my sister, and Father pointed at the books and said: All of them! They're all not coming with us!

So? Where will they go instead?

Nowhere! They're staying here.

And what good will they be here? asked my sister, and Father said: They'll lie around! Another book he set aside. This is one I care for, he said, this one is coming!

But how can it? said my sister. It hasn't got any legs!

Oh yes, the books know who I am, they come when I call!

They go to be by my side, said Father, who hadn't read anything in a long time.

Because my sister was so lacking in tact, she asked: And what will you do when Mother has married the Herkenschwein? but Father didn't hear her. He was still pointing at his books and saying: Mountains, mountains! Then he pointed to his bookcase, which wasn't actually all that big. (Later I got to see other, larger, altogether more imposing bookcases.) He thought a while and said: They will have been mountains! Then he went to the door, opened it quietly and looked down the corridor. He wanted to see whether Mother hadn't perhaps reconsidered and come out of her room. Maybe she wanted to talk to him again and ask him not to move away after all. But Mother hadn't come out again after all, and the corridor was quite deserted. Even my sister had no hope left, only she wouldn't admit it. She said: Maybe you'll talk to her again!

Yes, said Father, maybe!

Tomorrow?

Possibly tomorrow.

Or the day after?

Yes, perhaps the day after tomorrow.

You could write to her too.

Yes, he said, I can write to her! Then he pulled himself up. He had decided on something, we just didn't know what. He slipped into the green woolly cardigan that Mother had once given him. It just happened to be lying there. He looked like a huntsman in it. Then he shook his head again, but didn't say anything. When my sister asked: Why don't you go and say something to Mother? he said: What else am I supposed to say? and when my sister said: Something truthful! You should say something truthful! he asked: What other truthful thing is there left to say? She knows everything already! My sister had another think. Maybe she wanted to say: Why don't you tell her you love her? but then she didn't say that, because that always only made Father laugh. He put his beret on. Then he went to the door.

Are you going? asked my sister. Hey, are you going? She didn't want Father to leave all on his own. She was afraid for him.

I stood myself right next to him. May we come with you? I asked.

I want to go on my own, he said in a way that you couldn't argue with, and he went out into the corridor.

All right, said my sister, but where are you going? and I said again: We'll come with you if you like! We were standing either side of him, we had *framed* him.

Father shook his head. I'm going on my own, he said, and he ran out of the apartment. Who would have thought the fat old geezer could still run so fast! We watched him from the doorway, then we ran over to the window. Who would have thought the fat old geezer . . . He was already on the road.

You've forgotten something! called my sister. Father couldn't hear her, though, the windowpane was in the way. My sister cried: Look! This! and held his stick up in the air, but Father didn't see or hear her. He didn't look round either.

It was cooler than it had been in the morning, a breeze had got up. Midday, my last midday here, was long past. Because Father wasn't here any more, and Mother didn't have to worry about *bumping into him*, she came out of her room.

Well now, she asked, do you want something to eat? and my sister said: I don't know if I want anything to eat!

Mother poured us some milk and made us a sandwich. That

stood around for a long time. The birds in the garden were quiet. They had made their din for a long time, and now they were resting. Where there had just been sunshine, there was now shade. Where had Father run to? Why had Mother not taken him by the arm and kept him back? She was in her room again. She was on the heavy side, but she was fun! Now she was trying on shoes for Herr Herkenrath, who else? She was looking for some that would make her feet look slim, but that she could still walk around in. Ideally she would have floated everywhere. But she didn't have any floating shoes. And where was Father? I hadn't touched my sandwich, only my sister was eating. We were on our own again. We were standing at the nursery window, looking up the street.

Sometimes he just goes for walks, said my sister.

But not without us!

Yes, she said, sometimes!

Then why would he go without us today?

Because that way he'll think of more ideas for his book.

He doesn't need any more ideas, I said. He won't write any more books.

Yes he will, said my sister, he will, but only little ones.

But he didn't even take his notebook with him!

Then he can write it in his head.

Anyway, I said, and we were silent again for quite a long time. Besides, I said, he can't be going for a walk.

Why not?

He hasn't got his stick with him!

Why can't he go without his stick?

He'll have nothing to lean on.

He doesn't need to. He's not an old man!

But he soon will be.

No, said my sister, not for a long time!

Yes he will, maybe as soon as tomorrow.

Why tomorrow?

Because he's leaving Mother today. Anyway, I said, he'll be back very soon.

I don't think he will.

Do you mean he won't ever come back?

That's not what I said.

And what did you mean to say?

That he won't be back *immediately*, but later.

When it's dark?

Very dark.

Yes, I said, very dark! and we stood around again. My sister was bored again, she couldn't even say how bored she was. I would have been bored too, if I hadn't been so afraid. As soon as someone's afraid, he stops being bored, that's the good thing about it, Father would often say. For a long time we hoped something would happen, but nothing happened.

And what if? asked my sister, then paused for quite a long time, and I asked: What if what?

What if he doesn't come back?

You mean never?

Yes, never!

Of course he's coming back, I said. He's just going round the block.

Then why can't we see him if he's just going round the block?

Because he's going a different way to the way he usually goes!

Then why isn't he back yet?

Because he has stiff legs, I said. Plus he misses his stick. He can't walk so fast without it.

Even so, he ought to be back.

I'm sure he'll be back soon.

We stood around, some of the time in our room, some of it in Father's. We watched out of two windows. Outside, everything was the same as ever, only not quite so bright: trees, sky, blue air, but no Father, no Father! My sister asked: And why isn't he back yet?

Because he's making a loop.

Such a big one?

Yes, such a big one!

Then why didn't he say he was going to make such a big loop?

We didn't ask him.

But why didn't he say *anything*?

Let's go and see Mother, I said.

Because people were always looking up at us now, the curtains were often drawn in Mother's room as well. Then no one would see from outside whether she was there or not, and what she was doing. But it had never been as quiet as it was today. When Father heard the silence, he shook his head and said: Well, I'll be! Only the floorboards creaked quietly when we went in to Mother. We stepped up to her window, and remembered other times we'd stepped up to her window before. When it was raining, it was here that you got to see the best drops. Because Father and Mother were separating, I imagined the drops exploding on the pavement. When I put my hand out of the window, I could touch the rain. When I held it up in the air, the raindrops rolled down into my armpit, and my sister said: Look at you sweating! Our parents had now said all they had to say to each other, and there was nothing left. Mother took long, deep breaths. She was unhappy with her hair. It was supposed to *relax*, but it simply wouldn't! And it was so important!

How important? asked my sister, As important as a leg?

Oh what nonsense you do keep talking, said Mother. She didn't want anyone to know how thin her hair really was, and so she said: It's so fine! Then she took the comb and went over it, to *distribute it all fairly*. We were standing right behind her, thinking: Where has Father got to? Once, my sister became really cross and shouted: Where has that silly Father got to?

Is he not in his room? asked Mother. She didn't know he had disappeared.

He's not in his room, I said, and Mother said: Then he will have run off somewhere with his thick skull!

Fine, said my sister, but then why isn't he back yet?

Up till now, he's always come back, said Mother, plucking at her hair. Then my sister forgot about Father again, and pointed to the hair and asked: What are you doing that for? and Mother said: To make it lie nicely!

You've got such fine hair, said my sister, and Mother said: Now what are you after?

I'm not after anything, said my sister.

Mother had a cigarette in her mouth, that reduced her appetite. Yes you are, you're after something, she said to my sister, and rolled her cigarette between her lips. Father had forgotten his stick, but he was wearing his beret. My sister stood between Mother and me and asked: What am I supposed to be after? and I said: You're always after something!

He's squabbling again, she said, and Mother put down her cigarette and said: Today is a special day, and I don't want any squabbling!

I'm not squabbling, said my sister, I'm just watching you do your hair!

Of course you're squabbling, I said.

Mother was looking for her comb now, but the long fine one. She shouted: No squabbling! No squabbling! Then my sister started crying. I'm not squabbling, she said.

Of course you're squabbling, I said.

After we'd already given up on Father, he turned up. Because he was coming from the opposite direction than usual, we didn't recognize him to begin with. He wasn't even wearing his beret with the mourning ribbon, he was holding it in his hand. He smacked his thigh with it as he walked and Mother said: What a big baby! He needs something to play with all the time!

Look! I said. We were standing—where else?—by the window. We looked up the street.

My sister asked: Why do I have to look? and I said: Father!

For a long time she didn't see him, she was looking in the wrong direction. When she finally caught sight of him she said: Oh, I've seen him for ages, I'm not blind! She was so relieved that she laughed out loud. She waved to him. Father, with his bad eyesight, didn't see us for a long time. I almost waved myself, but I didn't want my sister to see how relieved I felt, and so I didn't. Instead I sent him a very subtle signal with my index finger. He'd only been for a walk! He still wasn't looking up at us, his thoughts were on something else entirely. Maybe he was writing a sentence in his mind, or crossing it out again. Finally he saw us. Even then it took him a while before he recognized us. He seemed to say to himself: Why, of course, my children! They exist too! And with that he got a grip on himself and *surfaced*. He threw away a little twig he had pulled off in his misery somewhere and carried about with him. Then he put on his beret and straightened his green cardigan. He made himself presentable for us and waved and was once more back among us.

18

Outside it was getting cooler now. It was getting darker as well. Father sat in the middle between us, but only very briefly. My sister put her hand on his knee, I kept my hand on my chair. Father looked up and nodded. He wanted to say something again, but we had to wait for it to come. When the day's at an end, he said, there isn't anything for a while, and then there's the other thing!

What other thing? asked my sister, and Father replied: Night!

With that he disappeared into his room, and I went on with my packing. When we'd stopped thinking about Herr Herkenrath, he appeared. My sister said later that she'd been the first to see him, but that wasn't true. I was the first to see him. I now had five shirts lying in my suitcase, there were getting to be more and more of them. Plus the jumpers, the underwear, everything had to go, everything! My sister stood right by the window, looking out. She had no idea. Because she was staying with Mother, that didn't matter. She would hear everything she needed to know from Mother. My sister's trousers and shirts were in the wardrobe as usual. My sister herself was hanging around, just as useless as she always was. Maybe she thought I'd always be around, and had forgotten that I was just about to go. But it was always like that with her, she never knew what was going on around her. She said: So. You're leaving! but she didn't understand what that *meant*. She pointed to my blue jumper and asked: Are you taking that? and I said: Yes.

What about the shirt?

That too.

And the socks?

I don't know, I said, I think so!

Suddenly my sister pointed to the street and cried: Here comes that stupid man, I think!

Of course I'd seen him long before, I just hadn't *said anything*. I went over to the window and looked out. It was Herkenrath, I could tell at a glance. He was wearing a shit-brown suit and a matching cap. Either the cap was too big for him, or his head was too small. He was carrying a briefcase, as though he was going to the office, and not to see Mother at all. He had a bunch of flowers. He was standing on the other side of the road, and didn't know where to go. He looked lost with his cap in front of our house where we'd *gone back and forth for a few years, and got older*, as Father said. The house belonged to the property owner Franke. He owned lots of houses. He didn't need them all, and still refused to let us have one. When Herr Herkenrath had stood around for long enough, he crossed the street towards our house. We had to tell Father—but quick, quick! Because Father finally wanted *to think over what was happening and grasp it*, he had locked his door, and I had to knock. So I knocked and called out that someone had come, and was standing around downstairs. Of course my sister had wanted to be the one to tell Father, and she started crying right away.

Oh go on, I said, you tell him yourself as well if you like!

But he already knows, she said.

Maybe he didn't hear me!

All right, said my sister, then let's pretend he didn't hear you, and I'll tell him again! and she shouted: The Herdenschwein is grunting outside!

We heard Father getting up off the cane rocker. What did you say? he shouted.

The Herdenschwein, the Herdenschwein! shouted my sister. Hurry!

Father swore. Then we heard his chair. He squeezed past it and unlocked the door. He was in his shirtsleeves, as before. How he would have liked to get on with his packing, if only he'd be left in peace! Then the three of us stood by the window looking down at Herr Herkenrath, who wasn't aware of us. Father had one hand behind his back, the other was resting on the window strut. Yes, he said, that's got to be him! He shook his head and said: What a prize twerp! She's gone for a twerp this time! Now children, be truthful: Isn't he ugly?

Ugly, said my sister, and I said: Very ugly!

Father could no longer understand anything. How can such a twerp dare to rest his eyes, his hands . . . He couldn't understand why Mother wanted to leave him and take Herr Herkenrath instead. I don't understand it, he said, do you?

I don't understand it either, said my sister, and I said: Me neither!

Unaccountable, said Father, and he took a breath and nodded. He was still looking down at Herr Herkenrath, he *couldn't take his eyes off him*. Slowly, on our last day, Herr Herkenrath approached our front door. He was stoutly shod. When he was directly below the window, he looked up. Maybe he had felt us looking at him, it's possible! We hurriedly melted back. Father plucked at his kerchief and said something. Unfortunately he didn't open his mouth and we didn't understand. Either it was: There he is, the man who's come to kill me! or: There he is, bringing me a double whiskey! When my sister asked him what he'd said, Father said we shouldn't ask any unnecessary questions, nor show our faces.

What about you, asked my sister, are you going to show your face?

He won't see me, said Father. As soon as he looks up, I'll leap back.

Can you actually leap? she asked, and Father said: Can I ever, I can do anything!

Herr Herkenrath's suit had loads of pockets, many more than a normal suit. It had yellow buttons. From behind, he looked a little bit like Father, but only a little bit. That's probably why Mother took him. Then she knew what she was letting herself in for, and didn't have to make any major adjustments. His trousers had a leather belt that kept everything together. Father didn't like the suit. Ridiculous, running around like that, he said. Simply ridiculous!

Why isn't he coming up the stairs? asked my sister, and Father said: He's got no guts! He needs to collect them all together, what little he does have!

Finally Herr Herkenrath did enter our house. Then we heard Mother's voice too, it sounded light and merry. Herr Herkenrath is approaching, children, she called from her room. Quickly, let him in!

I looked at my sister. She pressed her lips together and shook her head. Then I looked at Father. He had gone pale. And then his fist, his fist! He was holding it in front of his mouth, maybe he was even biting it. Then we heard Herr Herkenrath's footfall. He was slowly coming up the stairs. And there was the bell already, it was deafening. Neither Father nor my sister nor I went to the door, we wanted him to stay outside. We heard him pawing the ground with his boots, which were obviously nailed. Because we didn't open the door, Mother had to let him in. Of course that took a while, because it was hard for her to tear herself away from the mirror. (My sister said: un*glue* herself.) No wonder the bell rang again. Because we didn't make any sound, Herr Herkenrath didn't know whether there was any-one at home or not. He didn't want to ring three times, the third time he scraped at the door instead.

Would you be so kind as to open the door for me when I ask you to? Mother called from her room. Herr Herkenrath is waiting outside!

Father leaned against the door, nodding and smiling subtly. He hoped Herr Herkenrath would take himself off again if we left him waiting long enough. He wasn't going to open the door, and we didn't open it either. So Mother was forced to put down her brush and comb and open the door herself. We could see it all, but only in our imagination. Herr Herkenrath was blushing when the door opened. It looked as though he was going to say: Don't worry, I'll go away again! When he had come because he wanted to stay for ever! Mother had opened the door wide, so he could enter easily. Even though she'd been thinking about him incessantly and had been waiting for him, she pretended she hadn't been expecting him at all. Oh Benno, she said, this is a surprise! How nice of you to drop in!

Yes, said Herr Herkenrath, I thought I'd drop in!

I hope you didn't have too long to wait!

Oh, said Herr Herkenrath, I don't mind waiting for the odd minute or two! He was done up and dolled up because it was his first visit to us, and he wanted to make an unforgettable impression. You could smell him from the other end of the corridor. He smelled of male cosmetic. But it was a different kind than Father had, when Mother gave him some. She would have to give Herr Herkenrath a new kind.

We had stepped out into the corridor, me and my sister. Herr Herkenrath had taken off his cap and crushed it under his arm. His hair shone as soon as the least bit of light fell on it. It wasn't very thick any more, but at least he had some. Plus teeth and eyelashes and eyebrows, it was all still there! That must be why Mother loved him so much. There was nothing else to say about him. Because he was moving in, he took a good look around. Maybe he was wondering what side of the dinner table he would sit at and get outside whatever Mother would cook for him, like for example plum dumplings with run butter and sugar and cinnamon, because he has a sweet tooth, Mother had once told us. If he had looked in her former bedroom, he might have thought about what side of my parents' bed he would lie on, the left or the right. Then Mother would lie on the other side. Thank God I'd be gone by then! Gently, as though not wanting to break anything, he looked all round the corridor and said: How very gemütlich!

It's nice you've come, said Mother.

If I enter something in my diary, there's an end of it, said Herr Herkenrath, and Mother said: Oh, but something might have come up! Nothing that would have caused me to change my plans, he said. He wore ankle boots as well, but very different to Father. He had polished them too. You could smell them from the other end of the corridor too, it was just like the cobbler's. When he turned this way or that, you heard a creak. I'm not one to shirk duty in any of its forms, he said, I know how to behave, and Mother nodded. Strictly speaking, she hadn't known him all that long, but she had hit it off with him straight away. She was glad she had found him, so soon before the final whistle. Just as she was beginning to think that was it, he fell into her lap, Father had said one time. Now she took him for her happiness, and tugged at his sleeve. This way, Benno, she said, and she pulled him into her room. At the same time she signalled to us behind his back that we weren't to stand around, but come into the room with them. We didn't want to, though.

Mother had waxed the floor in her room on that last day. Naturally, we hoped Herr Herkenrath would slip and break something. But he didn't slip. He went around on tiptoe, so Mother would see how much he respected her floor. She led him to the green chair that we weren't allowed to sit in. She had pushed it right into the middle of the room, to show it off to good advantage. Herr Herkenrath looked at it reverently. Then he parted the coats of his jacket and sat down. That was the chair that Father had always sat in until Mother told him one day: You've got enough chairs of your own to sit in, you're too heavy for this one here! Then she had *exiled* him from that chair. When I or my sister wanted to sit down in it, she said: That's not for you! and she chased us away, and when my sister asked: Then who is it for? she said: For a visitor, in case I ever have one!

And what if you don't ever have one? asked my sister, and Mother said: Then it'll just have to remain empty!

Now, after a long, long wait—we had had no idea that Mother had been waiting all that time—the visitor had finally arrived. His hair was neatly parted. He still had his bunch of flowers in his hand. Because she didn't want to leave Herr Herkenrath on his own, Mother called for us again. Children, she called, where have you got to? We have a visitor! But we didn't go. So much for their obedience, Mother said to Herr Herkenrath. And they like to pretend they're shy! Come along, she shouted, the gentleman won't bite you—or? and Herr Herkenrath thought about it for a while and said: No, I suppose not! and we stood around again. Then I gave my sister a nudge and said: She won't let up, come on! My sister spat on her dress once more. She took my hand and we went into Mother's room, but softly, softly. My sister went in behind me and kept her eyes on the floor. I looked straight ahead of me and expect I looked the same as always. Mother was wearing her red blouse and was looking expectantly at us. She wanted to be nice to us, and called us *her rapscallions*. Well, so what have my rapscallions been doing with themselves? she asked, and made her voice all gentle and affectionate. Well, she said, wouldn't you like to shake hands with the gentleman and say good evening?

My sister and I stood in the doorway, whispering to each other. I told her she should have a good look at him. He's your new father, I said.

No, she said, he's yours! and I said: I'm going, but you'll be staying here with him!

Then she wanted to cry again, she already had her mouth turned down. But she thought about it, and ended up not crying.

Don't you want to come in instead of whispering in the doorway? said Mother. That's not going to lead anywhere, is it?

Then we took a deep breath and went in to Mother and Herr Herkenrath. She looked at us. Herr Herkenrath stood up, so we could take him in in his full stature. Close up, he was exactly the way I'd always imagined, only a bit seedier. Mother liked him though, even his face. She seemed not to have noticed just how seedy he was. She told Herr Herkenrath who we were. That was of course completely unnecessary, who else were we going to be? When she told him our ages, she made us both a year younger. We let her go ahead and lie. Then she said Father couldn't be with us just yet, because he was packing up the manuscript he was presently working on. He mustn't leave it behind, she said, otherwise he won't know what to do with himself, and will be quite at a loss in a place like Russdorf. On the subject of Herr Herkenrath, she told my sister that she would soon learn to know him and to love him. And now give him your hand, which I trust is clean, she said.

Even though Herr Herkenrath was newly arrived, Mother's room already smelled of him. We went into the smell and shook his hand. He looked at us sternly. Looking down at us like that, he looked thoroughly untrustworthy. His hands were damp, like Father's so often were. They were small and dampish and soft, also like Father's. Perhaps Mother liked men with hands like that? Neither of them did a proper job, they both preferred sitting around. Father did his sitting around at home, Herr Herkenrath went into an office to do his. Instead of putting his back into something, Father made up people who didn't really exist. He wrote down things for them to think and say to each other. Then he cried: No, that's wrong! and he crossed it all out again. Apart from that, he didn't do much. Herr Herkenrath, in his own way, probably didn't do much either. When she said hello, my sister didn't look at him. Mother seemed pleased with us though and had a double chin. She had white arms and elbows, all without hairs. They were plucked out on Sundays and grew back during the week. She was doused in perfume, God knows where all! Round her neck she wore her string of pearls that she kept plucking at. She'll keep plucking at it till it breaks, and all the pearls go rolling all over the floor, Father would always say, and my sister asked: And what will we do then? and Father pointed at the floor and said: We'll go crawling after them on our hands and knees! The blouse Mother was wearing was one she had bought for Herr Herkenrath. After buying it she'd gone up to the mirror and said to herself: This blouse makes me ten years younger, if not fifteen! Then she had put the blouse aside, to slip into it at some unexpected moment, and frolic towards Herr Herkenrath. Now the moment had come! Under it she wore her black skirt and nylon stockings that had cost a king's ransom. She still held Herr Herkenrath's flowers in her hand. That's a surefire way of killing off the stoutest blooms, Father always said when he saw Mother holding flowers. My sister wasn't crying, I could have done with that. Herr Herkenrath was sitting neither perfectly straight, nor bent. There was something the matter with his back. Mother asked him if it was playing up again, and he said no, it wasn't. Then she asked how long we intended standing around instead of sitting down. She said: There's no need to be shy, Herr Herkenrath doesn't eat children! That's the case, isn't it, Benno? she asked, and Herr Herkenrath thought about it for a moment, and then shook his head. His little finger had a long nail that looked like a shovel. Father had told us about the nail once when we were sitting at table discussing *personal foibles*. He had heard about it from Mother. My sister didn't know what a *personal foible* was, and she was doing the most talking. Suddenly Father said: Before I heard about this particular gentleman, I would never have thought anyone could have been so tasteless as to grow that nail so long!

How long is it actually? asked my sister, and Father said: Oh, it must be all of four inches!

Mother didn't want to mention Herr Herkenrath at all. But now she had to. She said: What nonsense you do talk! and Father said he was always truthful. Perhaps he needs it, he said, and when my sister asked: What for? he said: To crush his lice!

You should be ashamed, making such unfair remarks in front of the children about a distant acquaintance who never hurt a hair of anyone's head, said Mother, getting fearfully agitated.

So does Herr Herkenrath have lice then? asked my sister, and Mother cried: You see your wickedness bearing fruit in that innocent breast! and Father said: It's no secret that some people use their nails for that! There's no shame attached to it!

That's enough, cried Mother, and she ran off. And now, she said to Herr Herkenrath, I'm going to make us all a nice cup of coffee, and the children can have some tasty cocoa, because there are some things we need to talk about. Then she said we should sit down on our four letters and tell Herr Herkenrath something about ourselves, so that he got to understand what went on in our heads. And with that she went into the kitchen. Outside, darkness was falling.

When Mother had gone out of the room with her flowers, it suddenly got very silent. Herr Herkenrath was holding the armrests of his chair, and was presumably thinking: This is how I look my most relaxed! But he wasn't at all relaxed. His head and his arms might be, but his eyes and his feet weren't. We didn't know what to say, we all just breathed. Herr Herkenrath had a little paunch when he was sitting. When he stood up and walked around, it went away. That day, he didn't stand up, so we had the benefit of his paunch. He sat there and studied his toecaps, the left and the right. Then he looked from one of us to the other, and wondered what he could talk to us about. He didn't have any children, and he didn't know how to deal with them. My sister was plucking the hair out of her dolls. When she had pulled out one hair, she let it fall on the floor, it drifted so nicely from side to side. Then she trod on it, and plucked out the next one. She didn't speak. I might have said lots of things, but I didn't speak either. I preferred to go over to the window, where at least I wouldn't see Herr Herkenrath. Instead I looked across the road. It looked different again now. That was because it was getting darker and darker, and because I was leaving. The gardens looked different too, and the sky, and everything, everything. The trees and shrubs stood around peculiarly, like wild beasts. Some seemed to have humps. Some others had bits sticking out of the front of them, beastly bits. They didn't bark though. They stood quietly in one place, and didn't come nearer. Some of the houses had people walking around in them, others were empty and dark. Their inhabitants had left, but they would be coming back. In the kitchen, Mother stood her flowers in the vase, and thought how beautiful they are. She started making coffee, and ran the tap. Herr Herkenrath was still wondering what to talk to us about. Then he looked at his watch, and finally he said something. He said: Not long now, and this one'll be in the bag as well!

My sister stared and asked: Where will it be?

In the bag!

And who's going in the bag? asked my sister, and Herr Herkenrath said: The day! My sister waited in case there was more, but there wasn't more. Slowly she stood up. With her dolls under her arm, she walked in astonishment round Herr Herkenrath. He studied his fingernails. After another long silence, he spoke again. And then, he said, when this day's in the bag, there'll be the next one! And then he was silent again. We heard Mother next door, but quietly, quietly. Because she had been *up and about such a lot today*, she had sat down. We heard her grinding coffee. In a moment, we would be able to smell it.

Boring, said my sister and yawned. She took one doll's hand, and wiped the wall with it. She's cleaning, she said.

Herr Herkenrath looked at her in surprise. But she's getting dirty, not clean, he said, and my sister said: Then I'll just have to wash her again! Then she walked round the room again, but this time with a different doll. It was the one with one eye. The other one was in the wardrobe, it needed to be put back. Mother couldn't do it, she didn't have time for fiddly little things like that. Every day, my sister tugged at her sleeve and said: Will you fix her eye? and every day Mother said: Say it nicely!

Will you fix her eye, *please?* said my sister, and Mother said: I've got more important things on my mind today!

What about tomorrow? asked my sister, and Mother said: Tomorrow too, by the look of it. That's how it was with her. Now my sister went up to the window with her one-eyed doll and looked out into the dusk. But she already knew what the dusk looked like on this side, so she went over to the other window. But there was nothing there either. Herr Herkenrath passed his hand across his brow, he wanted to say something again. He was already opening his mouth, but then he forgot what it was, and he closed it again. Finally he did say it after all. The dusk, he said, is dragging on for such a long time, that you'd think the night would never come. And then, when you've forgotten the question again, and just happen to be looking out of the window . . .

Out of which window? asked my sister.

Ha, said Herr Herkenrath, that's the question! And then we were all silent again.

Why aren't you talking to them, Benno? shouted Mother, I can't hear you at all! You must get them to tell you something, she said, but Herr Herkenrath misheard her and asked: Sell me what?

Tell you! shouted Mother, To tell you something!

I know I should get them to tell me something, said Herr

Herkenrath. But they won't tell me anything! and Mother asked: Have you tried?

Yes, and they won't!

Show them your dog whistle, shouted Mother. Let them blow on it!

On my dog whistle?

Yes, your dog whistle!

All right! shouted Herr Herkenrath, I'll let them blow on it!

The first time Herr Herkenrath came to us for a bit of a natter— so you can hear his voice, as he's going to be your new father, Mother had said—he soon got into a muck sweat. In front of each stick of furniture, he asked himself: Do I keep this, or do I chuck it out? When Father was as excited, he began to sweat around the nose, and Mother would say: It's healthy to sweat! Would she say that to Herr Herkenrath too, when she was alone with him? Herr Herkenrath wiped his hands on his trousers so he didn't make any stains anywhere. Then he beckoned us over to him.

Would you like to see something? he asked, and my sister asked: See what?

Something interesting, said Herr Herkenrath.

In his top pocket he had a dog whistle, and he pulled it out for us. Earlier he had used it for his dog, but his dog wasn't around any more. One fine summer's day he had whistled to him and the dog had charged off, but at the same time a car had come along. The whistle was unhurt. Now all Herr Herkenrath's feelings were for Mother. He said: There! and he pulled out his whistle. It was short and stout and black and it rattled when you shook it. Herr Herkenrath put it in his mouth and blew into it quietly, so that nobody in the house could hear. After that, he whistled a bit louder, then he held it out to us. He didn't even wipe it. I said: No thank you! I didn't want to blow on it. I didn't even want to take it in my hand. My sister didn't care that it had been in Herr Herkenrath's mouth, all she cared about was that she was allowed to blow on it! First she blew on it loudly, then a bit more quietly, because Mother shouted: Not so loud, you dreadful creatures! from the kitchen. Ideally, my sister would just have gone on and on blowing. But there was Mother arriving with the coffee and the cakes, and my sister had to thank Herr Herkenrath for letting her have a go on his whistle, and return it to him, so he could put it back in his top pocket and blow on it himself some time the fancy took him. Then Mother spread the tablecloth, and we helped her with that. It was the last time we all sat round a table together and drank coffee and ate cake. We were all ready to tuck in, but now Father wasn't there.

19

He sat at his desk, and hoped Mother would call him. But she didn't call him. Why should she call him, everything had been said between them! Father held the stub of pencil in his hand, and wanted to write something. With his other hand, he groomed his beard. Each time he found an especially long hair, he said: This will be painful, but it has to be done! and he plucked it out. I knew it would be painful, he said, and he threw it on the floor. Then he picked up the thread of his thoughts where he had left it. In the apartment too, everything just went on, in town, in the rest of the world, they were ruthless that way. For instance Mother had laid the table. Seventeen years she had tried to train Father in the ways of order and cleanliness, and what had she achieved? I give up, she said. Let another woman torment herself with him, if he finds another.

Herr Herkenrath sat in his green armchair. He said he didn't know of one.

Well, said Mother, it's his business! Maybe he will. And now I've got to get him, because he won't come by himself! She took off her flowered apron. Then she went to Father's study and knocked on the door, we could hear it clearly. It's me, she called, and she pressed the handle, but Father had locked himself in. Mother called: I can't get in! You must have absent-mindedly turned the key! Then she said: Herr Herkenrath is here and would like to make your acquaintance quickly, before you hop on to the moving van! Then she corrected herself: Before you slowly make your way on to the moving van! He's in my room with the children, and he would like to talk over a few things with you still. Then Mother waited, but there was no reply. For a long time she stood and waited outside Father's locked room in her red blouse. But Father wouldn't open, he was quietly making a hard sound with his mouth. Perhaps he was grinding his teeth. Can't you hear me? cried Mother, and pressed her ear to the door. Herr Herkenrath would like to meet you quickly, she called. Won't you come and say hello to him, in the way any civilized person who uses a knife and fork would do? said Mother, but Father remained silent. If we hadn't known he was in his room, we might have thought he had already moved out.

Suddenly something in his room fell on the floor and he shouted: Goddammit! Then he picked it up and said: Tell him he can lick my ass, your Herkenrath! He'd better get out of here, before I come after him with the carving knife!

Mother withdrew her ear from the door in alarm and said:

Dear oh dear! Then she pretended Father had said something quite different, and nodded. All right, she said, if you're too busy packing, we won't bother you now, you can come when it suits you! We'll make a start, and have a bite or two without you. And of course I'll pass on your regards to Herr Herkenrath! I'm sure he'll understand.

Father growled. (Mother said: grunted.) He can bite my ass, somewhere in the middle, where it's nice and juicy! he said. Then he sat down on his cane rocker, we heard the creak. At least Father wasn't yelling any more, and Mother was quiet too. She came back to us. She put a hand to her heart, and she was blushing. She didn't want Herr Herkenrath to see how nervous she was. She smiled at him and said: He conveys his apologies, but he's even now packing up his manuscript. That's almost a religious act with him, and must not be disturbed. Words, words, exclaimed Mother, he'll choke on them one day! He hasn't even left himself the time to sit down with us and talk things over quietly.

I see, said Herr Herkenrath. He was relieved that Father wasn't coming. Good, he said, excellent!

So let's forget about him then, and fortify ourselves a little, said Mother. The little ones will be hungry. She brought the coffee. She brought the cake and the rolls and the sugar and the milk. For us she brought mugs of our healthy cocoa, and said: There, now you may begin! Whoever doesn't eat at the proper time will have to take his chances with what the others leave him! That's right, she asked, isn't it?

At our last meal at home I had a ham roll and then two pieces of cake, because I always eat savoury things first, and sweet things only afterwards. My sister had no self-discipline, and she went straight for the cake. She dropped crumbs on her napkin, and on her lap as well.

Look at the way you're scattering crumbs everywhere, cried Mother, and my sister said: I'm not scattering them, they're crumbling by themselves!

At any rate they're all going on your pretty dress, said Mother, and my sister said: No, some of them are landing on my shoe!

Mother had broad shoulders and a small mouth. As ever, she took little bites and ate slowly. It looked less greedy and it helped with putting on weight. She had her napkin on her lap and said: You should always eat slowly! Herr Herkenrath ate slowly too, but not *that* slowly. He looked over to the door quite often in case Father came in, seized him by the shoulders and threw him out. But he didn't. Herr Herkenrath kept saying what delicious cake Mother had sliced up and what delicious rolls she had bought and spread things on, just the kind he really liked.

Really? asked Mother, and Herr Herkenrath said: Yes, just the kind I really like! Instead of *eat* he said *consume*, and instead of *good* he said *tasty* or *wholesome*. Apart from that, there wasn't much talking, because at table everyone has to decide for themselves whether to eat or talk. We all wanted to eat.

When we were already almost done, we heard the cane rocker suddenly creak in Father's room. Then we heard Father's key turning in the lock, and the door of the study slowly but irresistibly opening. Now Father was standing in the corridor. Because we were all trying to hear him, we stopped swallowing. Mother was the first to speak. She held her finger aloft and said: There's a creature creeping out of its cave, because it smells coffee! All I can say is thank God I've made enough! Then the steps came nearer, the door opened, and Father stood in front of us. To prepare himself for his meeting with Herr Herkenrath he had had a little lie down. When the coffee smell (Mother: *the aroma*) had reached him, he had been unable to stay in his rocker any longer, and he had come and joined us, just like that. The cheek he had been lying on was rather pink. He hadn't even slipped into his jacket. His few remaining hairs were all over the place. Perhaps his face was so pink from seeing Herr Herkenrath in Mother's room, and eating cake. He didn't say anything though, only maybe growled a little. Maybe he growled: And now she's even feeding him! When Herr Herkenrath saw Father, he stopped chewing. To make sure his mouth was empty and ready to speak, he hurriedly gulped everything down, whether it was already chewed or not. Then he put his napkin on the table, and stood up. Mother looked from one to the other without coming to any decision. She had to say something now. So there you are, she said. To me she said: Don't just sit there, but go and fetch a plate, a big plate, for your Father!

Now, after such a long time, Father and Herr Herkenrath stood face to face. One was just in shirt and trousers, the other was in his Sunday best. One looked down at the floor, the other off into space. They left a lot of room between them. Each of them would have liked to run away, but they weren't allowed to. Outside, it was getting even darker. Lots of houses had their lights on, just like us. Father and Herr Herkenrath both let their arms dangle, and both were breathing a lot. Herr Herkenrath's breathing was mostly quiet, Father's was mostly not. When one of them had finished breathing in, the other breathed out. They were neither of them good-looking, but in different ways. If Father was missing most of his hair, Herr Herkenrath was stunted. Even Mother was taller. She sat there, loving one of them, having previously loved the other. Just as well his thick-soled boots contrived to make Herr Herkenrath appear a little taller, though still not tall enough, whereas Father . . . Even though he'd been suffering for weeks, he was still too fat. Probably he would remain too fat to the end, or even beyond the end. And then in the memory of those who had known him, until they too were no longer *extant*. Mother said: Well, so it goes! and positioned herself between her two men. Won't you say hello to each other? she asked.

But of course we'll say hello to each other, said Herr Herkenrath. Father said nothing for a long time, he seemed to be thinking it over. Once he had thought it over for long enough, he said: Well, why not? Then they each took a step towards the other, and held out their hands. Herr Herkenrath had to do all the squeezing and shaking by himself, Father didn't participate. Also, Herr Herkenrath tried to look Father in the eye, but Father wouldn't let him. He looked at the floor. Then Herr Herkenrath drew a deep breath and began about the weather.

Curious weather we were having today, with curious air, he said, and Father asked: What do you mean?

The whole weather position is curious, said Herr Herkenrath, and motioned with his hand in a sort of all-embracing way. While yesterday it looked like rain, but when I had a closer look, I thought: No, you're wrong!

And what time did all this happen? asked Father severely.

In the morning, I was just on my way to the office, said Herr Herkenrath. Unfortunately I didn't consult my watch.

You work in an office then?

That's right!

A large office or a small office?

More middle-sized really.

But at a desk?

Yes, processing my files!

Well, well, said Father, and that was it. Probably Father and Herr Herkenrath were racking their brains what else they could talk about, but they couldn't come up with anything. My sister looked from one of them to the other, probably thinking about which of them she would prefer as a father. She didn't decide one way or the other.

Perhaps we'll catch a drop or two tomorrow, but for the time being I'm not anticipating any major precipitation, said Herr Herkenrath after pausing long for thought, and Father said: Like me, just like me! Then he said: I'm going to sit down! and Herr Herkenrath said: And why not! and they both sat down. Then Mother poured cups of coffee for both her men. She was sitting smack between them and so could talk equally to either of them. She kept her hand on the coffeepot, so she could pour either of them a refill. She tried to get a conversation going between them, and to that end turned now towards Father and now towards Herr Herkenrath, but neither one of them was especially forthcoming. Thank God there was food on the table. Father didn't need a second—or perhaps even a first—invitation, he helped himself right away. He kept to the sweet things. Mother kept putting more cake on his plate, but each piece disappeared promptly. Father merely ate, he didn't talk. My sister looked from one to the other, she was quite unabashed, but so was Father too. If he needed to breathe, and wheezed a little, she listened closely. I didn't speak either, I was just think-ing. Everything was sad. I kept thinking: This is the last piece of crumb cake Father will ever eat here! or: This is the last cup of coffee Mother will pour for him, and so on. Starting tomorrow, Father and I would eat our cakes and our rolls in places we hadn't even seen yet. In spite of that, Father filled his boots. He made a lot of crumbs, of course, but he didn't let that bother him. He waited till all the crumbs were lying on the tablecloth. Then he said: Right! swept them up into his palm and tossed them into his mouth. Then he had a piece of cake that wasn't crumb, and that of course made far fewer crumbs. I watched the last piece of it vanish into his beard and not come out. Now he'll speak, I thought, but Father didn't speak, instead he helped himself to *another* piece. His hand shook slightly, his head too. Mother's hand wasn't shaking as it rested on the coffeepot. I knew now that there was nothing more to come, that it was finished. If somebody did say something, it would be nothing new. With that, I couldn't stand to be in Mother's room any longer. I got up and said I had something else to see to, before it got too dark. It wasn't true, I just wanted out. I saw Mother nod, and then Herr Herkenrath. Only Father didn't nod, he looked at me sadly. He begged me with his eyes not to leave him alone with Herr Herkenrath and Mother, but I couldn't help it. I threw him a glance that said I couldn't help it, and that I *had to* leave him alone with Mother and Herr Herkenrath. Then I ran out of my Mother's room, and out of my Father's house.

20

Father no longer had any hope that Mother would stay with him. I could see it in his eyes. He had gone to stand in a corner, to feel supported. He looked at his hands, as though surprised to find them still there. When I tried to distract him by asking him questions, he only replied yes or no. Often he got them wrong. When I asked him: Are you sure you mean no, and not the other thing? he said: I expect I mean the other thing! One time I touched his hand, but softly, softly. Then I felt he hadn't turned to stone, but was just cold, very cold. When I tried to touch him again, he pulled his hand away and said: Give me peace! One time I wanted to examine the sadness in his eyes, but then I felt ashamed of myself.

Curious, he said, and shook his head.

What is? I asked.

That she's taking Herkenrath now, and beginning all over again.

Ach, I said, never mind!

I have no other option, he said. Well, maybe this time she'll be happy. Maybe she'll have more children.

It was dark outside now. As he leaned against the wall in the light of the lamp, he looked older than ever. He was all ready for the move, inasmuch as a muddlehead like me is ever ready for anything, he said. His *two giant suitcases*—they weren't really as gigantic as all that—he had dragged to the door. I had helped him with them. I don't even know if I'll have a desk there, he said. Maybe I'll have to write on my knees. Then again, Thomas Mann is said to have done much of his writing on his knees, he said.

I'm sure you'll find a way to write, I said.

I wonder, he said.

With his beret on his head, he went up to the window. I stood next to him. Now we weren't looking into the light any more, but into the dark. Where there had been houses before, we had to guess at them now. Behind them we guessed were trees, the taxus hedge, the forsythia. They had always been here, and they had to be here. As so often, Father didn't know what they *were doing to him*. You won't credit it, but I'm a little mixed up, he said. Everything has hit me rather suddenly. Do you not find that too?

Yes, I said, I do too!

Then he said: No, not that! He hadn't meant to say that. He searched a while and said: I have plans! That was why he had crawled into his nice jacket. Into this one here, he said. He had said that many times, he had just forgotten it. He patted his jacket and said: Yes, this one here!

I had stood myself very close to him. I said: I know!

So here we are in our glad rags, awaiting the impending unpleasantnesses, he said, and I again said: I know!

Where has your little sister got to? he asked. Has she hidden herself from that gentleman? and again I said yes.

It is possible, he said, that I haven't been the best of all fathers, but at least she never had to hide herself from me.

No, I said, not from you!

Unfortunately, I had had to lie once more, my sister hadn't hidden from Herr Herkenrath at all. Nor was she in our room. Instead, she was in Mother's room, with Herr Herkenrath. Maybe she was perched on his knee. Maybe she was eating a piece of apple cake without holding her hand underneath. That would be the third. She was probably scattering crumbs like there was no tomorrow, without Mother saying anything to her. She would allow it today and only bring it up tomorrow, when everything would be back to normal, *only with a different cast.* Now Herr Herkenrath was probably laying his hand on my sister's head, and saying: Go on, eat, it's good for you! Then he would pause and say: You have such lovely hair! and my sister would probably be nodding and saying: I know! Then Herr Herkenrath would probably pop a liquorice pastille in her mouth and say: You're to suck it, mind, not chew! The rest of the pastilles he would put back in his pocket, frugal man that he was. I wonder what's keeping the moving van, he would ask quietly, and Mother would probably reply: Yes, it ought to be here by now! Then they would all not say anything for a while, but just suck and think.

When I looked over at Father again, he seemed completely different. He was a chameleon, and he didn't look so sad any more. He was standing with his feet apart, adjusting his beret. It made him look a little roguish or *raffish*. And then a thought came to him. You know, he said, one should, and then he smiled and didn't say what. Maybe he wanted a little bite to eat, a little glass to drink, to take a gander through the Hoher Hain, or put a long and elegant sentence that Thomas Mann might have used once, into whatever story he was working on at the moment. The important thing was, he was making plans again! Suddenly he said: Oh yes! took off his beret, and let me see his little bald patch. Then he ran the tip of his finger under the mourning ribbon and tore it off. That's the end of that, he said. He sniffed it, he wanted to know if it smelled of mourning. It seemed that it didn't. Father smiled at me and said: Would you like to have it?

Me? I said, taken aback.

As a souvenir, said Father, but I said: No, I don't want to have it!

Then I should get rid of it, said Father, and, being *an untidy person, quite impossible to have in the home*, he simply tossed the mourning ribbon under his desk. Let her pick it up and think about what she's done to us, he said. Then he put the beret, shorn of its mourning ribbon, back on, and fooled around with his walking stick. He made it whistle through the air, and called: There goes another head! And another! And another one! For all eventualities, he said, we'd better take this stick with us, in case the Russdorfers should take it into their heads to attack us! From behind, which is the way one is always attacked in this world! Because the moving van wasn't coming, he kept fooling around with his stick, but without much conviction. The box of books by the door was quite modest really. I don't need that much these days, said Father. I don't eat, don't drink, don't sleep, and don't read. All these things are being phased out. Most books he was *sated on*.

At about half past nine, the moving van finally came. It was short and stout and rolled up to the front of our house. It had probably got lost along the way. I thought: It's tiny! and wondered if we'd even fit into it with our things. But there were only two of us, and we didn't need much space. One of the neighbours had rolled up his sleeves and was looking out of the window. I carried my satchel up to the door and thought: Let's get out of here, let's go! Father guessed what I was thinking, and smiled at me sadly. I hope we've remembered everything, he said, and listed the most important things: his best shirt, the three books he sometimes leafed around in, the framed postcard he'd got from Thomas Mann, the damaged cane rocker, the braces that Mother . . .

What about my bicycle! I cried.

Yes, your bicycle! I hope we haven't forgotten anything, he said, because we can't turn round and collect it.

Why can't we turn round and collect it?

From the claws of a Herkenrath? cried Father, Never! Once more we were standing by the window. Well, I suppose that was it, he said.

Yes, I said, it was!

The driver of the moving van wore a cloth cap. He was pretty heavily built. He opened up the van doors, and made so much noise that the lights went on in the houses all around. It didn't seem to bother him. He liked doing overtime, it was well paid. Father was ready for that, and had a couple of folded-up notes in his purse. I hope this will cover it, he said. Right then, but no rush! One thing at a time. First . . .

Brush my teeth?

No.

Wash my hands?

No.

Say a prayer to the Almighty that nothing gets broken?

Nonsense, said Father, He's got other worries! He doesn't care about our move. First of all say goodbye to your Mother and your sister and if you must . . .

Why should I say goodbye to him? I cried. I don't want to . . .

Because you have to learn to be polite, said Father, and he led me past the lupins to the door of Mother's room. The lupins were dangling their heads, they were all dead. Father put his bags down. Now he would knock on Mother's door, which from tomorrow would be Herr Herkenrath's door. Fifteen or sixteen years he had lived here with Mother, one year more or less didn't matter afterwards, and somehow they'd all trickled away. Well, they weren't so bad, the first ones certainly, but now they're finished, and there won't be any more, he said and knocked.

It's open, called Mother.

She was sitting with my sister and Herr Herkenrath in the middle of her room. They took up space and used up oxygen. Before long we'll just take up space, Father often said. Slowly but copiously, Mother had drunk coffee and eaten cake. Her belly stuck out a little further. Perhaps she should have bought the red blouse half a size bigger! She and Herr Herkenrath had my sister between them, now she wouldn't get out. Nor did she want to, she liked being there. She and Mother and the new husband all breathed deeply in and out.

Excuse the interruption, Father said politely and took off his beret. He didn't know what to do with it, so he stuffed it in his jacket pocket. It made a lump against his hip. He put his little suitcase on the floor which Mother had waxed so nicely. He pointed at it. Jump, boy, not into it, but over it, he said to me. Mind you don't break a leg! You'll need them both so you can keep running away.

The moving van has arrived, said Mother.

What else could it have done, said Father, given that you ordered it!

I was just telling you.

I had known it was there, thank you.

Mother, sister and Herr Herkenrath were sitting close together. Mother had thrown her arm around my sister's shoulder, which meant: She belongs to me! Her arm seemed to be particularly long today, much longer than usual. It looped round my sister's neck as far as Herr Herkenrath, who was sitting on the other side of my sister. Because she thought: No one will see! Mother was toying with Herr Herkenrath's hair round the back of my sister with one finger. It was loathsome! Father didn't want to see it, he was smiling sadly. I was thinking of the way Mother was betraying us, and I wasn't able to smile. I was furious that Herr Herkenrath had been allowed to insinuate himself here. He had already settled into Mother's deep green armchair. He had lit one of Mother's cigarettes and was puffing away, quite indifferent to the rest of us asphyxiating. He brushed off the ash over the ashtray without bothering to look. He knew where everything was. He had slipped his shoes off to be more comfortable. Now he was in stockinged feet, no matter if they smelled! In the end he managed to rise out of the armchair and looked for his shoes. Quickly he slipped them on. He muttered something I didn't catch. Perhaps Mother did, perhaps she was already used to his mumbling. She was already used to his little coughing, his body odour, his hanging around her. She had stopped noticing that he was stupid and smelled bad. If I didn't leave quickly with Father, I would get used to it too. Lucky I was going!

You can sit down for a moment, if you like, said Mother, but Father didn't want to, and said: I'd rather stand!

What about you? Mother asked me, and I said: Thanks but no thanks! and I didn't sit down either. I wanted to get to the moving van, I knew what was going to happen next. In a moment I would no longer be in the room, and Mother and my sister wouldn't miss me. They would soon forget me, and Father too. He was still standing next to me, clenching his fist. He had clenched his fist so many times now, he wasn't even aware of it. As in all important things, everything now happened very quickly. The moving men were suddenly standing in the corridor in their work shoes. They followed Mother to Father's former study. Mother wouldn't even go in. She just pointed at the door and said: It's all in there!

Is that all there is? asked the moving men, once they'd looked around, and when Mother said: That's all he's got! they tied their belts around the boxes. They carried everything slung onto their backs and lugged it down the stairs and out of the house. They came back once for the bicycle that was on the landing, and then once for the chair.

Lift it higher! shouted one of the moving men, and the other shouted back: Won't go any higher!

Then put the bloody thing down! shouted the first of them, and the other shouted back: It'll go, but only just!

Then they went down with the cane rocker, one step at a time, till they had reached the bottom. Mother locked the door of the apartment behind them and said: That didn't take long!

Yes, said Father, it didn't take long!

Then he put his beret back on and picked up his suitcase and his desk lamp. He didn't even look back. He led the way down the stairs and out of the building. I had my satchel on my back. I didn't look back either. Then something odd happened. Or, because I hadn't slept for four or five nights, maybe I just imagined it. When I stepped out in front of the house with Father and Mother and my sister and Herr Herkenrath, but with generous spaces between us, to watch the moving men tossing Father's cane rocker into their van, I suddenly realized I wasn't alone. I was being observed. A few people had come up to the back of the moving van in the dark. They had come to say goodbye, I could see quite clearly. There was the teacher F. W. Förster with his wife, and Herr Schröder-Jahn with his dog, who couldn't have drowned in the Big Pond after all. Frau Jahn, who was otherwise always lying on her windowsill, had climbed down from her first floor on the Lessingstrasse, and Mariechen, with her hunchback and her heavy rings was right next to her. A little further back, but clearly visible, was Hutsche, looking a bit sheepish because Malz was leaning against him. He had been unfaithful to me with Malz longer than any of the others. Herr Schimmel the tobacconist was smoking a cigar, and thinking: I'll get a discount! But the odd thing wasn't that they had all come, I might have expected that.

The odd thing was that none of them were waving. They stood there, as though rooted to the ground, and looked at me silently. I raised my hand to wave, but when I saw them all standing there so dispassionately, I let it drop again. I was about to turn away, but then I said to myself: No, you mustn't leave here without a sign, after all you've put in a few years in this place! and then I did this. I gave them all, especially Hutsche, but even Malz, a little sign with my index finger, like this. It could have meant all sorts of things, like: I'm off! See you in the funny papers! or: Bye-bye blackbirds! or just: That was it! I don't know if anyone saw the signal, probably no one did. At any rate, no one made any signal back, no one waved. All right, if they've forgotten you, then you can forget them too, I thought, and I forgot them right away. I quickly walked to the moving van to say goodbye. Father was already looking for me.

Russdorf awaits, he said and nodded seriously.

Waits or won't wait? I asked.

Won't wait, said Father. That sounds better in this instance.

First I had to kiss my sister, then my sister kissed me. Then I had to kiss Mother, and Mother kissed me. What are your plans now? she asked. Will you sometimes think of me?

Sure, I said.

And will you read a good book from time to time, she asked. Or will you just sit around and stare into space?

I won't just stare into space, I said.

Father only kissed my sister. Your Mother and I, he said, have done all our kissing. Herr Herkenrath kissed no one at all, he just stood idly by. Maybe he kissed Mother, but only when no one was looking. He shook hands with Father and with me, and wished us "all the luck in the world". Father tugged at his beard and said: We'll see about that! and wished him nothing in return. Who knows how it'll end, happily or stickily, he managed to say. Something will turn up!

Nonsense, said Herr Herkenrath, nothing will turn up!

Oh yes, said Father, mark my words, it will!

Then we climbed into the moving van, Father and the moving men and me. It was hardest for Father. Because he found it so hard to move, he had difficulty getting up. So one of the moving men had to go round the other side, climb in there and pull Father up from the inside, while the other one pushed.

Easy, easy with this old antique, said Father. Maybe it'll turn out to be worth something after all!

What kind of antique, and what's it supposed to be worth? asked my sister, and Father said: In the eyes of the Almighty, perhaps, otherwise hardly! Then he settled into his seat and said: Future generations will be grateful to me for every book I fail to write!

Then he was ensconced. The moving man who had been pulling, slid over to the steering wheel, and the other went in the back. I sat between Father and the driver, because there I had the best view. There wasn't much to see, though, it was too dark. Father had his desk lamp and his bag of books on his knee. They are the ones I have fond memories of, and that I no longer look at to avoid disappointment, he said, and patted his favourite books.

Never again? asked my sister who was standing a long way below us, right next to Herr Herkenrath.

Never again, cried Father.

Then he straightened his beret, I don't know why. But then I didn't really know much about him, nor he about me. The engine started, and I didn't think about him any more. We drove away quickly.